"Ripe with sexual tension. . . . The fast pace, flawless narration, vivid and vital characters, sharp and witty dialogue, and an interesting and suspense-filled plot all make this book a must-read. Breathtaking!"
—www.RoadtoRomance.ca

"Steamy . . . sensual. . . . Readers will enjoy this book."
—*Booklist*

"Electrifying . . . provocative . . . lushly descriptive . . . a ripe and willing offering for romance readers who thrill over anything Scottish."
—www.RomanticFiction.com

DEVIL IN A KILT

"A lovely gem of a book. Wonderful characters and a true sense of place make this a keeper. If you love Scottish tales, you'll treasure this one."
—Patricia Potter, bestselling author of *The Heart Queen*

"As captivating as a spider's web, and the reader can't get free until the last word. It is easy to get involved in this tense, fast-moving adventure."
—*Rendezvous*

"FOUR AND A HALF STARS! This dynamic debut has plenty of steaming sensuality . . . a dusting of mystery. You'll be glued to the pages by the fresh, vibrant voice and strong emotional intensity. . . . Will catapult Welfonder onto 'must-read' lists."
—*Romantic Times*

Master
of the
Highlands

Master
of the
Highlands

Sue-Ellen
Welfonder

WARNER BOOKS

An AOL Time Warner Company

WARNER BOOKS EDITION

Cover design by Diane Luger
Cover illustration by John Ennis
Hand lettering by David Gatti
Book design by Giorgetta Bell McRee

Warner Books, Inc.
1271 Avenue of the Americas
New York, NY 10020

Visit our Web site at www.twbookmark.com

 An AOL Time Warner Company

Printed in the United States of America

First Paperback Printing: August 2003

10 9 8 7 6 5 4 3 2 1

For the love of wild places,
the roots in the land, and quiet moments.
For ancient yews, old stone, and Highland sunsets,
the splendor of golden afternoons.
And for a long-ago Highlandman,
Iain of Lochaber, whose lot in life should have been
as bright and shining as his noble and valiant heart.

Acknowledgements

As always with deepest appreciation and eternal gratitude for the intrepid heroines of my real life, my agent and friend, Pattie Steele-Perkins, for always being there, even in the storms; and my editor, Karen Kosztolnyik, who is so great of heart she'd make a splendid heroine in any Scottish Medieval. Ladies, I am indebted to you both.

And for my handsome husband, Manfred, my real-life hero, whose patience and support allows me to hide away in my turret and chase my dreams; and, too, for my own wee four-legged champion, my little dog, Em, who loves me despite my long hours at the computer and never fails to brighten my day.

Master
of the
Highlands

The MacLean Bane

Farther back in time than any living clansman would ever dare to question, two notable characteristics began distinguishing MacLean males, setting them apart from all other men: the fierceness of their heated blood and their ability to love, truly love, only one woman, the latter trait being either a blessing or a curse.

Depending.

And, willingly or unwillingly, in the early days of summer 1331, on the fair Isle of Doon, the most hot-tempered MacLean of them all was about to challenge tradition.

Chapter One

Baldoon Castle, The Isle of Doon,
1331

EXACTLY ONE YEAR TO THE DAY since his sweet lady wife breathed her last, Iain MacLean's black temper unleashed the disaster his clan had e'er dreaded, and neither the frantic labors of his kinsmen nor the deceptive beauty of the unusually calm night could undo his calamitous act.

The damage was too severe.

His family's private chapel would soon be little more than soot and ash, its much-praised splendor naught but a memory.

Guilt bitter on his tongue, Iain scanned the smoke-clogged great hall for a hapless soul to vent his wrath upon, but his clansmen dashed right past him, hastily filled water buckets clutched in their hands, each one paying him scant, if any, heed.

Iain's brows snapped together. He couldn't hasten anywhere. Fury and disbelief twisted through him, turning his legs to lead and rooting him to the spot even as all his darker emotions coiled into a cold knot of self-contempt deep in his gut.

Scarce more than a grim-faced shadow of the carefree man he'd once been, he raked shaking fingers through his soot-streaked hair and mentally prepared himself to glower at any poor soul foolhardy enough to glance his way.

Eager to reward any such effrontery with a blaze-eyed glare hot enough to wipe the disapproving mien off a gawker's face, he was sadly impotent against the fine Hebridean gloaming that sought to mock him by spilling its fair light through the hall's high-set window slits.

The wide-splayed recesses glowed with a soft, luminous gold, wholly uncaring of the torment whirling inside him . . . or the blasphemy he'd committed.

Iain blew out an agitated breath. He preferred stormy, cloud-chased skies, knew well the perfidy, the seductive illusion, of a placid-seeming summer's eve.

And naught spoiled the deception of this one save the acrid smoke tainting the air and the cold darkness in his own heart.

The emptiness.

That, and the harried shouts of his kinsmen as they fought to extinguish the flames of what, until a short while ago, had been the finest oratory in all the Western Isles.

The pride of the MacLeans . . . destroyed in a heart-beat.

"Tsk, tsk, tsk." A particularly annoying voice pierced the din. "You'd best hope for divine forgiveness, laddie."

Gerbert, Baldoon's seneschal since time beyond mind, thrust his bristly chin forward, clearly bent on pushing Iain past the bounds of endurance. "This night's sacrilege will cast a pall o'er every man, woman, and child who bear the name MacLean."

Making no attempt to hide his perturbation, Iain fixed his darkest look on the scrap of a graybeard who'd dared disrupt his brooding. "If the saints are as all-seeing as a certain white-haired goat e'er claims, they'll be wise enough to ken I alone shoulder the blame."

Gerbert matched Iain's glare, his rheumy blue eyes narrowed in unrepentant ire.

"Aye, the good Lord will be having His finger on you," he prophesied, swatting a knobby-knuckled hand at the thick tendrils of smoke drifting between them.

"His finger?" Iain scoffed, his vexation mounting. "Some would say He's burdened me with more than a finger."

Try having your wife fall prey to a power-hungry uncle, then live with knowing you couldn't save her, that she met her fate on a tidal rock, tied fast by her own tresses, and left to drown.

Iain's chest grew so tight he could scarce breathe. Ire pounded through him, the image of Lileas cold and still, seaweed entangled in her unbound hair, stirring his rage with all the fierce intensity MacLean males were said to experience upon recognizing their one true soul mate.

A ridiculous notion if ever there was one.

The only wildly intense emotions *he'd* e'er experienced were those borne of vexation, not mindless passion.

His blood heating, he squared his shoulders and

stepped closer to the seneschal, hoping his formidable height and hard-trained body would intimidate the clack-tongued elder, but the ploy failed.

The belligerent old rotter continued to bore holes in him with a decidedly pointed stare.

Iain drew a series of long, deep breaths until the tension beneath his ribs began to lessen. "Aye," he conceded at length, raising his voice to ensure the seneschal understood his every word. "Would the pearly-winged saints peer inside me this very moment, they'd find more than a finger weighing heavy on my heart."

"I've known you since before you could say your name, laddie." Gerbert's scrawny chest swelled with importance. "'Tis you, and you alone, heaping burdens on yourself."

Sheer weariness kept Iain from giving a derisive snort. "Think you?" he asked instead, the cool smoothness of his tone enough to send a less courageous man sprinting for shelter.

Gerbert nodded, his silence speaking worlds.

"And what else do you think?" Iain pressed, full aware he'd regret asking. The graybeard's unnerving perception could cut to the quick.

"What I *know* is that you've made your own sorry bed, and"—Gerbert poked at Iain's chest with a you'd-best-listen-to-me finger—"mayhap if it weren't such a cold and empty bed, you'd not be stomping about wound so tight you fail to see where you're heading."

Fail.

Iain cringed, the very word plunging like an expertly wielded knife straight into his heart.

He knew more about failing than all the men of the Isles and Highlands combined.

"A lass in my bed on this of all days? Have you gone addled?" He shoved Gerbert's thrusting finger from his ribs. "Wenching is the last—" he broke off, indignation closing his throat.

In another life, he would have laughed aloud at the absurdity of the thin-shouldered seneschal even mentioning such things as manly needs and bare-bottomed lasses.

But in *this* life, Iain MacLean, possessor of the loneliest heart in the Hebrides, had forgotten how to laugh. So he did what he could. He scowled. "Light skirts and lust-slaking." Leaning forward, he narrowed his eyes at the old goat. "What would you know of such pursuits?"

"Enough to ken what ails the likes o' you." Gerbert's face scrunched into an odd mixture of pity and reproach.

Iain stiffened, a vein in his temple beginning to throb. He wanted nary a shred of sympathy. Not from Baldoon's cantankerous seneschal, not from any man.

Nor did he need censure.

Or a lass in his bed.

Most especially not a lass in his bed.

In the year since his wife's passing, he'd become quite adept at stilling his baser urges. He scarce remembered what it was like to have his blood fired, much less feel his loins quicken with need.

He took a deep breath, wincing when the acrid air stung his lungs. "One year ago today, Lileas was stranded on the Lady Rock. She drowned there," he elaborated, carefully enunciating each word. "That, and naught else, is what ails me."

And not a one of the countless hours stretching between then and now had dimmed his pain . . . or lessened his guilt.

Be of great heart, his kinsmen were e'er harping at him. *Move on with his life,* they'd advise. He drew his brows together in a black frown. Of late, even the womenfolk had begun pestering him to take another wife.

Defeat clawing at him, he pressed the back of his hand to his forehead and glanced heavenward. Saints, but he was surrounded by witless, persistent fools, the lot of them unable to see the truth if it perched on their noses and winked at them.

Closing his eyes, he pinched the bridge of his own nose and repressed the urge to throw back his head and howl with cynical laughter.

He knew what his well-meaning clansmen neglected to comprehend.

Iain MacLean, renowned for his hot temper and master of naught, didn't have a life to get on with.

About the same time, but across the great sweep of the Hebridean Sea, past the rugged coast of the mainland, then deep into the heather hills and green glens of Scotland's heartland, Lady Madeline Drummond of Abercairn Castle stood within the hospitable walls of a friend's thatched cottage and braved her own night of turmoil.

The raw edge of her temper spurring her to desperation, she yanked hard on the worn cloth of the voluminous black cloak her common-born friend, Nella of the Marsh, clutched tight against her generous bosom.

"The robe is perfect," Madeline insisted, and gave another tug. "It will serve my needs well."

Nella shook her head. "Nay, my lady, I shan't let you

traipse about in rags," she protested, snatching the mantle from Madeline's grasp. She tossed it onto the rough-hewn table behind her. "Nor shall I let you traverse the land alone. Your life would be forfeit the moment you stepped from this cottage, and of a surety, long before you neared the first shrine."

Resting a work-reddened hand atop the threadbare cloak, Nella narrowed shrewd but caring eyes. "Penitents and holy men do not set aside their manly cravings simply because they've embarked on a pilgrimage."

Madeline flicked a speck of unseen dust from her sleeve. "I harbor no illusions about carnal lust. Men's or women's," she returned, fervently wishing the opposite were true.

Her heart ached to revel in the bliss of the unenlightened, longed to be filled with naught weightier than fanciful dreams of a braw man's bonnie smile.

The sweet magic of his golden words, the sensual promise of his touch.

But rather than a dashing suitor's seductive caress, his soul-stealing kisses and sweetly whispered endearments, cold shivers tore down her spine. "You needn't warn me of the darker side of lust," she said, more to herself than to Nella. "I am full aware of what spurs men to commit black deeds."

Her shivers now joined by a rash of gooseflesh, Madeline Drummond, reputed to be the loveliest maid in the land, moistened lips yet to part beneath the onslaught of a man's hot passion. *Lovely* they called her to her face. Madeline sighed, her virginal lips almost quirking with the irony.

She knew what they truly thought of her.

She was no more lovely than any other maid, but she *was* lonely.

The loneliest lass in the Highlands.

Lacing her fingers together to still their trembling, she slanted a quick glance at the nearest window . . . or rather, the crude opening in the wall that passed for one. Square-cut and deep, its view, were she to peer past the alder thicket pressing close to Nella's cottage, lent ponderous weight to her need to steal across the land cloaked in a postulant's robes.

"I am no stranger to men's greed," she said, another shudder ripping through her, this one streaking clear to her toes.

"Mayhap not," her friend owned, still guarding the frayed-edged cloak, "but you have been sheltered, my lady. Ne'er have you—"

"Ne'er have I lived," Madeline finished for her. She blinked, for some of the color of Nella's cozy cottage seemed to fade before her eyes, the stone-flagged floor seeming to tilt and careen beneath her feet.

Ignoring the dizziness beginning to spiral through her, she jerked her head in the general direction of the atrocities she couldn't bear to look upon. "My dear Nella, do you not see it is living that shall prove impossible so long as the perpetrator of yon blackness walks this earth?"

A world of objection swam in Nella's troubled eyes. "Will you not even listen to the dangers?"

"I ken the perils . . . and their consequences."

Madeline squared her shoulders. Were she not apprised of such things, her friend's boundless concern spooling through her, pulsing and alive, underscored the validity of Nella's disquiet.

And the curse Madeline carried with her since birth: the ability to feel the emotions of others.

Not always, and ne'er at will, but often enough. And always unbidden, bubbling up from some unknown depth in her soul to enfold her in the cares and wants of others as swiftly as a sudden mist could blanket the whole of a Highland glen.

It was a dubious talent, which had shown her the true heart of every suitor who'd ever called for her hand but, in truth, sought no more than her father's wealth and strategic lay of his land.

Clamping her lips together, she swallowed the bitterness rising in her throat and, instead, eyed the pilgrim's cloak draped across Nella's well-scrubbed table.

"A man would have to be sightless not to recognize your beauty and station," her friend declared, following her gaze. "Clothing yourself roughly will scarce make a difference."

"Not roughly," Madeline amended. "As a postulant."

Nella snorted. "I can see you now . . . the fiery and proud Lady of Abercairn seeking the veil."

"After I've done what I must, I will have no recourse but to plead God's mercy by gifting him with a life of servitude."

"My faith, lady, if you truly wish to spend your days in a sequestered existence, we can journey directly to the nearest abbey," Nella suggested, tilting her head to the side. "You've no need to traipse from one holy shrine to the next in search of Silver Leg. The gods themselves will smite him."

Silver Leg.

Sir Bernhard Logie.

By either name, the very mention of Madeline's nemesis reached a cruel hand through the evening's quiet to
snatch away her hopes and dreams and dash them upon
the charred pyres his men had erected before Abercairn's
proud curtain walls.

The crenellated defenses of a stronghold taken only
because her father's worst enemy had stooped to unutter-
able savageries: the burning of innocents.

One life for each refusal to throw wide the gates.

Compliance came swift, the drawbridge clanking
down without delay, but a blameless herd-boy still met a
fiery end, the ignoble deed repeated until three of Abercairn's most vulnerable were no more.

When Silver Leg's men escorted Madeline's father,
straight-backed and unflinching, to the flames, she'd fled,
seeking refuge from the unspeakable at Nella's door.

Her only sanctuary in a night gone mad.

A simple but good-hearted woman, Nella secured her
peace by allowing others to believe she possessed a talent
as unique as Madeline's own, a carefully chosen ability
daunting enough to keep most danger well at bay.

Few men claimed a stout enough heart to near the
dwelling place of a woman rumored to receive visitations
from the dead.

And it was Sir Bernhard Logie Madeline wanted dead.
Dubbed Silver Leg for the silver votive offerings, fash-
ioned as legs, that he e'er left at holy shrines in gratitude
for some obscure saint's intervention in healing his childhood lameness, the seasoned warrior knight best known
for his lightning changes of allegiance, gave himself a
devout man.

Madeline knew better.

She fixed Nella with a determined stare. "The gods and every ravening wolf in the land can do what they will with the man . . . after I've avenged my own."

Nella drew a deep breath, and Madeline could almost see arguments forming on the tip of her friend's tongue. Thus warned, she spun around before they could grow into full-fledged protestations. "He would have been wise to choose a better cause than to seize Abercairn," she said, and yanked open the thick-planked door.

Her heart pounded in hot anger as her gaze latched on the distant smoke still curling upward from blackened woodpiles she couldn't see but felt with every fiber of her being.

"You ken there is a well-honed dirk hidden in my right boot," she said, her voice tight. "I will not hesitate to use it once I find him."

Nella joined her in the open doorway. "Then let us be gone before they find you." She sent a meaningful glance at the evening mist already rolling down the nearby brae-side. "Rumors of my witchy ways will only stay them so long."

A jagged-edged bolt of sorrow, or mayhap regret, shot through Madeline, and she glanced sharply at her friend, but the sensation passed as swiftly as it'd come, and no sign of distress marred Nella's kindly face.

The wayfarer's cloak already swirling about her ample form, Nella offered a second, less worn-looking wrap to Madeline. "Can you feel him?" she asked, low-voiced, as Madeline donned the second mantle. "If his malice stirs you at all, we will at least have a lead and won't waste time journeying in a false direction."

"I feel . . ." Madeline began, but trailed off as quickly.

She did sense something, but the darkness closing round her heart held too much poignancy to hail from Bernhard Logie . . . and it came from too great a distance.

"I feel . . . nothing," she hedged, her chest tight and aching with a stranger's loneliness and guilt.

A *man's* loneliness, and of a certainty, not the guilt of a murderer.

'Twas a heart-wrenching guilt far too deep and intimate to be shared with another.

Not even dear Nella.

Cold, black, and laced with a bottomless yearning for vanished days and what-could-have-beens, the man's anguish seized her very soul. And squeezed so tight she could scarce breathe until his hold on her began ebbing away, slowly retreating to the far-off corner of the land whence it had come.

"You felt nothing, my lady?" Nella's doubt cut through the residual haze still clouding Madeline's senses.

"I . . ." Not quite sure *what* had swept through her, Madeline gave off trying to explain and leaned back against the doorjamb, her breaths coming in great ragged gasps.

"And, when he yet lived, I was the good King Robert's favored lady love," Nella quipped, peering hard at her. "Truth be told, you've gone whiter than new-fallen snow, so don't be telling me nothing's touched you."

Touched her.

That was the difference—she'd been touched, and deeply. The realization washed over her in a torrent of golden waves, freeing her from the last tenuous threads of the stranger's powerful grip. She grasped Nella's strong hands with her own, trembling, ones. "I *did* feel," she breathed, awed by the depth of the man's anguish, stunned by the fierceness of his longing.

"And what did you feel?" Nella prodded, giving Madeline's hands a light squeeze.

Madeline hesitated, not willing to share the stranger's pain, yet unable to conceal her wonder at the rest.

"Well?" Nella urged again.

"I felt love."

"*Love?*"

"Aye, love," Madeline repeated, suddenly quite convinced. The very word sent little tremors tripping across her every nerve ending. "Heart-pounding, thunderous, shake-the-very-earth-beneath-your-feet love."

The kind she'd dreamed of every night for as long as she could remember.

Shattered dreams, the remnants of which she'd cast to the four winds the instant she'd slipped into Nella's wayfaring cloak.

Murderesses didn't deserve to know passion, and nuns weren't allowed.

In his own far-off corner of the land, Iain MacLean stood amidst the chaos of Baldoon's great hall, his backbone steeled against the unpleasant awareness that every saint worth his wings must now be frowning upon him in fits of fine, feathered fury.

Assorted fragments of his deepest needs, all his longings and best-kept secrets, weighted his broad shoulders as surely as the billowing clouds of smoke still pouring from the ruined chapel swirled around him in a choking mantle of black reproach.

Bile thick in his throat, he struggled to ignore the seething frustration gnawing on his innards. A vein still throbbed wildly in his left temple, and his heartbeat pounded in his ears with such furor, he could scarce hear the pandemonium unfolding all around him.

Not that hearing the ruckus would tell him aught he didn't know.

The shameful aftermath of his carelessness stood carved on his conscience. Indelibly and, without doubt, dancing already on the flapping tongues of every prattle-monger in the Isles.

His jaw clenching, he drew a hand down over his face.

One fit of blind rage, an accidentally toppled cande-labrum, and all hellfire had erupted, its jeering demons clamping sharp-taloned hands around his ravaged soul in a foretaste of the damnation awaiting him.

Blinking against the sting of smoke, he drew a great heaving breath and tried not to cough. If the good saints possessed a shred of mercy, they'd let the raging inferno in Baldoon's chapel claim him as well.

Unfortunately, much to his vexation, his brother, Don-all the Bold, much-revered laird of the great Clan MacLean, had other plans.

Every inch as tall as Iain, and of the same impressive build and dark good looks, Donall MacLean aimed an as-sessing glance at the smoke-clogged chapel . . . and at the grim-faced warriors gathering ever nearer. Trusted kins-men, well accustomed to Iain's quick-tindered blood and how swiftly sparks ignited between the two brothers who resembled each other so closely that those meeting them for the first time oft mistook them for twins.

Keenly attuned to their laird's wishes, a near-imperceptible nod of Donall the Bold's raven-haired head was all the encouragement the loyal fighting men needed to form a tight, semicircular cordon behind him.

An impenetrable barrier between Iain and the fire licking its way up the chapel walls.

His handsome face set in bitter earnest lines, Donall MacLean whipped out his steel with the loud *zing* only the most lethal of blades can produce.

He aimed its deadly tip at Iain's middle. "Do not even think of going back in there," he warned, his dark-eyed gaze hard as ice-frosted stone, his deep voice equally cold. And so annoyingly contained, Iain's temper blazed all the more hotly.

Irritation pumping through his veins, he met his older brother's cool gaze with his heated one. "You think to stay me by the edge of your sword? Our own father's brand?"

Donall didn't so much as blink. "I have no desire to maim you. Enough ill work has been wrought this day, but, aye, I will cut you if I must . . . if you attempt further foolishness."

"Then have at me." Iain lifted his hands, palms out, in open challenge. "Think you I fear steel more than flames?"

"'Tis well I ken you fear naught." Donall slid another pointed look at the ruined chapel. "Fearless or nay, I'd counsel you to consider God's wrath after this night's sacrilege."

Iain fixed his brother with a steely-eyed glare, his own wrath ready to erupt in a welter of invectives. Battling such an outburst, he pressed his lips together and hoped Donall wouldn't notice the muscle jerking in his jaw.

Nor guess the depth of his turmoil, for he alone bore the weight of his wife's demise.

His entire body thrumming with agitation, he clenched his hands to white-knuckled fists. Had he loved Lileas as fiercely as MacLean men were legended to love their women, he would have sensed the danger stalking her that day, could have kept her from going anywhere near the Lady Rock.

But he'd sensed naught.

He hadn't even thought of her that fateful morn . . . until it was too late.

So he staunched his guilt the only way he knew: by braving his brother's censure with the bold arrogance few but a MacLean male can summon. "You dare say I ought consider the whims of a God so uncaring He allowed Lileas to be murdered?"

"The good Lord had nary a hand in her death, but I vow He will be mightily displeased to see you've set alight His place of worship."

Roiling anger rose in Iain's throat, his bitterness near choking him. "Aye, you're right, my brother. He had naught to do with the deed," he seethed, no longer even trying to contain his fury. "God and all His saints were sleeping that foul-dawning day, just as they slept when my own grief sent me wheeling away from the altar and into the accursed candlestand."

Bristling, he met Donall's measuring gaze with the calculated sizzle of a narrow-eyed glare. "Or would you insinuate I collided with the candelabrum a-purpose?" he ground out, unwilling to admit his deepest guilt even to the brother he loved above life itself.

"Think you I wished to set fire to the chapel?" he pushed, his voice louder this time.

Louder, and laced with crackling anger.

Donall studied him for a long, uncomfortable moment. "Everyone within these walls knows you've spent more time on your knees before yon altar than in your own bedchamber this past year," he said at last. "Why should you burn the one place you're e'er hiding yourself? Nay, my brother, I think your own torments and your unchecked ire blinded you."

"Torments and ire?" Iain's very toes tensed in outrage. "I'd say it is my fullest right to harbor both."

Grief, hot and all-consuming, coursed through him, but he'd be damned a thousand times before he'd give a name to his regrets. Or admit to the black void that darkened his every waking hour and shadowed his sleepless nights.

Donall lifted a brow, his silent appraisal more eloquent than words.

Drawing himself to his full height, Iain cocked a brow of his own. A *challenging* one. "You dare say I've no claim to those rights?"

"I say you forfeited any such claims the instant your temper caused you to knock over the candlestand."

"Some dull-wit moved the unwieldy apparatus," Iain countered, every fiber of his being daring Donall to state otherwise.

"Nay, you err," the MacLean obliged him. "The candelabrum stood where it's always stood."

Iain held his brother's gaze. "It scarce matters now."

"Say you?" Donall cast another quick glance at the

shouting kinsmen still battling the flames. "It matters to them."

And it matters to me! Iain's temper roared. *So much so that I see no purpose in living in the dark and chasing shadows all my days . . . subsisting as one ill wished.*

Or, less appealing still, pitied.

His mood worsening with each beat of his heart, he took a step forward, then another, until the sharp point of Donall's blade pricked his abdomen. Then, standing proud and straight, he risked a smile, his first in longer than he could recall.

And meant to be his last.

Keenly aware of his brother's scrutiny, Iain readied himself for a lightning-quick sprint into the flames. His decision made, the unaccustomed smile began to spread through him, not filling him with joy and light as smiles ought do, and not banishing the dark in his soul, but flooding him with blessed relief.

The sweet surety that his bone-deep aching would soon cease.

He heaved a great sigh . . . and blinked back the unexpected heat suddenly jabbing the backs of his eyes. "You err, brother mine, for I do know fear," he said, his deep voice husky and . . . tight. "I fear living and"—he made an impatient gesture—"I've grown mighty weary of it, too."

Realization flashed across Donall's face. "Nay!" he cried, flinging aside his sword. He lunged forward, throwing his arms around Iain in the same moment a strange prickling in the back of Iain's neck made him spin around.

His agility rewarded him with the surreal glimpse of a

bonnie raven-haired lass rushing him. Wild-eyed and screaming, she held a large earthen wine jug high above her head.

Its descent was the last thing Iain saw before a numbing darkness of a wholly different nature than he'd hoped for rose up to claim him.

Many leagues away, on the other side of Doon, ever-stronger wind gusts swept across the isle's high moors and boglands, but carefully skirted a particular cliff-top glade, not daring to bend a single blade of grass within its enchanted circle.

A lone thatched cottage stood there, thick-walled and silent. Perched precariously on the rugged edge of nowhere, high above the sea, sheltered by silver birch and rowan trees . . . and the magic of Devorgilla, Doon's resident crone and wise woman.

The *cailleach,* who, even now, as Iain slumbered in fitful oblivion, used her skills to borrow some of his darkness to cloak her own doings from the gloaming's luminous light.

"Not the time o' year for spelling," she muttered, carefully fastening a length of dark linen over one of the cottage's unshuttered windows . . . the last one to require such a blackening treatment.

Pursing her lips, she smoothed the cloth into place. Her most potent incantations had failed to conjure sufficient gloom, and no wonder, when *his* disbelief raged so strong it hindered her even while he slept!

"Harrumph," she scolded, shuffling across the cold, stone-flagged floor toward a rough-hewn bench pushed flush against the far wall. Her straggly brows met in a frown. "'*I want naught of your depraved chantings and even less of black cauldrons bubbling over with newts and bats' wings,*'" she mimicked him as she eased her bent form onto the bench.

Once settled, she allowed herself a well-earned cackle and pulled a large, wooden bowl filled with stones onto her bony knees. "Hah!" she scoffed, a familiar thrill tripping down her spine.

"Iain the Doubter shall have a more potent cure than tongue of newt and wing of bat," she informed the stillness, her concentration focused on the softly gleaming stones.

Special stones.

Highland quartz, mostly, though some came from sacred places throughout the Isles.

Fairy Fire Stones, rare and precious. Each one collected by her own two hands or gifted to her by those more appreciative of her talents than a certain dark-eyed laddie too closed-minded for his own good.

Humming to herself at his ignorance, Devorgilla began to poke through the stones with her gnarled fingers until their tips grew tingly and warm, and the stones themselves began to vibrate and glow.

With a deftness that belied the appearance of her knotty, age-spotted hand, she plucked *his* stone from the bowl and placed it on the bench beside her.

Her stone, the one she'd selected to represent Iain MacLean's true soul mate, was found with equal ease. And while his stone still felt cold to the touch, its core a deep and chilling blue, *hers* was growing warmer by the day.

Savoring its heat, Devorgilla set the female stone in

the palm of her left hand. Her wizened face wreathed in a knowing smile when a teensy point of reddish gold suddenly appeared deep inside the Fairy Fire Stone's core.

One be you, and one be she. When your lady's heart catches fire, you'll recognize her, she'd explained as she'd tried to give him the stones the last time she'd made the long trek to Baldoon.

A tedious journey she'd undertaken solely to offer him her assistance.

Clucking her tongue at the scowl he'd bestowed on her, Devorgilla placed his cold stone next to the maid's warm one and closed her ancient fingers over the two.

His lady's heart couldn't catch flame, he'd informed her, claiming her heart was cold as the grave and would ne'er warm again.

The *cailleach* cackled anew.

Her smile turning impish, she curled her fingers tighter around the stones, and fixed a self-satisfied gaze on the low, black-raftered ceiling.

Iain MacLean was sorely mistaken.

Though the flame in his true lady's heart might not yet be a blazing inferno, it'd already caught a fine, healthy spark, and was very much alive.

Very much alive indeed.

Chapter Two

IAIN CURLED HIS FINGERS DEEP into the tangled linens of his massive four-poster bed in a futile attempt to stop the oaken monstrosity's ceaseless spinning.

Unfortunately, with each agonizing moment of his slowly awakening consciousness, the whirling only increased, the bed now dipping and tilting in perfect rhythm with the fierce throbbing behind his forehead.

A clanging of discordant bells rang in his ears, and the backs of his eyes stung worse than the time when, as wee laddies, Donall had laughingly blown a handful of sand into his face.

Iain grimaced, the memory driving a white-hot spike of bitterness right into the middle of his pounding head. A low groan escaped his parched throat, and he tightened his grip on the careening bed.

When was the last time he'd laughed?

Truth to tell, he couldn't recall, and ne'er had he felt less inclined than now.

Compressing his lips against the massed pain assailing him, he cracked his eyes as much as he dared and squinted into the blinding brightness of a chamber far too sun-filled to be his own.

Some audacious whoreson had wrested open every last shutter, allowing the piercing afternoon light to flood his private quarters . . . a refuge all knew he purposely kept in cool and blessed shadow.

"By the Rood!" he thundered, fury propelling him bolt upright. "What depraved arse—?" He broke off at once, collapsing against the pillows, his indignation soundly capped by the sickly sensation of his head bursting into a hundred jagged-edged fragments.

"By-the-Rood," he repeated, the words barely audible this time, pressed as they were through gritted teeth.

In utter agony, he stared at the comfortingly dark underceiling of his great, oaken bed. Didn't the meddlesome miscreants who professed to care about him ken he had ample reason to ban the sun's golden rays from his life?

Was it not common knowledge throughout the Isles that appreciation of such pleasures belonged to a man he could no longer claim to be?

His jaw tightened as a wholly new thought weaseled its way past his ire and pain. Mayhap he only imagined he lay, aching and bleakhearted, in his bed.

Perhaps he *had* sprinted into the flames, and now found himself in the antechamber to Satan's own fiery pit? The glaring brightness stabbing his eyes, not the sun's streaming rays, but the leaping flames of hell itself?

Not as pleased at the possibility as he'd thought he'd be, Iain forced himself to endure the dazzling light long enough to survey his surroundings a bit more thoroughly.

At once, a strange blending of relief and vexation

welled in his chest. If he'd died and gone to hell, his most persistent tormentors had followed him. Each one claiming some privy corner of his chamber, and with absolute disregard for his pitiful state, his closest kinsmen and friends peered at him with such cold disdain it was a bonnie wonder they didn't have icicles hanging from their brows.

All save his raven-haired sister.

She stood a scant pace from his bed, wringing her hands, her dark eyes red-rimmed and swollen. Iain blinked, confusion dancing light-footed around the edges of his black and bitter mood.

His sister possessed a backbone of steel. Amicia MacLean wouldn't flinch if someone set a flaming pine knot to her skirts . . . and ne'er had Iain seen her weep.

"On my soul, ne'er would I hurt you," she said, her voice dulled by anguish. "But we . . . I thought . . ." Her words drowning in a choking sob, she swiped the back of her hand beneath her eyes. "Can you e'er forgive me?"

"Forgive you?" At her tearful nod, Iain cast a questioning glance at his brother, but Donall's stony visage and tight-lipped disapproval offered nary a clue to Amicia's distress.

A quick scan of the other intruders on his privacy proved equally fruitless. The old seneschal, Gerbert, returned his stare with a defiant look of sheerest reproach, while Donall's wife, the lady Isolde, hovered just inside the half-open door, her troubled gaze fastened firmly on her husband.

Gavin MacFie, Donall's most trusted friend, sat in one of the deep window embrasures, carefully wiping soot from one of Baldoon's prized reliquary caskets. A strapping, auburn-haired man well loved for his sunny disposition, he held Iain's stare for a long, uncomfortable moment before giving a sad shake of his head and returning his attention to the small bejeweled chest balanced on his knees.

Iain frowned. He hadn't missed the tinge of pity in Gavin's hazel eyes . . . eyes that usually brimmed with good cheer.

Thick silence stretched between the room's occupants, its weight lending an oppressive pall to the crisp salt air pouring through the open windows. The unnatural stillness magnified his sister's sniffling, and sent the first nigglings of ill ease slithering down Iain's back.

A second, *closer* glance at the narrow arch-topped windows sent a whole platoon of agitation to join the nigglings.

Someone hadn't just opened the shutters . . . they were no longer there.

"God's blood! Who dared—" Iain bit back the rest of a dark oath, his confusion dissipating with the sudden return of his senses. A myriad of images flashed through his mind, and the most telling one of all was his sister rushing at him, only to crash a wine jug full square on his head.

Wincing at the memory, he touched cautious fingers to the egg-sized knot on his forehead. The lump pulsed hotly and sent tendrils of searing pain streaking clear to his toes.

But its portent moved him, spilling light and warmth into a heart long consigned to darkness and cold.

Despite his bleak moods and perilous tempers, Amicia cared enough to seize any means to keep him from harm.

Even from his own wretched self.

Especially from himself.

Fighting the nausea even the slightest movement set loose, Iain pushed up on his elbows and drew a ragged breath. "Stop crying, lass," he rasped, appalled by the effort it cost him to form those few simple words. "I am not vexed with you."

"For truth?" Amicia's cheeks glistened with tears. "You are not wroth with me?"

"Nay," he assured her, making a brusque motion with one hand. "You have my oath on it. I ken why you did it, and I— . . . I thank you." He gave her a tight smile . . . a wee one.

The best he could manage.

And only for *her.*

Others present were about to taste the full measure of his wrath.

With a burst of energy torn from the very depths of his hardihood, he flung back the covers, swung his legs over the side of the bed, and held fast to its edges until the wild spinning lessened.

Then he raked every male in the room with a scorching glare.

That accomplished, he heaved himself to his feet and fixed his most formidable stare on the cheeky soul he held responsible for transforming his quarters into a sea of eye-gouging brilliance.

The grizzle-headed lout had even set a fire blazing in the hearth and lit every branch of candles in the room. The wall torches, heavy iron-bracketed nuisances long unlit and neglected, hadn't been ignored either. Each one hissed and crackled with well-burning flames.

Iain suppressed the urge to give a bark of cynical laughter. For all the stifling heat thrown off by the myriad sources of light, he might well have awakened in Satan's den.

With the most casual calm he could muster, he addressed the rheumy-eyed seneschal. "As I mind it, *Gerbert,* I've instructed you times without number not to lay a fire in here, to desist from lighting a single taper, and"—he paused for emphasis—"to leave the windows shuttered."

Not to be intimidated, the seneschal regarded him with a look of studied blandness, but gave away his discomfort by shifting his feet in the floor rushes . . . a sure sign of guilt.

Iain drew a deep breath, released it slowly, and, holding the old man's gaze, asked, "Where *are* the window shutters?"

Stiff-lipped silence met his narrow-eyed perusal, but he caught a flash of pity in the graybeard's hazy blue eyes . . . the same fleeting glimpse of commiseration he'd noted on Gavin's open visage just moments before.

And that great oaf avoided all further eye contact with him. The lumbering Islesman kept his shaggy, auburn head bent low over the jeweled reliquary casket, furiously polishing its silver casing . . . though not a single speck of soot remained.

The precious container for holy relics gleamed brighter than a bairn's newly scrubbed behind.

A wholly *un*-formidable glance at his sister-in-law reaped no more than a noncommittal shrug.

A shrug and a most eloquent glance at her husband.

Iain looked at him, too. The MacLean laird's rocklike

stance bode ill, but too fine a ferment brewed in Iain's gut for him to care. "'Twas you," he said, squinting in the sun's glare slanting in through the now-bare windows. "You ordered the removal of the shutters."

Donall the Bold didn't deny it.

Instead, he crossed his arms and set his mouth into a hard, uncompromising line.

Cold-edged pricklings of ill ease attacked Iain anew, only this time, rather than merely slide down his spine, they laid vicious siege to his every nerve ending, crashing over him in a tidal wave of foreboding as ominous as the missing shutters and his brother's grim-set countenance.

Ignoring the others in the chamber, Iain fixed Donall with an equally stern eye, but his brother didn't so much as blink. Nor did his features soften or reveal even a hint of the sympathy he'd seen on the faces of the others.

Iain's hands clenched at his sides, his nails cutting welts into his palms. Honor demanded he accept and abide by his brother's edicts. Donall was laird, not he, and ne'er had Iain minded his lot as younger son.

But ne'er before had Donall crossed the threshold to Iain's private quarters as *laird*.

Only as his good brother and friend.

That he'd do so now, and in such a dark hour, left a bitter taste in Iain's mouth.

Squaring his shoulders, he willed himself to ignore his wobbly knees, the thick and clumsy state of his tongue. "Think you I haven't bled enough this day?" he managed at last, his voice stronger now.

He made a broad, sweeping gesture with his arm, taking in the roaring hearth fire and the countless lit tapers.

"Would you see my quarters reduced to a charred wilderness as penance for my sins? Or"—he strode to the denuded windows, purposely avoiding the recessed alcove claimed by Gavin MacFie, then whirled around—"perchance you seek to blind me?"

Donall met his taunt with infuriating calm. "'Tis you who've blinded yourself." He slanted a quick look at Gavin, still busy polishing the reliquary casket. "We only seek to *un*-blind you."

"That may be," Iain acceded, fisted hands braced on his hips, "but I am none too keen on regaining my . . . *sight.*"

Turning back to the window, he gripped its cold stonework, holding fast to the elaborate tracery swirls. His pulse racing ever faster, he stared out at the vastness of the Hebridean Sea, his gaze going unerringly to the near-submerged islet where Lileas, his sweet lady wife, had met her doom.

The Lady Rock.

A seaweed-festooned hump of rock barely breaking the surface, its black-glistening crest deceptively benign in the sweet, golden light of late afternoon.

So near, yet impossibly distant.

His own personal nemesis, its ominous presence a grim reminder of another world, another life, and everything he'd lost.

All he'd done wrong.

A strangled groan rose in his throat, lodging there, as familiar talons of grief and guilt clamped cold round his heart, and a tight knot of pain formed in his gut.

With great effort, he tore his gaze from the tidal rock's jagged face and focused on the bright sunlight dancing silver across the endless expanse of blue-, green-, and amethyst-shaded water. Iced with white-crested rollers, the sea's beauty lanced his very soul.

At length, he turned back to the room. "Donall, you ken I would slay dragons for you," he said, carefully measuring each word. "Even walk barefooted over hot coals if you required it of me, but ne'er have you entered this chamber as aught but my brother and friend . . . until now."

Donall lifted a silencing hand, but Iain rushed on. "You mistake if you seek to press such a privilege. Name any penance and I shall tender it, but I will not abide your intrusion here, nor the desecration of my private quarters."

His protestation voiced, he slid a last pointed look at old Gerbert, then started across the room. "I shall expect the shutters reaffixed by sunup on the morrow," he declared, just as he meant to stride past Donall and into the blessed shadow of the corridor, but his brother's arm shot out, staying him with a viselike grip to his elbow.

"You will not be here on the morrow," Donall informed him. "My sorrow that it is so, but this time you went too far. It grieves me to—"

"To what?" Iain demanded, jerking free. "Cast me in the dungeon? Banish me to prowl the hills outwith Baldoon's walls? Send me naked into the heather and scrub?"

Donall pinched the bridge of his nose, drew a long, pained-looking breath. "Naught halfway so odious."

"What then? Shall I count the stones in every cairn dotting Doon's high moors?" Iain rammed a hand through his hair, winced at the sound of his blood rushing through his ears. "Come, man, have out with it!"

"Iain, please," Amicia pleaded from the far side of the room. "And you, Donall, can we not just leave him be?" She took a few forward steps, raised beseeching hands. "He's suffered enough as is."

"Aye, he has," Donall agreed, his tone grim. "And as his brother, my heart sympathizes, but my duty as laird demands I see him expiate his transgressions." He crossed his arms, his features growing visibly stern. "Mayhap in the execution of his penance, he will come to suffer less."

At a solemn nod from Donall, Gavin MacFie extracted himself from the window embrasure, and joined them, the bejeweled reliquary casket held reverently in his large hands.

Late-afternoon light reflected off the glittering gemstones embedded in the small casket's silver-and-enamel casing, each one shooting off rays of dazzling, multicolored light.

Rays that streaked straight at Iain's aching eyes.

He blinked hard, frowning as countless teensy dots of blinding color danced across his vision, but when his sight cleared, a cloud must have passed o'er the sun, for the room lay in sweet shadow.

His relief, though, proved fleeting. The pink stain on Gavin's freckled cheeks and the abashed look in his downcast eyes could only bode ill.

The redheaded lout knew something he didn't. Something Iain instinctively knew he did not want to be privy to.

Hot waves of wariness licking across his every nerve

ending, he glanced at the reliquary casket. For centuries the MacLeans' most prized possession, it contained a holy relic of inestimable value: a fragment of the True Cross.

At once, a horrible thought popped into Iain's mind. Steeling himself, he eyed his brother. "Don't tell me you'd see me martyred?"

Rather than answer him, Donall turned to a nearby table and poured himself a cup of wine, draining it in one long swallow. His face grim-set, he dragged the back of his hand over his mouth. "You would have to commit a more grievous sin than burning the chapel for me to pass such a harsh judgment on you."

He began pacing the chamber, his long strides taking him back and forth between the blazing hearth and the now-empty window embrasure. "Nay," he said at last, sliding a quick glance at Iain, "'Tis a pilgrim I would make of you, not a martyr."

"A pilgrim?" Iain near choked on the word. Ne'er had he heard aught more ludicrous.

All knew he was not a devout man.

Truth be told, he believed in scarce little beyond that the sun rose each day to plague him.

He stared at Donall, his brows arching ever higher. "I did not mishear you?" His already strained voice sounded two shades higher than it should. "You mean to make a *penitent* of me?"

The sort that roams the land in a heavy cloak and wide-brimmed hat, a wooden staff clutched in one hand, a beggar's bowl in the other?

The very thought froze his blood.

"A pilgrim and an emissary of goodwill," his brother confirmed, and Iain's stomach plummeted.

Gerbert snorted. "That laddie out and about, a-spreading goodwill across the land?" he spluttered, his cheek earning him a sharp glance from his laird. Unimpressed, the aged seneschal shook his white-tufted head. "'Tis a fool plan if e'er I heard one."

Donall stopped his pacing to draw a long breath. "The undertaking will appease the saints for the destruction of Baldoon's chapel and, with God's good grace"—he wheeled around, his granitelike countenance leaving no room for rebuttal—"help Iain to master his temper. I, and every man, woman, and bairn beneath this roof have tolerated enough."

"I—" Iain began, then swallowed the heated words, his dread temper and all his bitterness contracting to a tiny, icy ball of tightness somewhere behind his rib cage.

Some would say in the vicinity of his equally cold and tightly closed heart.

His anger and guilt locked soundly away, tied and bound by the truth of his brother's words.

Words he couldn't gainsay.

He *had* become the bane of his clan, fouling the mood and robbing the smile of anyone foolhardy enough to come within ten paces of him.

Consigned to a fate he could blame on no one but himself, he dragged a hand down over his face, carefully avoiding the still-aching lump pulsing hotly on his forehead. "Have done," he gritted, meeting Donall's eye. "I would hear more of my . . . penance."

Donall held his gaze. "I told you, 'tis more a journey of goodwill than aught else."

"Goodwill toward whom?"

"The deserving brothers of Dunkeld Cathedral." The words came calm and measured, but overlaid with a subtle warning.

One Iain caught and understood.

His refusal to embark on such an endeavor would not be tolerated.

At his silence, Donall continued, "You'll ken Dunkeld's status as an important reliquary church. More Columban relics are sheltered within its walls than anywhere else in the land. A foster brother of our father once served as bishop there, and Da himself was a great benefactor—"

"Could you not choose a more distant place?" Iain cut in, his stomach turning over. He stared at his brother, disbelieving. "Dunkeld lies in the very heart of the mainland. I would need two full cycles of the moon even to near its boundaries."

Donall gave him a hard look. "Time is not of essence. Nor the hardship of the journey," he said. "Dunkeld is needy. The English, and the Disinherited, those landless Scottish lords who serve them, have repeatedly fallen upon the cathedral and its holdings in recent years. They've ransacked and stolen, burned orchards, and even cut down canons in their sleep."

"Holy men, slaughtered whilst washing the feet of the poor!" Gerbert shook his head, clucked his tongue.

"So I am to lend them my sword arm?"

"Only if they fall under attack when you are there." Glancing aside, Donall signaled to someone outside the open door, and, to Iain's surprise, one of his brother's younger squires entered the chamber, two leather satchels clutched in his hands.

Two bulging satchels.

The red-cheeked lad deposited them at Iain's feet before near stumbling over his own in a hasty retreat.

Iain cocked a brow. "You are so eager to see my back that you've packed for me?"

"Those"—Donall gestured at the satchels with his thumb—"are gifts." He resumed his pacing, his hands clasped loosely behind his back. "Dunkeld has lost much to the marauders: silver cups and salvers, golden crosses, an illuminated manuscript with jewel-set bindings."

Halting beside his wife, he slung an arm about her waist and drew her near. "The thieving dastards even helped themselves to the revered *Cathbhuaidh*, the 'yellow battler,' St. Columba's own crozier."

"And we are to replenish their empty coffers?"

Donall nodded. "Our own panoply of relics and treasures is vast enough for us easily to restore a portion of their lost wealth. In doing so, we can attempt to"—he paused to rub his forehead—"atone for the sacrilege you committed by setting fire to the chapel."

Tight bands, cold as frozen steel, slid round Iain's chest, clamping hard and stealing his breath. "You'd send them our greatest wealth? So I am granted remission of my sins?"

So you can reclaim the life you should have had.

The words, feminine and sweet, came close to Iain's ear. Soft as a sigh, and in a voice hauntingly like Lady Isolde's lilting voice, but his brother's fair wife's lips hadn't moved.

Nor had she left her husband's side.

And Amicia still fretted across the room, far too hampered by sniffles to form a coherent word. A chill lifting the hairs on his nape, Iain turned back to his brother, only to find Donall's gaze resting on the precious reliquary in Gavin's hands.

Iain looked at it, too. And the longer he did, the more the tiny casket seemed to glow and pulsate, its glittering gemstones staring at him like so many multihued eyes, each one brimming with accusation.

Brought back from the Holy Land by a distant forebear who'd gone on Crusade, the casket and the holy relic contained within had been in the MacLeans' possession since time immemorial.

By all reckoning, two hundred years, if a day.

'Twas the clan's greatest treasure.

And his father and every MacLean laird before him would return from their graves in protest if e'er it passed through Baldoon's gates.

Some amongst the elders even claimed tragedy of untold proportions would be released if e'er it did.

"The tragedy has already come to pass," Donall said, confirming Iain's conviction that, at times, his brother could read minds. "A heavy sacrifice must be made lest greater ill befall this house." He paused, his dark eyes narrowing. "Or would you rather I commanded you put to the cliff?"

"So my penance is to deliver our family's most valued treasure into the hands of Dunkeld's canons?"

"Taking gifts—humble offerings—to Dunkeld to replace what they've lost is your duty as my brother, and son of this house." Donall regarded Iain for a long moment, then slid a meaningful look at Gavin MacFie. "He will accompany you."

"MacFie?" Iain glanced at the burly Islesman.

Not unpleasant to the eye, Gavin MacFie stood head and shoulders over most men, had an open, honest face, and warm hazel eyes. His thick auburn hair could be called a bit unruly, but he kept his beard neatly trimmed.

And at the moment, he shuffled his brogue-clad feet in the floor rushes and looked more uncomfortable than Iain had e'er seen him.

The bampot's ill ease fueled Iain's own. "Do the good saints have a score to settle with him as well?"

"Nary a one," Donall said, his voice sounding tired. "He goes solely to keep an eye on you, and"—he paused, a look very close to genuine sympathy clouding his face—"to make certain you heed your penance."

"So at last you tell me the whole of it." Iain folded his arms. He'd known there'd be more.

Donall released his breath on a resigned sigh.

Iain tensed, and waited.

Though, in truth, his brother's sigh, followed by a brief glance at the raftered ceiling, proved eloquent enough.

"I want you gone before daybreak," Donall said, his voice surprisingly soft for such harsh words. "On your journey to Perthshire, you shall draw halt at every sacred place you happen upon. Be it holy well or tree, stone cross or martyr's shrine, you are to prostrate yourself and pray to be purged of your temper."

"And you've charged MacFie with assuring I do?"

Donall gave him a tight-lipped nod.

The MacFie's face turned near the same shade of red as his unruly hair.

Cruel and swift, comprehension swept aside all remaining vestiges of Iain's befuddlement. He stared at his brother—now every inch his laird—the glimmer of regret in Donall's dark eyes smiting him more than aught else.

"Is that all?" he managed, his voice blessedly void of emotion.

Donall lifted a hand, and for the space of a heartbeat, Iain half expected him to reach for him, mayhap clasp him to his breast in a gesture of brotherly camaraderie—something he could have sorely used—but Donall lowered the hand as quickly.

"There is more, aye," he admitted, the words thick and choked-sounding . . . as if dredged from the most desolate corner of his soul.

Iain waited, his defenses already throwing up shields.

"Christ God, but I loathe that we've come to this," Donall vowed, his lairdly reserve breaking. A shudder ran the length of him, and when it had passed, he was once again all chief, his face expressionless.

He cleared his throat. "As the first rains of spring come gently, then gradually build to a steady, lashing downpour, so have we suffered your increasing foulness of mood"—he paused to draw a breath—"You must now brave the fury of the storm you've called upon yourself."

Iain braced himself and hoped no one else heard the roar of his blood, the wild knocking of his heart.

"You, Iain, younger son of the great house of MacLean, shall ne'er again set foot on Doon lest you adequately master your temper," Donall declared, his voice rife with finality. "As I and the Council of Elders have decided, so be it."

So be it.

Hours later, long after moonrise, the words still echoed in Iain's splitting head, and much to his annoyance, his every attempt to outstrip them proved a fool's exercise in futility.

The devil himself couldn't craft a more fruitless pursuit.

Nor one so maddening.

Salt wind whipping his hair and stinging his eyes, he spurred his shaggy-coated garron down Doon's wee strip of a boat strand. Faster and faster he rode, streaking past thatch-roofed fisher cottages and sailing over any impediments daring to rise in his path.

And still the shame of his banishment held pace with him, its black portent pounding through him in macabre rhythm with the drumming clatter of his horse's hooves on the pebbled beach.

Ne'er again set foot . . .

Iain frowned, a fresh tide of anger washing over him, his fiercest scowl powerless against the pursuing words. They tore after him with the persistence of sleuth-hounds fast on a scent.

Equally persistent, and even more troubling, came the uneasy sensation of being watched.

Observed by unseen eyes, his progress along the moon-silvered beach more than well noted and not by the auburn-headed lout riding so annoyingly close beside him.

Blinking against the lashing wind, Iain risked a glance

at his brother's friend—now his guardian—half-expecting, nay, hoping, to find the knave's hazel-eyed perusal fixed on him.

But Gavin MacFie appeared wholly concentrated on matching Iain's reckless pace whilst skirting, or jumping his own garron over the many upturned skiffs and coracles scattered about the narrow, crescent-shaped beach.

If anything, the easy-mannered oaf seemed intent on *not* looking at him.

But someone—or something—was. He could feel it in the chills rippling up and down his spine, the ill ease seeping into his bones.

And whoe'er, or whate'er it was, probed relentlessly.

The sensation sent a maelstrom of icy shivers speeding over his nerve endings and deeper: unholy tingles twisting through him in search of a chink in his armor, a way past his barriers for a glimpse at his soul.

His heart.

An organ so withered and forsaken, even he didn't care to examine its depths.

Warier by the moment, Iain shot a quick look at the wind-tossed sweep of the curving bay where full two score of MacLean galleys rocked at their moorings.

Their sails neatly furled, the single masts and up-thrusting sterns and prows made black silhouettes against the pearl gray sky. Each warship banked twenty-six oars, though a few boasted forty, and one or two only had sixteen.

Swift and feared at sea, this clear and windy night the galleys lay impotent and silent, their rocking slumber guarded by the enclosing headlands, the lot of them at peace . . . save one.

His brother's prized birlinn, a sleek twenty-six-oared beauty, the pearl of the fleet, waited patiently for Iain. Already drawn halfway onto the strand, seamen swarmed all over and around it, busily preparing for a hasty departure.

A knot of dark-frowning crewmen struggled with two packhorses, their attempts at cajoling the poor beasts into stepping over the vessel's low-slung side reaping little more from the frightened animals than white-eyed snorts of protest.

Humblies, full-bearded and naked of chest, stood waist deep in the foaming surf, the open sea behind them, each man ready to hurl his all into pushing the birlinn into the deeper, wider waters. Others, seasoned MacLean seamen, bustled about on board, clearly eager for the shipmaster's order to raise the great square sail.

But Iain scarce noticed the scrambling men, hardly heard their shouts and chants . . . and took even less heed of someone's repetitive beating on a metal-studded targe. His gut clenching, he focused on the ship's long row of vacant-eyed oarports.

Every last one of them seemed to bore holes straight into him.

Disquieting stares, accusing and cold, but by no means penetrating.

Nay, *that* particular nuisance came from a much greater distance than the soon-to-be-launched birlinn.

That much he knew.

Cursing beneath his breath, he dug in his heels, urging his mount into a full gallop, but the instant his beast obliged, surging forward in a great burst of speed, *it* found the sought-after chink.

A wee but patently vulnerable fissure in his heart, a crack narrower than a hairbreadth, but a weak spot all the same, and so well hidden he would've ne'er believed it existed.

But it did, and all his senses roared with the knowledge, the impact loosing a fresh tide of the strange tingles.

Tingles no longer cold and menacing, but fluid and warm.

Heated and beguiling.

And spilling unchecked into long-neglected areas of his body, the prickly sensation now a stunningly golden warmth. Dangerously seductive, and spiraling round his nether parts . . . much like a woman's gently curling fingers.

Nay, more like the swirling tongue of a well-skilled temptress.

A very well-skilled temptress.

"Dia!" Iain near shot off his saddle, his maleness set afire, tightening in immediate and direst response to the exhilarating waves of tingling heat whirling across and through his groin.

He did slip, lurching crazily to the left and almost losing his seat.

"Before you!" Gavin MacFie cried, his shout slicing through the madness.

The spell shattered, Iain grabbed his saddlebow, righting himself just in time to hurtle round a looming mound of broken creels and barnacle-encrusted drying nets.

Barreling up beside him, Gavin seized his reins, jerking Iain's steed to a skittering halt. "Have you run mad?"

he panted, his eyes wide, his face pale beneath his freckles. "You near plowed straight into that stinking pile."

Iain only stared at him, his hands clutching the saddlebow so tightly his knuckles gleamed white. He couldn't have answered if his life depended on it ... his throat had completely closed and his mouth felt drier than cold ash, his tongue withered and more useless than the tarse he'd believed good for naught but relieving himself.

Aye, I've run mad he wanted to shout, his inability to do so vexing beyond belief.

He'd run full mad and then some, for the golden warmth that had sluiced through him with such a vengeance had done more than stir his long cold vitals ... it had begun to melt the outermost edges of his heart.

Yanking back his horse's reins, he stared up at the heavens, utter turmoil whirling through him, the last aftertremors of the strange, crackling heat still rippling the length of him, curling through his limbs.

He blew out an agitated breath, indulged himself by tossing a glower at Gavin.

How could he 'lose his hotheadedness' when he might well have lost his mind?

His quandary heavy on his shoulders, he kicked the sides of his still-heaving mount and, leaving MacFie to follow or nay, spurred down the remaining stretch of beach, the familiar cold already stretching its icy fingers back round his sorry excuse for a heart.

And several nights later, as his brother's well-manned birlinn sped him across the silver-glinting waters of the

Hebridean Sea, a wholly different kind of cold plagued Madeline Drummond.

Many miles distant, she tossed and moaned in a fitful sleep. The best she could hope for in the dubious shelter of an abandoned cot-house. Fist-sized chinks in the walls bid entry to the knifing wind, while the cold damp of the earthen floor seeped with ease through her borrowed cloak.

Beneath two nubby-wooled plaids, Nella's generous warmth pressed protectively against her, but even that well-meant comfort failed to banish the chill.

Nor ease the darkness of the anguished heart hammering so fiercely in her breast . . . a heart not her own, but clinging to hers in need. As it had done each night since she and Nella had left Abercairn.

'Twas a strong-pounding heart, a man's, and a *good* one.

Just badly damaged and in direst need of repair.

The succor of light and warmth.

Another blast of icy wind whistled through the gaps in the wall, sending more shivers down Madeline's spine, a fresh bout of gooseflesh across her chilled skin. But neither the cold nor her troubled dreams kept her heart from reaching for the pained one seeking such desperate union with hers.

So as she slumbered, even long after the blustery night had calmed, some needy part of her own deepest self sent the shadowy man of her dreams all the golden heat and brightness she could summon.

And hoped upon hope that if good fortune hadn't abandoned her completely, one of these nights she'd reach him.

Chapter Three

"ALMS! FOR THE SAKE OF good St. Kentigern, have mercy!"

The raised voices of the wretched grated on Iain's ears as, a fortnight later, he swung down from his garron before the crowded steps of the west entrance to Glasgow Cathedral.

Scowling, he tossed his horse's reins to one of the two young but well-muscled seamen his brother had deigned to send with him, and tried in vain to close his nose to the foul reek all around him.

Quarreling dogs and the cries of peddlers behind their market stalls added to the general confusion, while the smells of raw meat, ale, and new bread blended with the stench of the slow-moving torrent of humanity, the whole proving a malodorous blight against the day's brilliant sunshine and cloudless skies.

A strong gust of wind whipped at his cloak, the brisk kind of wind that would have been clean and fresh if blowing across the rolling moorlands of his Hebridean home, but here . . .

Shuddering, he set his jaw and silently cursed the need to inhale. Ne'er had he seen such an assemblage of miserables. Naught he'd encountered thus far had prepared him for the teeming mass of the luckless pressing into the cathedral.

Each hapless soul, worthy or unworthy, crept, crawled, or limped forward, a motley gathering of cure seekers eager to perform devotions at the saint's tomb.

All hoping for a miracle.

Or a dole.

An old man hobbling along on one leg blundered past him, a dark swarm of humming flies buzzing about open sores on the unfortunate's arms and neck. Bile rising in his throat, Iain leapt out of the man's way only to find himself jostled by filth-encrusted children and a gaggle of witless women. Mumbling disjointed prayers and nonsense, they trailed after a young lass with a withered arm and a face cruelly marred by the pox.

Half-afraid of losing what scant victuals he'd imbibed that morn, he scanned the full-packed closes and wynds opening off the crowded High Street, desperately searching for a swift escape route and finding none.

Lest he wished to scale the well-guarded walls of the nearby canons' manses and risk a wild dash through their sequestered gardens. Frowning, Iain cast aside the notion as quickly as it had come.

Any such action would only give MacFie a new scandal to report to his brother.

Nay, flight would not prove easy.

Still, a fierce instinct for self-preservation drove him to dig in his heels and keep looking. Sadly, to his great regret, he saw only chaos.

Monks and friars milled about, selflessly lending what aid they could to the lame and the needy, their well-meant efforts repeatedly hindered by scamps and charlatans faking the direst ailments in hopes of an obol.

Some of these latter even writhed on the cobbled pavement, the bubbling foam on their lips smelling more like sharp-scented soap than the froth of the truly diseased.

Iain pressed the back of his hand against his mouth and nostrils. Very soon, *he* would be diseased—sorely afflicted of stark, raving madness—if he didn't find an immediate way to procure himself out of this stinking sea of calamities and cutthroats.

"Nay, nay, nay. A thousand times nay." Bracing his legs in a defiant posture, he folded his arms and leveled his most resolute stare—one of firm refusal—at Gavin MacFie. "A score of mean-tempered, whip-wielding fishwives couldn't persuade me to take another step. And I care not a merry whit what you report to Donall, nor how blessed the good St. Kenti—"

"Your brother laid particular worth on your paying proper homage to St. Kentigern," Gavin cut him off, his voice infuriatingly smooth. With a show of determination every bit as hard-bitten as Iain's, he slanted a telling glance at the second young seaman . . . the one guarding the two sumpter beasts and their precious cargo.

The one who, though a mite lack-witted, stood a few inches taller than the good-sized MacFie himself—and packed more muscled might in his wee finger than Iain's, Donall's, and Gavin's irrefutable brawn combined.

"The choice is yours, my friend." Gavin watched him, his usually sunny face set in solemn lines.

Slowly stretching his arms above his head, he cracked

his knuckles . . . and had the poor taste to appear as at ease as if they stood in the middle of the sweetest spring meadow, and not elbow to elbow with the unwashed, unkempt, and diseased. "Go peaceably as befits your station and your purpose here, or . . ." He lifted broad-set shoulders, the simple gesture more eloquent than any further threats.

Spoken or unspoken.

Iain glowered at him, then slid a furious look at the seaman, secretly suspecting MacFie of feeding the mucker sweetmeats or mayhap wide-legged lasses just so the oversized lout would e'er do his bidding.

And do it unquestioningly.

Too vexed to concede—yet—Iain squared *his* wide-set shoulders and drew himself to his full height . . . an imposing tallness all but a scant hairbreadth short of Gavin's own. "I am your laird's brother," he declared, trying to lay authority into the words. "Save Amicia, his closest kin."

"You are doing penance," Gavin returned with an all but imperceptible nod at the well-muscled giant.

The young seaman stepped closer.

Heat inching up the back of his neck, Iain ignored the implied threat and narrowed his eyes at his unsmiling companion. *His gaoler.* "You wouldn't dare."

Silence answered him.

"You would."

Gavin cocked an impervious brow. "If you leave me no other choice, aye."

For a long tension-filled moment, Iain pressed his lips together, frustration, hot and seething, coursing through his veins. "Then lead on," he ground out at last, with a quick upward glance at the impossibly blue sky. "*If* you can plow a way inside."

Looking confident enough to forge a path through a wall of granite if need be, Gavin MacFie strode off for the cathedral steps, every pilgrim, pious or otherwise, springing out of his way. Like lemmings fleeing a rat catcher.

Iain stared after him, opening and closing his fists in mute objection before he grudgingly forced himself to follow. "Drones and parasites," he muttered beneath his breath of the jostling mob. "Ply your wares elsewhere," he snapped at a greasy-haired bawd who'd loomed up from nowhere to block his path and rub her breasts against his arm. "I've no interest."

Biting back a harsher rebuttal, he jerked free of her clinging hands, readjusted the fall of the woolen pilgrim's cloak slung loosely about his shoulders . . . and wished the almost-gone knot on his forehead hadn't chosen that moment to start aching again.

His vexation now complete, he searched for, but caught no glimpse of Gavin MacFie's shaggy-maned head. Iain frowned. Without doubt, the long-strided varlet was already on his knees before the shrine.

Very likely praying for new and inspiring ways to bedevil one Iain MacLean.

Eager to have done with the whole sordid business, he started forward again, but each step proved a gruel. For his ill ease mounted in alarming degrees the nearer he came to the cathedral's great arched entrance.

'Twas the most unpleasant of sensations, and one that had naught to do with his splitting head, his wrath at MacFie, or his patent dislike of smelly places.

Something was staring at him again.

And might St. Kentigern and his host of holy cohorts preserve him, for the strange tingles were upon him, too . . . descending with a vengeance to whirl all through him, and igniting a firestorm of most unwelcome bestirrings in his vitals.

The same odd pricklings that had beset him so oft of late. Heated, and not entirely unpleasant . . . just undesired.

And whate'er unleashed them waited for him inside the hallowed depths of Glasgow Cathedral.

That he knew.

The queer tightening in his chest and the fierce pounding of his heart told him so.

For the third time since entering Glasgow Cathedral that same morning, Madeline Drummond tried her best to examine the jumble of ex-votos, crutches, and other assorted paraphernalia of the sick and needy adorning the elaborate metal gates enclosing the raised sepulcher of St. Kentigern.

Countless lit tapers threw flickering golden light across richly carved reredos panels and into the shrine itself, but the brightly painted columns supporting the tomb's vaulted canopy cast inky bands of shadows across the votive-hung gates, making many of the offerings indiscernible.

More frustrating still, and again for the third time, a sharp-eyed sacrist thwarted her attempt to slip out of the slow-moving line of pilgrims and edge nearer to the tomb's well-guarded enclosure.

"Ho, sisters, keep to the prescribed processional route," he admonished, just as she and Nella of the Marsh completed yet another tedious round of pilgrimage stations and reapproached the feretory bay behind the high altar.

Particularly harried-looking, the pallid young man trailed after her, shooing her along with his pasty white hands. "Good maid, might I suggest you return in winter—on St. Kentigern's feast day when we open the shrine—if you are so desirous of a closer look?"

Agitation beginning to heat her cheeks, Madeline resisted the urge to argue with him. The sacrist's haughty tone made her sorely regret her postulant garb and the limitations it put on her tongue.

Casting her gaze to the stone-flagged floor as a true sister-in-waiting would have done, she swallowed her annoyance and moved on with naught but a humble nod. "Faith, but I weary of this," she bemoaned to Nella as, a short distance from the tomb, they paused to genuflect before a side altar. "Pinched-face stick of a man! *He* shall be remembered without charity."

"Shhhh . . ." Nella reached for her hand, squeezed it. "The postulant's robe will fool no one if they hear you brandishing the peppered end of your tongue. He doesn't ken your true purpose and only sought to—"

"I don't care a toad's behind what his intent was, how many saints' bones he can produce, and even less when they are to be put on display. I only—" She quickly snapped shut her mouth and assumed a suitably devout expression as a pult of psalm-chanting monks hushed past. "'Tis Silver Leg's wee trinkets I seek and naught else," she blurted the instant the cowled brethren slipped from hearing range. "That, and to see my stomach cease churning."

"Your stomach?

"Nay, the freckles on my nose."

Nella shot her a reproachful look. Leaning close, she whispered, "I believe I may have glimpsed one of Sir Bernhard's little silver leg votives the last time we passed the shrine. I—"

"Are you certain?" Madeline almost forgot the discomfort roiling through her belly. "Where was it?"

"Hanging from the gate enclosure on the east side of the shrine, fairly close to the floor. I spotted it just when the sacrist made us move on. I cannot say for a surety, though. It was half-hidden behind the larger cast of a real-looking foot."

Excitement shot through Madeline, joining the tumult of strange emotions whirling inside her ever since they'd left the last side altar. "Why did you not tell me sooner?"

"Because I did not want to disappoint you, my lady." Nella's brow creased as she peered at Madeline. "I wanted to wait until I'd seen it again, and was certain."

Wrapping her arms around her waist, Madeline dug her fingers into the rough-spun wool of her borrowed cloak. Someone else's revulsion, anger, and boundless frustration filled her breast to such a degree she could scarce breathe, much less continue upright down the crowded side aisle.

She swallowed hard, fighting to ignore the sensations. "Can you find it again?" she managed, straining to keep her voice steady.

Ever attuned to Madeline's moods, Nella's gaze turned sharp, but she nodded.

"Then let us make haste," Madeline urged her friend,

barely able to get out the words, for her own heart had begun to thunder out of control.

Hurrying, she stumbled on an uneven flag in the stone flooring, barely catching herself before the roaring pulse in her ears welled to epic proportions . . . as did the wealth of love swelling the stranger's heart.

Nay, *his heart*—her shadow man's—and the sudden recognition nearly brought her to her knees, for his emotions no longer came to her from a great distance.

He was here.

Within the cathedral walls.

And nearing her by the minute.

His heart pounding ever stronger, hers skittering wildly out of beat. Forcing herself to keep placing one foot before the other, she moved onward. Praise be they'd almost reached the shrine again.

It was one thing to wax romantic about a man's depth of feeling—his capacity to love—and send him light and warmth in her dreams, and something else entirely to stand before him.

To face him.

In especial, *now,* when she'd committed herself to an undertaking the successful outcome of which condemned her to ruin and a life of piety behind cloistered walls.

A rush of heat suddenly pricking the backs of her eyes, she grabbed Nella's hand. "Come, let us look for the ex-voto and be gone from here," she implored, already pushing forward, dragging her friend through the crowd.

In as much a miracle as those wrought by sacred relics, the little band of hawk-eyed sacrists had all hands full assisting a pilgrim who'd fallen into a state of writhing blessedness on the far side of the feretory.

Seizing the opportunity, Madeline hurried to the spot Nella indicated, dropping to her knees in front of the tomb enclosure before propriety or watchful sacrists could stop her. Near-crazed by the intensity of the emotions spinning in her breast, she thrust her hands into the cluster of offerings hanging from the metal-wrought gates.

And the instant her fingers curled around the little silver-cast leg, *his voice* joined the chaos, filling her head and heart as surely as he would have filled her ears had he truly spoken the words.

A beggary votive thief! A postulant and a cutpurse.

Madeline shot to her feet, the swift movement, or mayhap her shame, shattering his hold on her, the wild racing of her heart now truly hers alone, the panic inside her no one's but her own.

Forgetting Nella, the sacrists, and the wee silver leg pressing icy-cold against her dampening palm, she hitched up her skirts with her free hand and searched for the surest place to push through the solid-packed, prayer-murmuring throng.

Half-afraid her knees would buckle before she could get away, she tried to block her shadow man's voice, but it slid through her, its rich timbre every bit as deep, husky, and beautiful as she'd known it would be.

Unbearably seductive and maddeningly distracting, it imprinted itself on the very fabric of her heart, doing the strangest things to her senses, and fully muddling her ability to think.

Beggary. A cutpurse.

Her breath came fast and shallow and she scarce heard

the words . . . only the golden warmth of his mellifluous voice.

"A sticky-fingered postulant." The words slipped from Iain's lips, though how they had, he scarce knew, for his jaw had to be brushing the cold stone of the cathedral floor.

His astonishment complete, he stared at the plain-frocked, travel-stained lass—the very one he'd just identified as *it*—as *she*.

The source of his weeks of discomfiture.

The reason every fiber of his being had inexplicably tightened, his loins all afire and setting like stone, the nearer he'd come to the cathedral.

To her.

A would-be nun and votive thief!

Iain stared at her, too stunned by the unlikelihood of his discovery, the immeasurable intensity of his heart-pounding reaction to her proximity, to draw breath, much less step forward and challenge her to hand over the wee whate'er-it-was he'd just witnessed her pluck from a cluster of ex-voto offerings affixed to the gates of St. Kentigern's shrine.

Nay, stricken as he was by his unaccountable reaction, he stood wholly flummoxed—in truth, fully *undone*—and hoped none of the wild and base urges thundering through him showed on his face.

His honor, tarnished though it might be, forbade even one such as he to flaunt carnal lust in the presence of priests and the pious.

And his pride, sore-battered or nay, cringed at the lustful urges inspired by the lamentably unattractive lass.

He hadn't been *that* long without a woman.

Then she whirled his way, her snatched treasure clutched in a fisted hand pressed against fine, high-set breasts, and Iain's heart swelled to bursting. Truth to tell, it slammed so hard against his ribs, the shock near felled him.

He'd erred greatly in assuming her plain.

Light green eyes, huge and panic-filled, locked with his, for a split second widening even more, their gold-flecked depths mirroring something uncannily like recognition—as if she, too, reeled from the crackling attraction sizzling between them.

A single curling strand of glossy copper-gold hair slipped from beneath the cowl of her cloak, tumbling over her left eye before coming to rest against the sweet curve of her cheek. Looking more like a startled doe than a brazen-hearted relic thief, she blinked, moistening lips he would have claimed in a heartbeat if only he'd glimpsed them when his honor had been intact . . . his life his own and unsullied.

She drew a deep breath, and her breasts, well-rounded and full, rose beneath her cloak, its travel-worn folds emphasizing rather than disguising their lushness.

Though he would ne'er have owned it possible, Iain's body tightened even more. His throat closed at once, his mouth going so dry he couldn't even give himself the paltry relief of wetting his lips.

Bitter regret swept through him, washing away his lust and replacing it with an emptiness so all-consuming its bite hurt worse than the cutting edges of a dozen wickedly honed blades.

In another eerie echo of his own shackled longing, a look of deepest anguish flashed across her beautifully expressive face, then she was gone—bolting through a sudden break in the throng, and taking the whole of his heart with her.

His MacLean heart.

The selfsame one he'd thought had withered and died but now knew had only ne'er been truly wakened.

Not by his late wife, Lileas, the saints bless her sweet-natured soul, and not by any other lass e'er to cross his path or share his bed.

Adrift in a roiling sea of disbelief and a glaring truth he could no longer deny, Iain squeezed shut his eyes and, lifting a none-too-steady hand, kneaded the back of his hot, aching neck. Several long moments later, when he reopened his eyes, they looked out on a different place.

A new world, and one through which he'd have to tread across very rough ground, for one of his staunchest beliefs had just been soundly toppled.

He, Iain MacLean, younger son of the great House of MacLean, master of nothing, and sometimes dubbed Iain the Doubter, could ne'er again scoff at the notion of MacLean men being fated to love, truly love, only one woman.

The legend wasn't just a *sennachie's* tale to be told round the peat fires of long and dark winter nights.

The legend was true.

He now knew it with a certainty that resonated with every thudding beat of his heart, every ragged breath he drew, for *his one woman*—a votive thief and a postulant—had just looked him full square in the eye.

And the repercussions of having to admit it ripped him to pieces.

*   *   *

A few scant hours later, but far removed from the splendor of Glasgow Cathedral, a darker, more ancient kind of magic than saintly relics and plainsong brought a smile to old Devorgilla's lips.

Cozily ensconced within the thick, whitewashed walls of her thatched cottage, Doon's resident crone hummed a merry, if slightly off-key, tune as she peered closely at her precious assortment of Fairy Fire Stones.

A sizable collection, the charmed stones nearly filled a large wooden bowl she kept on the little oaken table near her hearth. And although all the stones possessed their own immeasurable value, only two held her rapt attention.

His stone—Iain MacLean's—and his lady's.

His *new* lady's.

The lass meant for him since time beyond mind.

Clucking her tongue, the crone shook her grizzled head. Much grief would ne'er have come to pass had not men, with their fool meddlings into things best left alone, procured Iain the Doubter a political marriage to benefit the clan rather than the needs of his own braw heart.

For sweet-natured and comely as Lileas MacInnes had been, she wasn't *The One*.

And none of the powers-that-be at the time had heeded Devorgilla's discreet reminders of the MacLean Bane, the Legend. Neither Iain's late father, nor his Council of Elders. Nary a one of the better-knowing graybeards had listened to her.

Even her more dire warnings had fallen on deaf ears.

There'd even been threats to banish her from Doon if she didn't cease what they called her foolish prattle.

Her brow furrowing at their benightedness, the crone

banished the lot of them to the farthest reaches of her mind. Greater powers than hers would be needed to undo ill-made choices of the past.

A wiser move would be to help along the future.

To that end, the *cailleach* curled knobby-knuckled fingers around the edge of the wooden bowl and dragged it across the table's rough-planked surface until it rested at the very edge.

Leaning forward, she brought her wizened face to within inches of the bowl.

Just to be certain her eyes hadn't deceived her.

They hadn't.

Both stones, smooth and glistening Highland quartz, glowed with a finer luminosity than e'er before.

Not yet the blinding brilliance she was hoping for, but with a goodly portion more shine and inner fire than she'd expected to see this day. And they vibrated . . . Devorgilla even fancied a faint humming sound came from deep within their pulsing depths.

At once, sheerest pleasure stole over her. The giddy, breathless kind better suited to starry-eyed young lasses with all their days yet stretching before them.

But a gladness warm enough to do her bent frame a world of good nonetheless. And with no one but her napping grandson, Lugh, and her tricolored cat, Mab, to see her lapse of dignity, she gave an uninhibited cackle of delight and clapped gnarled hands in glee.

Indulging herself, she touched a fingertip first to *her* stone, then to his. For, at long last, the male stone had lost some of its chilly blue tint, and like the female stone, now showed a slowly spreading point of pulsating reddish gold at its core.

Equally telling, its flawless surface warmed her finger.

More than satisfied, the crone lifted her hand away from the bowl and straightened, for once not cringing at the creaks and pops of her aged bones.

Then, assuming a more suitably solemn mien, she recited the *spelling* words. "One be you, and one be she. When your lady's heart catches fire, you will recognize her."

At once, and for the first time ever, the wee glow deep inside the female stone seemed to first contract, then burst, spindly rays of bright red-gold shooting outward, some even reaching the very edges of the stone before retracting.

An erupting firestorm by no means, but enough.

The time had come, and they'd met.

There could be no denying it, for Fairy Fire Stones always spoke the truth.

Blinking hard, for a good *cailleach* ne'er shed a tear, Devorgilla patted her wiry white hair and allowed herself a trembly-lipped smile.

Her magic was working.

Iain the Doubter was a doubter no more.

Chapter Four

"GOD'S GOOD MERCY, BUT I cannot take another step." Her cheeks pink with exertion, Nella of the Marsh flung herself onto the grassy bank of the fast-moving Molendinar Burn. Breathing heavy enough to flood Madeline with guilt, she glanced over her shoulder at the whin and broom-studded abbey hill rising steeply behind her. "Will not take another step," she amended. "My feet would rise in rebellion should I even try."

"My apologies," Madeline offered, lifting her hands. "We will pause here until you've caught your breath. A rest will surely favor us both."

"I am fine. 'Tis you causing me worry," Nella panted, tugging off her calfskin brogans. "Grand or nay, my lady, a shrine holds naught but the dust of old bones," she declared, rolling down her stockings.

She turned a keen eye on Madeline. "Do you wish to speak of the reason for such an ignominious flight?"

"Nay." The swift denial drew a frown.

And before Nella could read even more into her hasty retreat from St. Kentigern's tomb and her wild dash down the sloping braeside, Madeline fixed her gaze on the thick growth of birch and juniper scrub edging the riverbank.

Tendered explanations could wait until her heart ceased hammering and her blood cooled.

If such were even possible.

Another wave of frustration began heating its way up her neck, so she swatted at the little bits of twigs and bracken clinging to her cloak ... tenacious flotsam to remind her of her foolhardy flight and the futility of expecting the tension thrumming inside her to ease.

A thousand tomorrows wouldn't suffice for such a wonder.

Not unless her shadow man's mellifluous voice relinquished its hold on her, ceased spooling its richly timbred warmth so seductively round her heart.

"I' faith!" She sniffed, her patience with herself near flown. Half-convinced some snag-toothed witch-wife had charmed her—and on *his* behalf—she gave her skirts a vigorous shake, but the twigs and bracken remained. They clung to her just as stubbornly as the tall, powerfully built pilgrim lingered in the periphery of her mind.

Nay, lingered everywhere, for his darkly handsome face seemed to hover in the leafy green shadows of the burnside copse, his haunted eyes, a rich peaty brown, beguiling her from the shelter of the trees.

Holding her fast in his golden-voiced spell, and as firmly as if he'd strode right up to her, closed strong fingers upon her chin, and simply let the smolder in his eyes compel her to his will.

Madeline swallowed, a tingling cascade of shivers rippling her length. Seductively delicious tingles prickling every inch of her ... including her most private places.

Feeling almost besieged, she stared up at the cloud-fleeced sky, bit her lower lip until she tasted blood.

Romanticizing about her shadow man had been . . . sweet.

Proximity to the dark-eyed stranger outside the bounds of her dreams proved dangerously perilous.

Even if she ignored the allure of his strapping build and great height, an inherent aura of power and depth simmered beneath his dark good looks, his intensity speaking to her, and calmly winding its magic around each uncharted corner of her femininity.

Truth to tell, everything about him shouted loud contrast to the shuffle-gaited, staff-clutching pilgrims she'd grown accustomed to seeing on the road.

Her braw shadow man—for he could be no other—proved unlike any man she'd e'er seen anywhere.

Pilgrim, common man, or lordling.

And that knowledge sank her heart, for ne'er had there been a darker hour for a man to stir her interest . . . make her burn to see him again.

Closing her eyes, she took a deep, cleansing breath of the cool, damp air. And another and another, until she'd filled her lungs to bursting with the pungent scents of gorse, pine, and rushing water.

But such measures helped not a whit.

All the clean woodsy air in Scotland wouldn't be enough to wash away the desperate yearning he'd ignited inside her. A profound need, deep beyond measure, raged through her like an all-consuming firestorm, and once awakened, she feared nothing would quell her thirst to taste the kind of fierce, undying love carved so indelibly into the walls of his heart.

Her own heart twisted with impossible longing.

She'd *felt* the boundless wealth of his emotion, its pounding intensity near bruising her ribs as, night after night, her accursed abilities delivered him into her dreams, revealing not just his pain but his never-to-be-severed bond with one single woman.

A faceless female he cherished beyond measure, and who now bore Madeline's mounting resentment because for one cast-her-cares-to-the-wind moment she envied that woman.

Wanted to be she.

And so fervently her insides tightened with a winding, relentless ache, sheerest need spiraling from the top of her head to the tips of her toes and back again.

"You've gone pale, my lady, and you tremble." Nella's concerned voice rose above the sound of the burn's rushing waters. "A plague on moldy relics and mumbling monks if sharing the air with such exalteds taxes you so."

Madeline blinked, the pilgrim's sway over her vanishing at once, his bonnie face fading from the shadows until only the hard thumping of her heart remained.

A bruised heart turned topsy-turvy, and the unsettling sense of something infinitely dear and precious spinning out of reach.

"I would not run from a whole phalanx of pasty-faced church worthies," she huffed, dusting her skirts again, the true reason for her distress tucked securely in her heart. "Nor do moldering bones frighten me. Saintly or otherwise."

Nella looked skeptical. "Then did the pain of some piteously cursed miracle seeker drive you to flee the cathedral?" She peered at Madeline from the shallows of the burn, her skirts hitched above the white-foaming water, her hazel eyes alight with keen interest. "Surely Madeline of Abercairn would not—"

"The Lady of Abercairn is no more," Madeline said, examining her broken fingernails. "She was extirpated on the same blazing pyre that now holds my father's ashes. His, and those of innocents whose sole crime was being too young to defend themselves against the killing swords of a turncoat Scotsman and the marauders who follow him."

A wholly different kind of passion—dark and roiling—swept her. But its heat strengthened her, too, allowing her to straighten her back and lock away her grief. Her anger. Clenching her hands to tight fists, she bolted every hurting ounce of pain into the most inaccessible corner of her mind.

Her father's honor, and her purpose, would be better served if delivered with a cooled temper and a steady hand.

She opened her mouth to remind Nella—and herself—of the purpose of their journey, but a loudly trilling curlew swooped out of nowhere, near clipping her head in its swift ascent to the rowans lining the abbey hill.

Almost a hedge, the red-berried trees flanked the buttressed wall of the Bishop's Palace, while behind it, the cathedral's bulk loomed proud and grand, its pointy spires piercing the sky, and soaring taller than the palace's loftiest turrets.

Madeline's gut clenched at the sight.

Had she truly burst through the palace gates, dodging the bishop's own guardsmen, and giving poor Nella no choice but to tear after her? Had they really careened through orchards and herb gardens, sprinting past startled lay brothers, and clambering over walls and other obstacles like common riffraff?

Like beggary thieves?

Aye, they had, and the truth of it blasted heat onto her cheeks and lay like a cold, hard clump in the pit of her belly.

Shuddering, she leveled her most resolute look at Nella. "Do not speak of 'the Lady of Abercairn' again."

Nella snorted, her brows shooting heavenward. "If the Lady of Abercairn is no more, then who was in such a fine ferment o'er a certain pinched-faced sacrist not so long ago?"

"Oh, bother!" Madeline blew out a gusty breath and eyed the swift-moving burn. A wade in its icy waters would cool more than her aching feet. "Certes, I am still . . . me," she capitulated, struggling to yank off her right boot. "I fled because . . . ." she paused to catch her balance. "It . . . it was him again."

Nella's eyes rounded. "Your shadow man?"

"Aye." The boot came free. "And more powerful than e'er before," she added, pleased when her left boot slipped off without a fight. "Between his emotions welling inside me and the hawk-eyed sacrists crowding our every step, I could scarce draw breath."

"In mercy's name," Nella breathed, tucking a damp-frizzled lock of red-brown hair behind her ear. "Now I see, my lady."

I pray you do not, Madeline almost blurted.

She didn't want Nella to see, wasn't quite ready to reveal she'd actually glimpsed the man.

Or risk having her friend guess the smooth richness of

his voice had spelled her ... especially when the few words he'd uttered had been anything but flattering.

For a very brief moment, other unflattering words, other masculine slurs echoed in her mind. Scornful voices expressing what they truly thought of her and why they'd come to Abercairn seeking her hand.

Cruelties she'd suffered repeatedly o'er the years, hearing them not with her physical ear but with her heart, thanks to her unusual talent ... a plaguey gift surely bestowed on her by the devil himself.

The taunts, uttered by past suitors, still cut deep enough to send waves of emptiness and cold regret tearing through her.

Breasts resembling the udders of a milk cow, one marriage candidate had scoffed.

Hair so glaring a red, gazing upon it would blind a man, another insisted, incensing her further by declaring her curls too unruly for even an iron-tined comb to address its tangle-prone masses.

Lips as wide as the River Tay.

And most mortifying of all: passable enough to bed if a man simply dwelt on the depth of her sire's pockets.

One by one, they'd crushed her confidence and stomped without mercy over her femininity until she'd wanted naught but to be left alone ... perhaps even to seek the solitude and blessed peace of a veiled life.

And now, for good or nay, she must.

Madeline blinked, furious at how deeply her shoulders had dipped upon recalling the slurs, discomfited more to discover Nella's sharp, perceptive stare on her.

"You were not meant for cloistered life, my lady," the other woman commented with all the quiet confidence

Madeline lacked, and so admired in her well-loved friend.

"Nay, verily I was not," Madeline agreed, her gaze on a long series of splashing rapids. "Nor is it even close to what I'd once wanted of life."

She sighed, wishing the cascading waters could carry away the remembered barbs.

And her dreams, for recalling them hurt far worse.

Especially now that she'd come face-to-face with the manifestation of those dreams.

She turned back to Nella. "I ne'er wanted aught but to be loved, truly and passionately loved, and for myself," she said, the admission an ache on her tongue. "Not falsely, and not for my father's fine keep and plentiful coffers of gold."

"And you think to find such a man behind cloistered walls?"

"You ken why I shall take the veil," Madeline said, folding her arms tight against her ribs, hugging her waist as she spoke. "And it scarce matters, for a man capable of such loving does not exist except in the songs of bards."

Nella tilted her head. "Or in dreams, my lady?"

"Aye, in dreams, too," Madeline admitted, looking aside.

In dreams . . . or at the sides of the privileged women who held their hearts.

As her shadow man's heart was held.

Wholly and irrevocably, just as hers was inextricably bound to his.

Tied to him by invisible cords of golden silk.

The strange bond leaving her to suffer a dull, throbbing ache for what she intuitively knew could have been so dear if only they'd crossed paths in another time and place.

Unfolding her arms, Madeline pressed her hands against the small of her aching back and heaved a great, weary sigh. Such disturbing notions were best examined later, when she was no longer quite so tired, hungry, and dispirited.

Perhaps after she'd avenged herself on Silver Leg and whiled safe and secure behind the shielding walls of a suitably remote and obscure nunnery.

But even as she shrugged off her cloak and gathered up her skirts to join Nella in the burn's chill waters, a tiny voice somewhere deep inside her laughed aloud at the flimsiness of her intentions.

In a different but not too distant corner of the same teeming bishop's burgh, frustration gnawed on Iain's dwindling patience with ever-increasing vigor. Gritting his teeth, he wished himself anywhere but in the midst of the noisome, tight-packed throng pressing through the arched pend of Glasgow's busy Trongate.

A stench of unidentifiable foulness clung to the crowd, the unpleasant odor rising up from the jostling wayfarers to hover beneath the low stone-vaulted ceiling. The rank smell soiled the air in the pend as thoroughly as the refuse-strewn cobbles paving its length posed hazards for even the most surefooted Highland garron.

Iain coughed, near choking on the smoke of two pitch-pine torches sputtering wildly in iron-bracketed holders in the middle of the tunnel-like passage. He blinked and dragged the back of his hand across his eyes, the biting sting of the acrid air making them water and burn.

Swinging about, he glared at the shaggy-maned Islesman riding close behind him. "By the mercy of God," he said through tight lips, "let us be far from here by nightfall."

The quintessence of calm, Gavin MacFie made no change of expression. "With His good grace, we shall be."

"Be warned, MacFie, for I cannot account for my actions if we are not. I have not the stomach for—" Iain broke off when his garron lost its footing, its iron-shod hooves slip-sliding on the muck-slicked paving.

He should have iron-shod nerves!

Biting back a litany of craven mumblings, he tamped down his vexation long enough to soothe the garron, but the moment the beast calmed, Iain swore.

Just one quick oath, and muttered beneath his breath, but black enough to curl the devil's own toes.

Feeling a wee bit better for letting loose such a prime epithet—and trying not to inhale too deeply—he urged his steed around a large pothole brimming with a particularly vile-smelling liquid.

Vile-smelling, and topped with slime.

Iain grimaced. "Ne'er in all the four corners of the world can I imagine a fouler place," he groused. "Forging a path across a well-slagged peat bog would prove less trying."

"A bairn's work by any comparison," Gavin agreed, his mild tone making subtle mockery of his supposed commiseration.

Iain's tightly held composure at grave risk of unraveling any moment, he drew a leather-wrapped wine sack from within his cloak and helped himself to a healthy swig . . . to wet his parched throat and, if only for a moment, camouflage the reek of the pend's dank, grime-smeared walls.

A blessedly short pend, praise the saints.

But his eyes widened in dismay, his mood worsening the instant he rode through the gatehouse arch. Instead of lashing his mount's sides and putting Glasgow's stench and chaos far behind him, he was forced to rein in, an even greater swell of humanity effectively barring the way.

Slack-jawed, he surveyed the open cobble-paved area abutting the gatehouse, and saw naught but shoving, shouting rabble, litter, and squalor.

Pilgrims, badge- and potion-peddling hawkers, women and children, barking dogs and scurrying pigs hurried about, their incredible number overrunning the streets and clogging the narrow rutted road stretching away toward St. Thenew's Well, a lesser shrine some miles distant, and dedicated to St. Kentigern's mother.

The next station on his journey of penance . . . as prescribed by his brother, and enforced by one Gavin Mac-Fie.

A man who believed himself descended of the seal people, and now Iain's own gaoler.

Iain's brows snapped together.

Selkies!

He had no time for such drivel and nonsense.

Frowning, he shifted uncomfortably in the hard seat of his saddle and seriously considered the merits of throttling the bland-faced varlet.

Sorely tempted, he slid MacFie his darkest glare, but the unfazed lout maintained his placid mien, returning

Iain's stare as calmly as if he scarce noted the cacophonic chaos brewing all around them.

Iain ground his teeth in irritation. If he didn't know better, he'd swear the mild-mannered bastard practiced schooling his features into blank-faced expressions of neutrality.

Without doubt, he swallowed broomsticks to keep his back so straight. Almost unconsciously, Iain squared his shoulders and began straightening his own spine . . . until he caught himself.

Compressing his lips into a taut line, he stared at the pandemonium ahead of him, refusing to further acknowledge the annoyingly even-tempered churl.

Aye, ridding the world of Gavin MacFie was tempting, but with innumerable lackwits, pilgrims, and scoundrels surrounding them, his chances of having done with MacFie and breaking away before his brother's brawny-armed guardsmen set upon him were about as great as one such as he sprouting angel's wings.

Donall's grim-faced henchmen sat their own mounts a scarce lance length away, and on his brother's orders no doubt, the dastards ne'er took their eyes off him, even taking turns tagging along when he went about his most private affairs.

So Iain MacLean, Master of Nothing, heaved a great sigh, swallowed his anger, and turned his mind to matters of more immediate import . . . such as the little silver-legged ex-voto resting in the small leather purse hanging from his waist belt.

Her stolen treasure, plucked off the cathedral steps by the ever-observant MacFie after it had slipped from her fingers when she had bolted into the crowd.

Resting a hand over the pouch, his fingers sought and found the hard outline formed by the votive. It pressed against the soft leather and, pray mercy be his, but his loins began to tighten and twitch even at that dubious connection to the large-eyed lass.

Large-eyed *postulant*, a gleefully malicious voice from his darker side reminded him.

Full-bosomed, sweet-lipped, and every fair inch of her, his . . . if he dared for once trust his instincts.

Nay, his *should-have-been*, his MacLean heart amended.

"The devil himself couldn't brew a greater travesty," *he* muttered, and loud enough for any who cared to turn an ear his way.

Sore beset, he squirmed, the tightening of his male parts besieging all consideration of sticky fingers and nunhood, the unwanted bestirrings a greater nuisance than his aching throat, smarting eyes, and the jammed roadway combined.

Equally perturbing—nay, alarming—he couldn't seem to lift his hand from his leather purse. His fingers stuck fast as if spelled, the image of the little silver-cast leg dancing before his mind's eye, its significance perplexing him.

Abandoning his resolution to ignore MacFie, he slanted a sidelong glance at the bastard. "A question," he began, his voice scratchy from the threads of smoke wafting out of the pend's archway and seeming deliberately to curl past his nose.

"Aye?" Gavin returned, *his* voice smooth as a fresh spring morn.

As casually as he could, Iain voiced his concern. "The

ex-voto the postulant dropped . . . such offerings represent a body part in need of healing, do they not?"

Gavin eyed him strangely, but inclined his head. "So it is believed. Or else whate'er part of the body received a healing, in which case they are tokens of appreciation to the miracle-spending saint."

"Can you think of any other use for such votives?" Iain pressed, his fool hand still affixed to his purse.

"Not in holy places," came Gavin's swift reply.

Iain nodded agreement. He couldn't think of any other use either . . . not wholesome ones anyway.

He swiped at his smoke-stung eyes again, blew out an exasperated breath.

No matter how he turned it, neither of the most logical possibilities fit the lass. Naught on her indicated a troublesome leg. Far from it, the quick glimpse he'd caught of her trim ankles and lower calves as she'd hitched up her skirts to sprint away, bespoke legs of the shapeliest sort.

Lithe, well formed, and bonnie enough to haunt his waking dreams for days.

And make his nights pure torture.

Especially when he wondered if the nest of curls at the juncture of such succulent limbs would prove the same coppery-gold as the single lock of glossy, curling hair he'd seen tumble from beneath her head veil in the Cathedral.

At once, Iain's mouth went bone-dry, a fusillade of lascivious images bombarding him.

Could her lower hair possibly gleam as bright as that one bouncing curl?

Or carry a scent as sweet as the light, heathery one that had teased his senses when she'd sped past him?

Would *those* curls be lush and plentiful? Soft and damp beneath a man's questing fingers?

His fingers—Iain thrust away the thought before it could expand into even more treacherous musings. His misery complete, he yanked his hand from the leather pouch with sheer brute force.

But any relief at winning that small victory proved short-lived when the still-receding lump on his forehead began throbbing with renewed vengeance . . . and in net-tlesome rhythm with the continued pulsing in a much more bothersome part of his body.

The mood of the smelly, shabbily clad masses altered subtly as well, shifting to an affable, almost celebratory air.

Iain slanted another glance at Gavin, then loudly cleared his throat when the other failed to notice him.

"Did you not say St. Thenew's Well was a less-frequented shrine?" He lifted his voice, the whole of his perturbation, every head-splitting throb at his temples coloring his tone. "It would seem she is a larger draw than her son, God rest his sacred bones."

Gavin shrugged. "Some would deem it heartening for a little-known saint to attract such a crowd."

"The pious mayhap, which I am not," Iain snapped, nonetheless praying for the pain in his head to subside, and most especially for the itch in his groin to cease and leave him be. "Nor do I see a shred of piety walking amongst this mob of cutthroats."

A shadow crossed the MacFie's open face, his

renowned patience clearly cracking. "The most are holy men and cure seekers. Have a look about—"

"The holy men and cure seekers I see appear anything but devout." Iain rose in his stirrups, made a great sweeping gesture with his arm. "Burghers on their way to a market fair, is how they look," he said, his gaze lighting on a tall stone cross by the roadside, its age-pitted face carved with Celtic symbols.

The scores of MacFie's pious hurried past the ancient way marker without a single reverent glance.

Iain looked back at Gavin, the explanation for the crush apparent.

"Off to partake of some form of jolly entertainment, they are," he said, quite certain of it. "Hair-shirted humblies hoping for a saint's merciful intervention in their woes? Nay, nay, and another nay."

"Mayhap they rejoice o'er some new wonder recently worked by Thenew," Gavin suggested. "A great miracle that has filled their hearts with hope? It could be."

To Iain's astonishment, an unaccustomed smile began tugging at the corners of his mouth. He glanced about, the underswell of jollity amongst the scurrying throng now almost palpable.

"Shall we see which it is?" he asked of MacFie. "Fair or piety?"

A brief flash of reproach flitted o'er Gavin's freckled face, but Iain ignored it and studied the passersby until he located the most shifty-eyed wayfarer within hearing range.

"Ho, good fellow!" he called to the man, delighting in the way Gavin blanched at his choice.

The weasel-faced wayfarer wheeled around, his darting glance filled with suspicion. "Aye?"

Clearly a man of ill living.

The sort who favored skulking in shadow . . . and peddled useless tinctures at market fair stalls.

Ointments and wonder herbs guaranteed to allay all maladies known to man.

Iain resisted the urge rub his hands together. He did allow his smile to spread a bit. He could feel MacFie's disapproval coming at him in waves. He cleared his throat. Saints, but it felt *good* to needle the righteous bastard.

To ken he was about to set him on his gullible chin.

"Sooo! What goes on here, my friend? What is all the bustle?" Iain asked the weasel. "Is there a fair hereabouts? A grand lord's wedding mayhap?"

"None of that," the stranger gave back, already moving away. "'Tis a far greater entertainment we hasten to see."

"Wait, you!" Iain tried to stop him, his rusty smile fading before it'd even come close to maturity, the strangest nigglings of ill ease tickling his nape. "What manner of entertainment?"

"A burning," the man tossed back, and was gone.

Iain's stomach turned over. He'd had enough of flames to last twenty lifetimes.

"Sweet holy saints." Gavin's eyes flew wide. "The burning of a living person?" he asked of no one in particular, his ruddy complexion paling. "At a stake?"

"Aye, sir, but in a tar barrel," a young lass answered, flashing him a bright smile. "Though some say her hands are to be cut off," she added, her eyes alight with excitement. "A thief, she is . . . caught stealing from the shrine of St. Thenew, and the worst of it"—she paused to cross herself—"they say she's a—"

"Postulant," Iain finished for her, his blood turning to ice.

The lass nodded. "Have you e'er heard worse?" she breathed, her voice dropping to a conspiratorial whisper. "Make haste, good sirs, for they may have already begun," she urged, then spun on her heel and sped away.

Iain stared after her, the girl's ominous tidings turning the boisterous tumult into a faceless red blur until he saw naught before him but two wide-set green eyes.

Wide-set, somewhat slanting, and filled with panic.

Eyes he wasn't about to let glaze over with the sightless chill of death.

Somewhere deep inside him, a long-forgotten sense of steely purpose stirred and wakened. And unlike the other times tarnished bits of his old self had sought to surface, this time Iain MacLean, Master of Nothing, seized firm hold of the tenuous threads of his neglected honor.

His vision clearing, his wits sharper than in months, he whirled about and grabbed MacFie's arm, determined to save the lass, consequences be damned.

He would, too . . . and preferably with Gavin ne'er-tell-a-lie MacFie agreeing to Iain's decidedly deceptive plan.

Such a measure would help immensely.

From nowhere, but feeling oh so sweet, Iain's smile returned. Just a wee uptilt at the very edges of his lips, but heady enough to flood him with renewed vigor and lend a bit of sheen to the rusted edges of his valor.

Drawing a deep breath, he tightened his grip on

Gavin's arm and leaned toward the lout's startled ear, eager to divulge his ruse.

And Gavin MacFie would comply.

Iain MacLean, the feeling-almost-his-old-self Iain MacLean, would not accept otherwise.

A world away from Glasgow's crowded wynds and closes, amidst deep green woods, heather moorlands, and silver-glinting lochs, the proud strength of Abercairn Castle graced the very verges of the Highlands, its curtained walls and turreted towers rising tall against the gently rolling hills.

Drifting sheets of thin, drizzly rain blew in from the east, occasional gusty winds tearing leaves off the trees and rattling shutters, while heavy, rain-swollen clouds descended ever lower on the mountainsides, their gray-tinted gloom stealing the color from a landscape awash with sweetest luminosity on fairer days.

But inside Abercairn's impressive central keep, gloom of a different nature—a black-browed, glowering sort— permeated the laird's bedchamber and anteroom, the castle's most sumptuously appointed quarters.

Tapestry-hung, warmed by a fine-smoldering peat fire, and occupied very much against the true laird's will by Sir Bernhard Logie, a tall, rawboned usurper of middle years. Dark, hood-eyed, and, much to his private dismay, possessed of an increasingly bald pate.

A staunch leader of the *Disinheriteds,* the Scots barons once exiled by the late Robert the Bruce, King of Scots, and now returned in Edward Balliol's tail, and with Edward of England's support, to attempt foisting Balliol on the Scottish throne and regaining their lost lands.

Or, in Silver Leg's case, as Logie was commonly known, adding the lands and riches of others to his own less-illustrious ex-holding.

A man of little virtue and many vices.

A proscribed outlaw in the eyes of everyone but himself and those who bowed to his whim.

And his whim at the moment verged on thunderous. Narrowing a furious glare on the two men before him, he smashed his fist on the fully laden table, the impact jiggling the rich spread of victuals and wine he'd been feasting on and the assorted mounds of Abercairn loot he'd amassed since seizing the stronghold.

Treasures he trusted nowhere but within a sword's length of the place he laid his head at night.

Reaching across the table, he grabbed a heavy, jewel-encrusted candlestick before it could topple over. Righting it, he placed it on the exact spot where it had been, then turned his wrath back on his men.

"Explain yourselves," he seethed, leaning forward in the massive laird's chair. "Tall as she is, and with hair so flaming red, she cannot have vanished into thin air. Someone must have seen her."

The older of the two men fidgeted, his feet shuffling on the furred animal skins strewn thickly upon the wood-planked floor. "By God's own breath, my lord, no one has," he owned, looking more miserable by the moment. "We've asked everywhere."

"*Ask?*" Silver Leg's eyes near bulged from his dark-frowning face. Dismissing the first, he pinned the second man with a narrow-eyed stare. "And you? Are you sashaying about the land asking the lassie's whereabouts, too?"

The man's face turned as red as the clump of hot-glowing peat popping loudly on the hearthstone.

Silver Leg stared long and hard at them both, his ill humor seeming to fill the room. He began drumming his fingers on the heavy, oaken table.

"Persuade them to speak is the way of it," he said, snatching up a handful of silver coins. "With a wee spot of artful assistance from Laird Drummond's coffers."

He glared a challenge at them until the first man, the older one, stepped forward, his hand outstretched.

"That ought loosen a tongue or two," Silver Leg declared, slapping the coins into the man's palm. "Scour every inch of the heather for hidey-holes if you must, search the most remote cot houses, or trudge the length of every wynd and alley in every burgh in the land. I care not how you find her, just bring Madeline Drummond before me, and alive."

"Aye, sir," the men chorused, bobbing their heads, the younger man's uncomfortable gaze dropping to the watchful greyhound curled at Silver Leg's feet.

"Only she can tell me where her tight-lipped father hides the bulk of his treasure. The fool refuses to speak and may well perish of his own stubbornness before he comes to his senses," Silver Leg said, visibly calming as his dog began licking the bared knee of his once-trouble-some right leg. "Now be gone with you, and do not come before me again lest the lass is with you."

Still nodding their acquiescence, the two men backed from the room, near colliding with a set-faced serving-woman just stepping through the opened door, a basket of freshly cut peat bricks clutched in her arms.

Ignoring the scuttling men, she placed the basket beside the hearth. But rather than seeking retreat, the grim-faced woman dusted her hands and eyed the greyhound at Silver Leg's feet . . . and the second one, equally large, sprawled comfortably across Laird Drummond's four-poster bed.

Sprawled there, and gnawing on a well-meated foreleg of roasted mutton . . . full atop the laird's finest bed linens!

Following her disapproving stare, Silver Leg reached down and stroked the first beast's rough-coated head. "Have you ne'er seen a dog, wench?" he asked the moment a particularly loud crack of thunder rumbled to an end. "They will not harm you . . . lest I order them to do so."

"Dogs make Laird Drummond cough and sneeze," the woman said, not a single sign of timidity in her voice or in her rigid-backed stance. "I vow we'd have enough of them running about otherwise, and I, Sir Bernhard, am far beyond the age of being called a wench."

Silver Leg's lip curled, but then his mood changed. "Mayhap so, but your bosom is as generous as the bawdiest wench e'er to grace my bed." Lifting a hand, he toyed with the tips of his beard, his gaze sliding over the serving woman's generous figure. "Are your legs as shapely?"

He leaned forward, filled a second chalice with wine. "Are you of a mind to show them to me? Your legs, and other sultry . . . charms?" He slid the chalice toward her. "Is that why you haven't yet exited my presence?"

"I am here because I would ask you to spare a clump of peat or two for the good laird," she said, ignoring the wine, her voice as firm as her lifted chin. "He ails, see you, and the chill of the dungeon will soon be the life of him."

Silver Leg eyed the finely woven Drummond plaid the knee-licking greyhound lounged upon. So many of the beast's hairs covered the once-proud plaid, the colors of its weft could scarce be discerned.

"The dungeon is cold, eh?" He sat back in the elaborately carved chair, allowed himself an indulgent smile. "If you fret for Drummond's health, then pray help yourself to his plaid," he suggested, flicking a hand at the ruined length of wool. "And if you are willing to warm *me* a bit"—he paused to glance toward the bed—"I'll send along yon mutton bone to fill his empty belly as well."

Her face flushing as red as his man's earlier, albeit for another reason, Morven the serving woman pressed her lips together, her gaze sliding to the iron poker leaning against the wall near the hearth.

Silver Leg followed her gaze. "Enough, *wench*—away with you now," he ordered her. "Lest you desire to feel an iron-hard poker of a wholly 'nother sort deep, deep inside you!"

Her bravura besieged at last, Morven whirled around and flew from the room, Silver Leg's lewd laughter chasing in her flustered wake.

Chapter Five

𝒜YE, IN A BLAZING TAR BARREL!" A high-pitched female voice rose above the other cries, the woman's glee joining the massed excitement of Madeline's tormentors, the whole of their fired-up eagerness to see her burn whirling so quickly in her breast its wild spinning made her dizzy.

"That'll teach her to steal from shrines," another voice boomed from the crowd, a man's this time.

"Thieving, and light-skirted, too, no doubt," a thin-faced woman sniffed. "A brazen whore a-hiding in nun's trappings."

The taunts came from all directions, as did Nella's ceaseless shouts at their captors as she struggled to break away from the two burly men restraining her.

Swallowing hard, Madeline closed her eyes to the sea of leering faces. The cacophony of jeers pounded so loudly through her head she feared it would burst asunder before they even shoved her into the pitch-lined barrel.

Her eyes snapped open when rough hands yanked her arms behind her back, and a man's large, calloused fingers began tying her wrists together with a length of coarse, flesh-abrading rope.

Biting her lip until the coppery taste of her own blood filled her mouth, she fought the rising urge to spit in the hard-staring faces of those pressing nearest her.

Or to ruin their pleasure by thanking them for sparing her a life of withering away behind cloistered walls.

A life without love.

But Drummonds died with dignity, the men with a bloodied sword in their hands, the women without complaint.

She would not defile their honor by being less bold.

So she held her tongue, kept her back as straight as she could, and prayed for a swift passing.

Blessedly, the increasing chaos in her head and the dizziness soon blocked out the taunts, and the tumultuous mob and even St. Thenew's little stone chapel and the nearby well shrine faded into a welcome haze of soft, thick gray.

A cloaking mist shielding her from all but the fierce hammering in her temples, the deep rumble of approaching thunder, and the undulating ripple and wave of the earth beneath her feet.

Cushioned her from an oddly familiar fury, black-roiling and ferocious enough to sweep her length and banish every last peal of the mob's jeerings from within her beleaguered breast.

Madeline's heart skittered a beat, something inside her recognizing the shape and color of this man's anger.

A maelstrom of rage aimed not at her but those who'd do her harm.

Her eyelids flickered open, the gray haze beginning to

thin, the trembling of the ground and low growl of thunder by then identifiable as the drumming of horses' hooves nearing at swiftest speed.

"Sweet holy Mother," the onion-breathed man tying her wrists cried out behind her. "'Tis the devil hisself come to fetch his own!" he shrieked, shoving her from him with such force she slammed headlong into the hard and rocky earth.

Brilliant white pain exploded inside her, her breath leaving her in a great *whoosh* of air, the scrabbling man near tripping over her in his blind haste to hie himself from the scene.

Stunned and windless, the dizziness back with a vengeance, Madeline lay where she'd fallen, the ropes binding her wrists and ankles preventing any movement even if she'd possessed the breath to try.

"'Fore God, what goes on here?" *his* voice pierced the haze. "Lay a further hand on the lass, and I shall see the lot of you dangling from a gibbet before nightfall," her shadow man roared, plunging his foaming mount straight into the screaming, fleeing mob.

Scattering them, he reined up in a welter of fury and wild-eyed, shrieking horseflesh, his garron rearing high, its lashing hooves a lethal threat to any fool not swift enough to spring aside.

Neighing protest, the beast pawed the air. Madeline's shadow man flung himself from the saddle before the garron's hooves struck ground. His handsome face thunderous as a storm cloud, he threw back his cloak and whipped out his steel, a gleaming, vicious-looking brand he clearly knew how to wield.

He strode toward her, tearing off his mantle as he

came, his dark eyes flashing scorn at the gawking burghers who hadn't yet fled. "Reveal to me who amongst you ripped her gown, and I shall emasculate the bastard," he challenged, hurling his pilgrim's cloak across her bared breasts.

Madeline went cold at his words, flinching as the cloak's rough-woven warmth settled onto her naked flesh . . . she hadn't realized they'd ripped her clothes, hadn't known she'd been so exposed.

That all and sundry—her shadow man, too—had glimpsed her too-full breasts.

Large as milk cow udders, one of her suitors had once sneered, not realizing she'd heard. The remembered slur shot through her mind, its ugliness bringing a new sort of shame. . . .

She glanced at the tall pilgrim. He'd taken up a fighting stance, and now loomed above her, standing so close, the hard edge of his booted foot pressed against her hip. His wrath rolling off him in great, black waves, he swept the gaping onlookers with a scorching glare.

"Cease ogling her this instant, or your best amends will not keep you from the cutting edge of my sword," he vowed, his outrage a loud crackling hum in Madeline's ears.

He stepped over her then, his hard-muscled legs protectively straddling her. "The man who thinks I jest can greet the morrow from beneath his headstone."

Still dazed, Madeline stared up at him, his earthy, masculine scent, a heady blend of woodsmoke, leather, and wide-open spaces, filling her nostrils and reeling her senses with each ragged, indrawn breath she pulled into her burning lungs.

Nella dashed to her side then, her own clothes badly disheveled, but untorn. Dropping to her knees, she cradled Madeline's head in her lap. "Oh, dear saints, what have they done to you?" she cried, horror standing in her face.

She ran trembling fingers across Madeline's brow . . . they came away smeared bright red.

A fresh wave of churning nausea welled in Madeline's stomach at the sight of the blood dripping from Nella's fingers. She opened her mouth to speak, to assure her friend she was only dizzy—merely queasy—and not bleeding to death, but her tongue wouldn't form the words.

"'Tis more than a few drops o' blood she ought lose for stealing from a saint," a hostile voice called out, its anger breaking the crowd's restraint.

"Thieving postulants don't deserve mercy," another agreed.

"And 'tis for mercy you'll be pleading when I cut out your tongue," Iain called back, scanning the throng for the first man bold enough to step forward.

Searching, too, for the long-overdue MacFie.

The lout should have ridden up minutes after Iain even if he'd kept his mount's pace to a trot merely to underscore his displeasure with Iain's plan.

A mousy, stringy-haired woman darted from around the side of the holy well and tossed a little silver-cast leg at Iain's feet. "Stole that, she did," the shrew scolded, raking the prone beauty with disdain. "I saw her take it with my own two eyes. We all did."

Iain's fingers tightened on the hilt of his blade.

He glanced around again. If MacFie didn't arrive

forthwith, the redheaded Islesman would be the first to get a taste of Iain's full temper . . . even if he ne'er glimpsed Doon's bonnie shores again.

The underswell of grumbles coming from the crowd increased until a handful of bull-necked ruffians edged forward. One brandished a pitchfork, another cracked meaty knuckles, and the rest just glowered their malcontent.

The brawniest-looking one, a great black-bearded bear of a man, cocked a bushy brow at Iain. "And who be you to come between God's own justice?"

"Someone so forsaken by Him that I make my own," Iain shot back, his contempt for the hulking churl so rife he could taste it.

His gaze lit on the little silver leg lying in the dirt. "The lass is not a thief . . . she is my wife," he said, the lie ringing with amazing authority, the words streaking through the shifting haze to squeeze Madeline's heart so fiercely it could scarce beat.

His wife, he'd called her.

His.

And oh but she was, the vanquished shadows of her hopes and dreams rejoiced. One by one, they rose from the darkness to stretch greedy arms toward her heart until her befuddled wits set them on their ears, squelching their daring as swiftly as they'd exercised it, banishing them to their proper lodgings—locked securely behind well-barred doors—and leaving only confusion and pain to plague her.

But even in her dull-edged state, a secret part of her thrilled with the certainty that her shadow man's bold rescue had thrust them both onto a playing ground from which there could be no easy retreat.

"Your wife, eh?" one of the ruffians sounded his disbelief.

"A strange husband, you are, pilgrim," another chimed in, casually tossing a battle-ax from one hand to the other. "Or is it the style of you to let your lady wander about the land unattended?"

Once more Iain eyed the little leg votive . . . and silently cursed MacFie.

"We became separated some days past," he lied again, the untruth falling from his tongue with disturbing ease. Casting further caution to the wind, he took his attention off the ruffians long enough to take a few steps forward and swipe up the ex-voto.

He held it aloft. "If you caught my wife with this in her hand, she was not stealing it but searching for me. My friend and traveling companion is lame and—"

"You'd best hope you have some friends, brother, spouting such drivel," the ax swinger cut him off. "I, for one, do not believe you."

"Nor I," came a chorus of denials from the crowd.

"He speaks the God's own truth," another voice boomed, and Iain wheeled around to see MacFie riding into the kirkyard.

His expression as clouded as Iain knew his own to be, though likely for a wholly different reason, Gavin dismounted, giving an exaggerated wince as his feet hit the ground.

Relief flooded Iain.

The e'er upright MacFie had managed the jump o'er his scruples.

Limping forward, Gavin dragged his left leg conspicuously behind him. He waved a little silver leg ex-voto at the gog-eyed bystanders as he came. "Yon lady kens I leave the ex-votos at every shrine we visit," he recited the agreed-upon words. "She will have but sought the way back to her liege husband by using my votive offerings to trace our steps."

The grumbles amongst the crowd dwindled until one cheeky soul called out, "And the other lass? Be she *your* wife?"

Iain's heart dropped to his feet.

He'd not thought far enough ahead to include the fiery-haired postulant's tall, generously made friend into his plans.

Indeed, he'd clean forgotten her until her sudden appearance at the beauty's side.

His blood running cold, Iain glanced off toward the distant foothills of the Highlands. He couldn't, just couldn't, look at MacFie.

Or the two women.

Heavy silence stretched taut over the uncomfortable gathering until the comely-featured woman herself pushed to her feet and ran to Gavin MacFie's, near knocking him down in her exuberant greeting.

The crowd drew a great collective breath.

Iain held his.

And Gavin MacFie played along, setting her gently from him, but keeping a very husbandly-looking arm slung low about her well-rounded hips.

"Anyone still doubt this lady is my wife?" Gavin challenged the onlookers, drawing the lass even closer against his side . . . and winning a good piece of Iain's gratitude.

Nigh giddy with relief—and some other best-unnamed emotion—Iain raked the crowd with the iciest glare he could muster. "And I, good fellows and ladies, would now see to my own wife," he said, dropping to one knee beside her.

"Without an audience," he added, glancing at the lass, his heart twisting at the waxy pallor of her creamy, lightly freckled skin.

He smoothed a softly curling lock of bloodied hair off the side of her face with more tenderness than he'd shown a woman in years—including the one who'd been his true wife.

A gesture he hoped would soothe her . . . and stay her questions until the crowd dispersed.

To that end, he gave them one more warning. "Be gone with you now," he called over his shoulder, "and be aware that just because I kneel does not mean my steel cannot be at your throat in a heartbeat if you linger."

None did.

Even MacFie and the beauty's friend moved away, strolling toward a stone bench placed against the far kirk wall, the Islesman still dragging his leg, though not quite so flagrantly as before.

And to Iain's greater surprise, the two appeared to be conversing most companionably.

As he would love to do with the beauty stretched at his feet if only she'd crossed his path a lifetime ago.

At a time when he would have been able to greet her with pride and woo her with grace rather than a simple show of muscle and a farcical ruse built on lies.

A faint hint of her clean, heather scent wafted past his nose just then, and Iain swallowed, his reclaimed bravura already showing the first cracks.

Willing them not to worsen, Iain unsheathed his dirk and cut the rope wrapped tight around her ankles. The same slender and delicate ankles that had so fired his blood in the cathedral, now making his gut churn with sheer, roiling anger when he saw how the rough-hewn rope had marred her tender flesh.

"Sweet Jesu," he swore under his breath, biting back a more volatile oath as he eased away the rope as gently as he could.

"Who are you, sir? I would thank you," she spoke at last, her voice weakened from her ordeal, but sweet enough to fell him with its pleasing, musical lilt . . . its softness.

A Highland lass.

"Nay, my lady, it is I who must thank you," Iain managed, still looking at her ankles. "A man on pilgrimage doesn't oft have the privilege of aiding a fair damsel in need."

And I would thank you for making me feel alive again.

Alive in ways that went far beyond the fine heat she ignited in his loins.

Saints, but he wished she'd speak again . . . simply for the enjoyment of listening to her lilting, honey-toned voice.

Iain squared his shoulders, the full gravity and mass of everything he'd ever heard about the Bane of the MacLeans—the Legend he'd scoffed at all his life— whirling through his head as if a full score of powerful-voiced *sennachies* stood singing the romantic fluff right into his ear.

He touched his fingers to the almost fully receded bump on his forehead, its persistent throbbing less important than his fervent hope she wouldn't notice.

'Twas his vain hope the lump didn't mar too badly the looks that had ne'er failed to catch the lassies' favor in the days before he'd forgotten how to smile.

"You are gallant, sir," she spoke again, the compliment going right beneath his skin and melting a good bit more of the ice packed so thick 'round his heart.

"But I would know who you are," she added, the faint quiver in her voice affecting him more than he would have believed.

"And I you, lady," Iain returned, dabbing away the blood on her ankles with a strip of linen torn from the hem of his shirt. "Will you grace me with your name?"

"I am Madeline," she said, a wee trace of sadness dimming her voice.

"Simply Madeline?" Iain pressed, wanting, *needing*, to know more.

"Aye, simply Madeline," she echoed, a note of finality coloring her response.

A slight furrow crinkled Iain's brow, but he tamped down his desire to learn more about her and left her her peace. He, too, had secrets, and darkness best left unveiled.

Setting aside the bloodied cloth, he ripped off a new strip to wipe the blood from her abraded wrists. Blessedly, less raw than her ankles, he tended them with equal care.

And as he did so, he steeled himself finally to look—truly look—at her face.

When he did, he near lost himself in the luminosity of her steady perusal.

Ne'er had he seen such lovely eyes.

Ne'er had a woman's mere gaze made him feel as if he'd been transported into the land of dreams and fancy . . . as if the very earth tilted and swayed beneath him.

She locked gazes with him, meeting his full on from incredibly large eyes of the same light green of spring's newest leaves. Thick-fringed brown-black lashes made them appear even larger, while tiny gold flecks within their depths caught the afternoon sunlight and seemed to reflect its warmth straight into every shadowed corner of his heart.

The rest of her undid him, too.

She'd lost her head veil, and the curly spill of her coppery-gold hair tumbled in fetching disarray about her shoulders, its bright gloss making his fingers itch to scoop up great handfuls just so its silkiness could stream across his palms.

So he could bury his face in the curling, glossy skeins and sate himself on its light, heathery scent.

She wet her lips—sensually full lips—lusciously ripe-looking, and just seeing the wee tip of her tongue moisten them had his entire body tightening with a ferocity that stunned him.

A lust-stoked rigidity so shockingly fierce its potency left him half-afraid he'd splinter if he but moved his little finger.

She did move, pushing up on her elbows now that he'd

freed her arms, and the motion caused his cloak to slip a bit, giving him a wondrous glimpse of the top swells of her lush, creamy breasts.

A low groan—nay, in truth, more the growl of a starving predator—rose in Iain's throat, but he battled it back, disguising it as best he could behind a pitifully lame excuse for a cough.

She peered at him, something in the depths of her green gaze giving him the uncanny sensation that she knew his cough had been a ruse.

That perhaps she knew as well that everything about him was a ruse.

Knew, too, saints forbid, that he struggled against a raging desire to yank his cloak from the well-rounded globes of her breasts, exposing their sweetness to his full viewing pleasure.

Indeed, the urge to do so made his hands tremble.

But if she suspected, she glanced discreetly aside, and Iain used the moment to squeeze a much-needed gulp of air down his constricted throat.

Her throat tightened with equally intense emotion, hot, painful, and bitterly sweet, for his daring rescue touched her more profoundly than she ought allow. His tender ministrations to her wounds poured warmth of purest, molten gold straight into her heart and pricked the backs of her eyes with scalding heat.

Biting her lip, Madeline stared hard at the distant blue line of the Highlands, and willed the unshed tears not to spill. At length she turned back to him, her vision once more clear, but still far too vulnerable to long-unquenched needs inside her for her own good.

Far too vulnerable to him.

She stared up at him, saw his own struggles mirrored in the tense set of his jaw and the slight narrowing of his peat brown eyes. Her gaze not letting him look away, she lifted a shaky hand to the well-worn warrior's hauberk he wore over a finely woven linen tunic.

Finely woven, and of highest quality . . . as was the leather of his hauberk, despite signs of wear.

More the trappings of a braw Highland laird than what he seemed.

Watching him carefully, she withdrew her fingers . . . but not before lighting them briefly on the finely tooled sword belt slung low on his hips. The belt, like his padded leather hauberk, appeared well worn but of superior craftsmanship.

"You are no ordinary pilgrim, sir," she said, not surprised when a brief flare of pain flashed across his handsome face.

A faint smile, a sad one, flickered over his lips. "And you, sweet lass," he began, gently skimming his knuckles down her cheek, "are you a true postulant?"

"I am on my way to enter a nunnery, aye," Madeline confirmed, a shiver of regret rippling through her at his evasive answer and the necessary half-truth of her own.

"Will you tell me your name if not who you are?" she asked, not wishing to prod too deeply, bespelled or nay.

Not when she held her own silences.

"I am Iain," he told her, the smooth richness of his voice spooling through her, entrancing her just as thoroughly it had in the cathedral . . . and her dreams.

"Iain . . . ?" she urged, so beguiled by his golden warmth, his dark masculine beauty, and the mysterious yet so compelling air of sadness surrounding him. She could almost believe he'd manifested from some silver-tongued bard's fireside tale of legend and romance.

Her gaze dropped briefly to his handsomely tooled sword belt again, lighting, too, on his equally fine waist belt, then the buttery-soft leather of his dusty but well-made boots. "You are Iain of . . . ?" she encouraged, for to possess such fineness—and his innate aura of power and grace—he could only hail from a very great house.

He looked away without answering her, and the humming silence stretched so taut its tension crackled in the cool afternoon air.

Madeline cleared her throat. "Please, good sir, I would know but who—"

"I am just Iain," he said, glancing back at her, the flatness of his tone revealing far more than the few spoken words. "I've no style to tag on to my name, lass."

Lest you wish to call me Master of Nothing.

The unspoken words hushed past Madeline's ear, swift as the wind and lancing her heart.

"Then I shall give you one." The sudden urge to do so welled up from the very roots of her soul. "A very fine style."

He cocked a skeptical brow. "Say you?"

She nodded. "Aye . . . to honor your gallantry and valor."

Another shadow passed over his face. "I must warn you, lass, nary a soul walks this earth who'd call me either gallant or valorous."

Madeline bristled, the pain behind his words making her simmer with anger at whoe'er or whate'er had embittered him. "And heed you, sirrah," she informed him, all fire and energy, her own cares momentarily forgotten,

"Madeline of— . . . *I* am not a maid to be swayed by common opinion. I gather and hold my own."

"Then, sweet lassie, you are not just fair to look upon but also of good and generous heart, and I . . . thank you," he said, a faint but unmistakable catch in his deep voice. "So what style shall you give me?"

Madeline glanced away, her mind whirling. She stared out across the heather to the long, unbroken line of distant hills. Her own beloved Highlands, resplendent in the late-afternoon light. Away on the horizon, they stared back at her, blue, shadow-chased, and gilded with palest gold.

A fine, warm gold.

Madeline smiled.

"I have it!" she announced, turning back to her shadow man. "I shall style you Master of the Highlands."

Chapter Six

"*MASTER OF THE HIGHLANDS?*" Gavin MacFie's astonishment hung in the air. He rubbed his bearded jaw, somehow managing to appear flummoxed, amused, and reproachful in one. "Did I hear aright? You do not jest?"

Iain ignored him.

His own face hard-set, he leaned broad shoulders against the cold gray stone of St. Thenew's Chapel and peered up at the wispy clouds scudding across the late-afternoon sky . . . his fate and the fine mess he'd made of it taunting him from across the now-deserted kirkyard.

Drawing a deep breath, he turned his attention on the small, yew-enclosed burial ground. *She* whiled there, safely ensconced within its green-shadowed quiet, her fairness shielded from view by the broad-spreading branches of the ancient, sheltering trees.

Iain crossed his arms, his awareness of her so palpable he could taste it. His pulse a steady roar in his ears, he imagined her there, partially or wholly unclothed, even now washing the blood and horror from her sweet limbs with buckets of water he'd drawn for her from the holy well.

Her presence stole across the little kirkyard to spool all around and through him. She fired his senses, numbed his wits, and posed a ceaseless thrumming challenge not just to his manhood, but to the very beats of his heart.

Every last one of them.

Each single breath he drew.

His mouth suddenly dry, he pinched the bridge of his nose and squeezed shut his eyes, seeking the familiar solace of darkness . . . if only for a moment.

Sakes, but he even *scented* the lass. Her light, heathery scent wafted about him, bewitching him with all the subtle mastery of a queen of the fey.

Clenching his fists, his eyes still tightly closed, Iain tossed back his dark head and knew the full power of the Bane of the MacLeans. Its formidable might rode him hard and furious, roaring through him, almost a living, writhing thing, its crackling intensity unnerving him more than little else had in all his days.

Even the tinkly, splashing sounds of her hasty ablutions flooded his mind with a barrage of images searing enough to have the punctilious MacFie sputtering in shock if he dared reveal their piquancy.

His own dark side, the heated one left so long unattended, reveled in the images, clinging in particular to a most delectable one of sparkling water droplets netting the lush, red-curled abundance he knew he'd find at the juncture of her shapely thighs.

When his mind's eye parted her legs a bit, and encouraged one glittering drop of water to break free of the red-gold curls and trickle slowly down the tender flesh of her inner thigh, Iain's maleness jerked and leapt, the whole aching length of him stretched and filling to near bursting.

God's eyes! He meant to cry out, his capitulation to the clan Legend underscored by the choked groan that escaped his throat instead.

Clearly believing him seized by a bout of shortness of breath, Gavin thwacked him on the shoulder. "Master of the Highlands?" he repeated, dutifully hammering Iain's upper back with the flat of his hand.

"Folly, pure folly, such a title, and I think you've gone full addled if you expect anyone to heed it," he declared, the words and his infernal shoulder pounding shattering the sensual haze, blessedly breaking its witchy spell.

Iain glared at him. "And I think your ears are stuffed with wax," he shot back, his chest tightening with vexation.

"I told you I did not style myself thus, *she* did," he sought to explain, relieved to detect no sign of a quaver in his voice. "She claimed she wished to honor me for my valor and gallantry."

MacFie's russet brows lifted, but drew together just as quickly. Scratching his beard, he peered at Iain as if he wished to say something but, thinking better of it, chose to hold his tongue.

Iain met his narrow-eyed perusal with a scowl.

"Rest assured I informed her I can lay claim to neither quality," he said, tight-voiced, the truth of the admission a lance jab to his tattered pride.

He turned aside, drew a hand over his mouth and chin. Gavin's astonishment irritated him more than it should have. Until recently, he hadn't cared a whit what anyone thought of him.

Truth to tell, he *liked* the style and wanted to savor the sentiment behind it if only for a wee bit. It'd been so long since a lass had paid him a compliment or looked on him with wonder and awe brimming in her eyes.

Regret coursing through him like a deep and sullen river, Iain studied the lichen patterns on a nearby dry-stone wall until the ifs and might-have-beens in his life ceased mocking him. The instant they did, he slid Gavin a long, pointed glare.

A blazing-eyed one piled high with all his frustration. "I am not some brazen cockerel out purposely to deceive hapless maidens with false tales of valor and prowess."

Heaving a great sigh, he ran a finger beneath the neck of his tunic, wondering at its sudden tightness. Pondering, too, the fiery-haired beauty's startling impact on him.

MacLean Bane or nay, he found himself torn between letting her admiration spill through him like warm and golden sunshine after days of cold, dark rain or cursing himself for having slung an ever-tightening noose about his own fool neck.

"Claiming the lass as your wife before all and sundry, and saddling me with one as well, puts us in a fine predicament, my friend," Gavin asserted, pacing the grass, his words mirroring Iain's own concerns. "The lasses, too."

Iain rammed an agitated hand through his hair. "Think you I am daft?" he fumed. "Unaware of the consequences wrought by my own impetuous tongue?"

A tongue fair aching to tease and taste the sweetness

of the bonnie maid's creamy skin, his not-to-be-checked MacLean heat embellished.

In especial the lush rounds of her breasts.

A tempting array of delight mayhap this very moment, naked, wet, and glistening . . . her hands moving gently o'er the succulent fullness as she washed herself.

His loins firing yet again, he fixed his gaze on the green birchwoods and gently rolling braes stretching beyond the kirkyard, struggled to shake off the lust gripping his vitals. He failed miserably.

Too deep, too all-consuming was his desire.

A frown settling on his brow, he strode after the pacing MacFie, easily catching up with him. "Have a care, lest you push me too far," he hissed, hurtling the whole of his annoyance at the unsuspecting MacFie. "I am many things, and most not particularly worthy, I know, but I am not without conscience."

"I ne'er implied otherwise," Gavin spluttered. "Nonetheless, I cannot stand idle and see you endanger two unprotected women."

"You may strike me down here and now if that was my wont." Iain bristled, a fine and frothing white-edged fury roiling inside him. "I sought but to *save* them . . . and did. I ne'er meant to cause them harm."

"But you have, willfully or nay." Gavin sighed. "Have you considered how they are to continue on their way after your bold claims?"

Iain opened his mouth, but snapped it shut immediately, his objections toppled before they'd left his lips. He *had* thought about such things . . . but not until after he'd declared the lass his wife.

Wife.

His wife.

Icy iron bands clamped round Iain's chest, the implications behind the two harmless-sounding words squeezing the breath from him, and even stealing the light and warmth from the sun-dappled afternoon.

A cold shudder slithered down his back, its chill reaching inside to blast his conscience with blackest frost. His thoughtlessness had already cost one wife her life.

Imperiling another—his in truth, or nay—was out of the question.

"I spoke with the older one," MacFie was saying, his voice coming as if from a great distance. Iain blinked, tried to listen. "Nella is her name," Gavin droned on, seemingly unaware that an invisible bank of lowering clouds had blotted out the sun. "Nella of the Marsh, and she tells me they are indeed journeying to a nunnery, though she did not reveal which one."

In a rare showing of distinct agitation, Gavin kicked at a tussock of grass. He wheeled on Iain, his hazel eyes snapping with reproach. "If they encounter any who witnessed your posturings this day—and you know they must—and we two are not at their sides, appearing to be their husbands, they could fall prey to all manner of ill-wishers."

Iain blanched, the chill inside him spreading to coat his innards and freeze his bones. Saints, he actually felt the blood drain from his face.

But then a strange rumbling, almost liked muted thunder, rose hot in his throat, sweeping away the cold on a torrent of angry, heated words. "God's blood!" he roared, planting fisted hands on his hips. "Think you I am so blinded by my own trials I cannot see hazards of the road?"

Two swift steps brought him nose-to-nose with the Islesman. "Pernicious cutthroats bent on rapine and other vices, ravening wolves and packs of long-fanged wild boar!" he railed, not bothering to cap his fury. "They all lie in wait for the unsuspecting, and 'tis well I know it."

Gavin spluttered something, but Iain waved him silent. "Och, aye, such terrors abound at every bend in the road, and two unescorted females make easy prey," he seethed, not caring if his wrath singed the other's neatly clipped beard. "Do you truly believe I am too thick-skulled to ken I've compounded their vulnerability?"

To his amazement, he would have sworn he caught a wee quirking at the left corner of MacFie's lips, but the twitching—or whate'er it'd been—vanished in a flash.

Gavin folded his arms, rolled back on his heels. "So what will you do to make amends to them?" he wanted to know, his tone calm as the sea on a windless day, his freckled face once more the pinnacle of blandness.

Blandness, and something most disconcerting that Iain couldn't quite put his finger on . . . and didn't really want to.

"Amends?" he stammered, the single word sounding more like the wheeze of a strangled man's last breath.

Gavin nodded. "We cannot leave them here, nor can we send them on their way." He cast a sidelong glance at the yew-enclosed graveyard. "Not with good conscience."

"Nay, we cannot," Iain ground out, massaging the back of his neck. Saints, but his skin felt hot . . . feverish.

He felt feverish.

Wholly besieged . . . condemned and damned to meet his fate face on, even when everything he'd lived and learned hitherto screamed in warning protest at the very idea of keeping the beauty at his side, letting her into his life.

His maligned, worthless life.

But the only one he had, and if he meant to salvage what honor remained him, he'd deny it no longer.

Indeed, the prospect of reclaiming his life held surprising appeal. More, in fact, than aught else he'd considered in a good long while.

Feeling as if he no longer teetered quite so close to the edge of a dark abyss, Iain drew a deep, rejuvenating breath, doubly pleased to note the air held a wee hint of heather.

He almost smiled.

"So-o-o, MacFie, we've come to a crossroad, it would seem," he said in a steely-smooth voice that would accept no rebuttal. "The lasses remain at our sides—for propriety's sake, as our wives—and we shall escort them to the nunnery of their choice."

Gavin arched a brow. "And then?"

Iain shrugged, surprising himself when he didn't bark at MacFie for posing the question.

Perhaps his temper *was* lessening.

If so, he'd credit any such improvement to the distraction of the flame-haired beauty rather than any oblations he'd spent the countless shrines they'd visited on their journey across the land.

Still, he didn't want to consider "and then" just yet.

Instead, he strode hotfoot to his horse and began

hastily undoing the fastenings securing his fool pilgrim's staff to the back of his saddle.

"I agree we must keep them with us, but have you forgotten we meant to sleep at the MacNab's this night?" Gavin reminded, coming up beside him. "He is a close enough friend of Donall's to ken you have not taken another wife."

Wife again.

The word chilled Iain anew and brought Lileas in all her fragile and tender beauty to the forefront of his mind . . . but not for long. Another image, a vibrant, bolder one, vanquished her with ease. The vision of a green-eyed minx with a tousled mane of fiery red curls and creamy, coral-crested breasts lush enough to harden a eunuch's tarse.

"Nay, I have not forgotten MacNab, nor that we sent on Beardie and Douglas to await us there," he snapped, blinking away the image.

Not quite able to shake the guilt that had come with it.

Guilt, too, for thinking of the stash of MacLean treasure hidden in the saddlebags Donall's two burly seamen guarded with their brawn and steel.

Iain frowned, his fool fingers freezing on the saddle ties.

His forehead began to throb again.

Woman of his MacLean heart or nay, he *had* seen her steal the votive . . . rob a holy shrine.

At once, the dread iron bands snaked round his rib cage again, and he struggled to banish the thought, to thrust what he'd seen from his memory as a dog shakes off water. Then, much to his amazement some deep-seated knowing rose from the darkest fastnesses of his soul and met his suspicions with scorn.

Scattered them before they could take root.

Determined to ignore his doubts and trust his instincts, he wheeled to face MacFie full on, pinned him with his best brother-of-the-laird look. "*You* shall ride on to the MacNab's with the older lass and make my excuses—I care not what," he said, waving away Gavin's protest. "The younger one stays with me, and we'll join you by eventide on the morrow along the road, north some ways beyond the MacNab's holding. The old Fortingall yew would be a good meeting place. Do you know it?"

"Aye." Gavin nodded. He stepped closer, and clamped a firm hand on Iain's shoulder. "But as your brother's man, I am loyal-bound to mind you of the treasures we carry," he said, his troubled gaze mirroring how little enthusiasm he held for raising the concern.

Iain went still. He narrowed his eyes at MacFie, half-believing the bastard had seen the selfsame thought emblazoned across his own forehead just moments before.

Flushing bright pink, Gavin lowered his voice. "If she is a thief, she could be tempted if she learned of such goods, could pose a threat—"

"She poses no threat." Iain winced at the glaring untruth the instant the words left his tongue.

The well-curved lass posed a tremendous threat.

But one that had naught to do with bejeweled reliquaries and golden chalices.

She imperiled his ability to control his baser urges.

Imperiled it greatly.

"I will only ask once, and thereafter consider my duty done," Gavin began anew, flushing a deeper red but undoubtedly taking his role as Donall's most trusted too seriously to desist. "Do you trust the lass?"

"Aye, I do." Iain blinked, stunned by the speed of his answer, rocked even more by the absoluteness of his certainty. "With my life, and with the entire stores of the MacLean treasury."

"I am glad to hear it," MacFie said, clearly relieved. He lifted his hand from Iain's shoulder. "I trust her, too, and think you'd be much mistaken to doubt whate'er reason she gives you for taking the ex-voto . . . if she deigns to tell you."

"She will tell me," Iain said for his ears alone, the need to know suddenly burning as fiercely as his physical lust for her.

Consumed, he glanced at the yew trees, staring hard at them for a long moment in a vain attempt to peer through the leafy green barrier and catch a sweet glimpse of her creamy skin or mayhap a quick flash of her red-gleaming tresses.

What he did catch—imagined or nay—was another faint whiff of her heathery scent. It wafted past him, a silken caress on the late-afternoon breeze.

Just a wee hint of her fragrance, barely there and already fading away, but potent enough to fire the fiercely carnal side of him that—he now knew—had ne'er truly wakened until he laid eyes on her.

And oh how he burned to address those newly discovered needs.

To slake them every one.

His, and hers.

Especially hers.

His loins setting like granite, his pulse thundering in

his ears, he turned back to his garron and set his annoyingly clumsy fingers to unfastening the remaining saddle ties.

A twig snapped behind him then, and the wind sent another scent to tickle his nose . . . but a decidedly masculine one this time. Unpleasantly familiar, and a dubious blend.

"Must you e'er lurk so close at my shoulder?" he ground out without turning around.

"We must speak of your penance, too," came Gavin's response.

Iain gritted his teeth and counted to ten.

Snapping at the bastard that he was beginning to remind Iain of his long-dead mother would only give him more fodder to relay to Donall.

Not that Iain really cared.

Not now when the shores of Doon seemed less inviting than the welcoming arms of a certain bonnie lass.

Squaring his shoulders, he drew a long breath and expelled it very slowly. "Take heart in knowing that, too, has not slipped my mind," he said at last, yanking free the hated pilgrim's staff. To his relief, the wide-brimmed hat and beggar's bowl gave him less resistance.

He gave Gavin a tight smile. "I shall continue to pray for easement of my worst vices at whate'er holy site we happen upon," he conceded, kneeling to place the items on the stony ground at the base of the chapel wall. "But I shall no longer disguise myself as a pilgrim, nor shall I deny my name."

Straightening, he shot MacFie a defiant look. "In especial before the lass."

Gavin cocked a doubtful brow. "And if she questions

why you are no longer a pilgrim? Why you continue to kneel before shrines?"

"I shall tell her truth of the whole sordid tale before she can ask," Iain declared, the assertion knocking a few more clumps of rust off his corroded pride. "At least the most of it," he added beneath his breath.

And regrettably, loud enough for MacFie to hear.

Gavin leaned toward him, looking as if he wasn't about to relinquish his good office of gaoler and Clan MacLean's highest-ranking lairdly tattler. "And just what part of it will you keep from the lass?"

The most damning part, Iain's shame answered.

"Exactly why I was so distraught I knocked over the candlestand," *he* amended, taking his plaid from its place of concealment within his leather travel pouch and flinging it boldly over his shoulder.

He'd tell her, too, that were she wise, she'd have done washing the grime from her limbs and use the shelter of the yew trees to scramble over the kirkyard wall and hasten away.

Seize the moment and run for her sweet life.

Run a thousand miles before her Master of the Highlands forgets his blighted touch and claims her for his own.

Claim her for his own.

The words shot through Madeline, a tingling hot streak of sizzling, molten gold, freezing her in her tracks before she'd taken more than a few steps into the open kirkyard, then spinning away before she could even catch her breath.

Almost reeling, she fought to regain her balance, but

the heated passion crackling behind those few words she'd caught still eddied through her, making her dizzy.

As did the man himself.

Even Nella gawked at him . . . or at least Madeline *thought* she did, for her friend stood equally still beside her.

Madeline stared, too, her heart tilting dangerously while some small corner of logic deep inside her nodded in satisfaction at having recognized the master beneath the dusty pilgrim's garb.

Those rags—and the accompanying trappings—lay forgotten in the dirt, discarded and exchanged for the proud plaid now slung so casually across his wide-set shoulders. A pilgrim no more, he seemed to tower above his auburn-haired friend, though Madeline knew the other to be a hairbreadth taller.

His hair glistened in the sunlight, no longer pulled back from his face, but spilling loose over his shoulders, full black and silky-looking, shimmering as a raven's wing, and making her fingers itch to touch the gleaming strands.

Madeline swallowed, stared hard at his hair. Dear saints above, its sleekness fell near to his waist. Just *looking* at it set her to trembling, turned her knees liquid, and stirred her to such a degree she had to remind herself to breathe.

She swallowed again, wholly captivated by his dark beauty, enthralled by the aura of barely contained masculine power emanating from every inch of his tall, well-muscled body.

Were she less overwhelmed, less startled by the transformation, she would have smiled, for nary a man could walk the earth who better fit the style she'd given him.

But she could only stare, too awed to do aught else.

The man—whoe'er he truly was—was simply irresistible.

A vibrancy, a *living* intensity, such as she'd ne'er seen a man—or anyone—possess, rolled off him in dark waves burnished with gold, his sheer presence filling the little kirkyard, beguiling her senses, and surely branding any female within a hundred miles as his own.

If he cared to claim them.

For one laming instant, Madeline's pounding heart thumped out of beat, her palms growing cold and clammy, as her damnable gift sent his words echoing faintly through her once more.

Claim her for his own, he'd said or thought . . . and Madeline had caught the sentiment. She'd felt its blazing need to the roots of her soul . . . and wished so fervently he'd meant her and not the one woman whose heart he carried within his own.

Wished, too, she could shake off her disappointment, free herself of the thrall he'd seemed to cast o'er her, and stride forward to greet him fairly—her true Master of the Highlands—rather than hang back in the shadows and make moon eyes at a man she desperately wanted but could ne'er call her own.

Determined to ignore Gavin's gog-eyed perusal, Iain blew out a gusty, frustrated breath and made a bit of a show of smoothing his plaid's fine, woolen folds into place as best he could until he calmed enough to search his bags for his sadly misplaced brooch.

That, too, grated on his nerves, so he indulged himself by tossing aside the thin leather band Gavin was e'er pressing him to use to tie back his long hair, insisting a man with hair nigh to his arse would ne'er make a believable pilgrim.

Enjoying the feel of his hair spilling unhindered down his back once more, Iain tossed his head and bit back a near-irresistible urge to shout out loud with the sheer glory of this wee, but to him important, reclaiming of his freedom.

He *did* level a deliberately dark look on MacFie, half-expecting the gawking bastard to take advantage of the eye contact to admonish him to confess his sins to the lass in their damning entirety, but the Islesman merely cleared his throat.

More than once, and quite affectedly.

So exaggeratedly, in fact, Iain wasn't at all surprised when the fine hairs on his nape prickled, and he spun around to find two limpid green eyes fastened on him.

She stood but a few scant paces beyond the yews, her friend hovering protectively at her elbow, and he'd been too caught up in thoughts of ravishing her and defying MacFie to notice her approach!

And most mortifying of all, her green-gold gaze flew from him straight to the discarded accoutrements of his sham pilgrimhood, then back to him, drifting over his plaid and his unbound hair, the widening of her eyes and the paling of her creamy-smooth skin sure enough signs she'd guessed all.

Knew before he could tell her that he was anything but a common miracle seeker.

An unfortunate turn of events any way he twisted it,

but one he knew he could have easily mended were it not for the grim set of her beautiful face, the hint of disappointment clouding her lovely eyes.

Rampant disappointment lest along with his tarnished honor and rusted pride, his ability to read a woman had waned as well.

Hoping it wasn't so, he straightened his spine and captured her gaze, holding fast to its startled loveliness until he could peer deep enough to be sure.

And when he did, his heart plummeted, for it was indeed disappointment he found.

Biting back his own, Iain steeled himself to cross the kirkyard to her side. But before he went, he turned his back on the sweet vision she made and stared up at the brilliant blue of the sky, blinking a time or two until his frustration ceased poking hot needles into the backs of his eyes.

And wondering, too, why the saints, good fortune and fate, and mayhap the devil himself, had chosen such a bonnie, sun-filled afternoon to steal away his slowly burgeoning happiness and make him feel like a Master of Nothing once more.

Chapter Seven

MADELINE DRUMMOND, once known as Lady of Abercairn Castle, dutiful and grieving daughter, flame-haired avenger of the weak, mostly fearless, cursed with a witchy gift she loathed and hopelessly attracted to a man who loved another, stared across the stony ground of St. Thenew's kirkyard at the object of her affections and wondered if perchance her Master of the Highlands was also an accomplished practitioner of the darker arts.

The old ways revered by their Celtic ancestors.

Tall, dark, and brooding as a storm-chased night, he'd turned his broad back to her, and her mouth went dry at the sight.

For truth, she near forgot to breathe.

His unbound hair, sleek and blue-black, spilled unhindered to his waist and powerful muscles in his neck and shoulders bunched and rippled as he threw back his head to stare at the heavens, his strong profile revealing how tightly he'd clenched his jaw, how grim-set his handsome features.

The proud way he wore his plaid and his wide-legged

stance marking him as a man well accustomed to getting his way.

For one heart-stopping moment, the very air seemed to come alive. It crackled and snapped around her, the brilliant blue of the sky suddenly appearing slate gray, and boiled with thick, shifting mist.

Madeline shivered, chills racing up and down her spine, raising gooseflesh and lifting the fine hair on her skin, but she couldn't for the life of her tear her gaze from him.

Ne'er had she seen a more beautiful man.

Nor a more intensely powerful one.

"There is a man with the might and vigor to bend others to his will," Nella whispered beside her, instinctively or nay, placing a steadying hand on the small of Madeline's back.

Madeline nodded in awed agreement. Reaching for her friend, she latched cold fingers around the warmth of Nella's wrist and held tight, for a chill wind had shrieked into the kirkyard, its frigid breath lashing at her skirts and even tossing the great yews.

Their rustling leaves and creaking branches made an infernal din, a hellish din unholy enough to curl her toes and convince her all the more that her shadow man—whoe'er he truly was—was working some ancient pagan spell designed to isolate them in time.

A queer magic to plunge them into a harsher age and place than their own . . . a world where none would dare challenge the whim and wishes of one such as he.

But just when she feared the howling wind and night-dark sky would plunder every shred of courage she possessed, a quicksilver flash of melancholy slid across her heart.

His, she knew, for the familiar sadness wound through her, following its usual path and laced as always with loss and despair. But then he lowered his head and the impression—and accompanying darkness—was gone.

Vanished as swiftly as it'd come ... and so thoroughly, she suspected no eyes and ears but her own had perceived the storm.

Her flesh still chilled from the biting wind, she glanced at Nella only to find the older woman looking awed, but far from unsettled or frightened.

Faith, she didn't even look ruffled.

Not in the least.

Nor did her shadow man's friend appear troubled or concerned.

Indeed, the man called Gavin MacFie was already crossing the grass, heading long-strided for Nella, a quite ordinary smile spreading across his open, bearded face.

Only *he* bore remnants of what she'd seen, for the edges of his plaid curled as if still lifted by a fierce, whipping wind, and his magnificent hair tossed and rippled as if caught up in a wild and spirited dance with the elements.

Then he swung round, his dark gaze claiming hers as he strode forward, and Madeline Drummond, unlikely candidate for nunhood and not particularly fond of sacrists, had to struggle with a near-overwhelming urge to cross herself.

He closed the distance between them with astonishing speed, reaching her before she could catch her breath much less recover her wits. She moistened her lips, strove to regain her calm. Mercy, but he towered over her . . . and she was a well-grown woman, taller than most.

She angled her chin to look up at him, her heart pounding a frantic beat, the wild-edged emotions whirling inside her, hers alone and no one else's.

Breathing deep, she met his gaze, but if her accursed gift sought to absorb whatever thoughts lurked behind the determined glint in his peaty brown eyes, her Master of the Highlands had thrown up impenetrable shields, leaving her no choice but to guess his purpose.

And that alone was all she could discern—that he had a purpose . . . and wouldn't be swayed from it.

Uncomfortable beneath his intent scrutiny, Madeline lifted her hand to the enameled cairngorm brooch she'd borrowed from his cloak, pressed her fingertips against its smooth coolness.

She dug the fingers of her other hand into the cloak itself, clasping its warmth tight against her waist as if she could draw a portion of his strength and bravura from the worn and travel-stained cloth.

Strength and courage she needed, for her own seemed to be cowering behind her.

She sneaked another glance at Nella, who sat atop the drystone wall some paces away, deeply immersed in conversation with the auburn-haired Islesman, the two seemingly oblivious to aught but themselves.

Madeline's brow knitted.

The Master of the Highlands smiled . . . if the wee upward lift at the left corner of his lips could qualify as a smile.

"Fair maid," he addressed her, the richness of his

molten gold voice weakening her knees. "It would seem our companions are becoming rather . . . *friendly.*"

Madeline cleared her throat, half-afraid her own voice would fail her. "Nella does not usually warm to strangers, most especially men. Gavin MacFie must be an exemplary man to win her trust so quickly."

"My brother would heartily agree," her shadow man ventured, and threw a quick glance at the couple. "I am relieved they get on."

Relieved?

Madeline blew a curl off her cheek and studied him, tried to see behind the dark of his eyes. He'd made that sound as if it were of great import that Nella and his friend understood each other.

His mention of a brother caught her interest, too.

But before she could question him, a slight change in his expression, something in the way he was looking at her, stole her breath.

Her heart responded, knocked wildly against her ribs.

"I would that we, too, understand each other," he said, and a little thrill of excitement tripped through her. Again, his mellifluous voice flowed into and all around her, its smooth deepness charming her as easily as he'd bespelled the blue of the sky.

Madeline wet her lips. "Understand each other?" she echoed, her own voice an embarrassing squeak by comparison.

He inclined his dark head. "Shall we begin with my apologies for withholding my full identity?" he suggested, making her a small bow. "I am—"

"You are my shadow man," Madeline clapped a hand o'er her mouth.

Now she knew he'd bewitched her. Dear saints, she'd almost blurted the intimacies they'd already shared . . . his nightly appearances in her dreams and his own heart's deepest secrets.

Everything her accursed gift had shown her.

He was watching her closely, one dark brow casually lifted, something bold, unsettlingly ravenous, and oddly knowing glimmering in the bottomless depths of his rich brown eyes.

Catching her hand, he brought it to his lips and placed a gentle but searing kiss against her knuckles.

A kiss she felt clear to her toes.

A kiss like no man had e'er bestowed on her.

Truth to tell, she'd ne'er been kissed at all.

Not properly.

"Allow me to correct my earlier omission," he began again, releasing her hand. "I am Iain MacLean, my lady." The words tumbled from his lips in a startling rush.

Surprising, too, because a hint of nervousness discolored the burnished gold of his beautiful voice.

"Not simply Iain," he added, almost as if he needed to convince himself. "My name is Iain MacLean."

The easiest part of his task now behind him, Iain drew a great shuddering breath but immediately regretted it, for in doing so, he'd filled his lungs with the wildly distracting essence of her.

And he already knew her scent could be his undoing.

Delicate and fresh, its heathery lightness held the faintest note of musk, just enough promise of woman to spin headiest magic all around him, befuddle his senses, and—almost—make him forget she'd called him gallant.

A myriad of emotions flickered across her lovely face,

some disconcerting, yet others so inviting he ached to flash her a seductive smile steeped with all the heart-winning charm he'd once been capable of summoning in the blink of an eye. But as he'd known would befall him, the best he could muster was his usual half smile . . . one he suspected lacked the dazzle to enchant even the most easily impressed of lasses.

So he simply squared his shoulders and hoped she'd not change her mind about his valor and gallantry now that he'd forced himself to stride across the kirkyard, dredge up more courage than he'd need in a good sword fight, and confess his name to her.

And in especial that she'd not blanch—or seek to scratch out his eyes—when he revealed the rest.

"MacLean?" she echoed his name, seeming to test its feel on her tongue.

A flare of hope sparked in Iain's breast. Not bold sparks but promising nonetheless . . . and hale enough to breathe warmth onto the outermost edges of the cold dark inside him.

She was peering at him, her light green eyes brimming with interest, so he summoned another rusty smile and inclined his head. "Aye, that is my name, lass, and I would that you know it."

That, at least, I can share without shame.

"MacLean of the Isles?" she prodded, tipping her head.

"Nay, of Baldoon on the Isle of Doon in the Isles," he corrected, and knew a moment's uneasiness—a ridiculous tide of nerves washing o'er him that perchance his calamitous reputation or even his most recent act of sacrilege had somehow found the way to her ear.

But she merely nodded, her greenish gold gaze flickering o'er him, the disappointment he'd noted just before crossing the kirkyard now replaced by open curiosity.

She looked past him to where his pilgrim's gear lay discarded on the stony ground. "I knew you were not a pilgrim."

"A pilgrim, nay," Iain agreed, "but on a similar path."

A journey of penitence, his conscience urged him to add, but he glanced aside instead.

He'd tell her the rest—the most of it—later.

After he'd found suitably respectable lodgings for them for the night . . . and perhaps, too, after he'd plied her with a wee dollop or two of fine and fiery *uisge beatha,* a good Scotsman's "water of life" and thought to be a cure-all for every ailment known to man.

Hopefully, too, for averting disenchantment.

Unable to help himself, he gently tucked a loose curl behind her ear.

Something he'd burned to do ever since she'd stepped from the burial enclosure, his cloak and her badly torn head veil clutched in her hands, her red-gold tresses no longer hidden but wound in satiny-looking plaits above her ears, a riot of bright-gleaming curls tumbling sweetly about her face.

He swallowed hard, the cool silk of that one wee curl, the satiny-smooth warmth of her cheek beneath his fingertips sending arrow bolts of keenest desire streaking through him.

She regarded him with an unblinking gaze, but a faint pink tinge colored her cheeks, and he would've sworn a light shiver traversed her length at his touch.

Endeavoring not to disillusion or frighten her, Iain

lifted away his hand, struggled to keep his gaze from dipping to the torn bodice showing beneath her unfastened cloak.

Two brooches held the ruined gown together, her own and his, for he'd forgotten he'd secreted the heavily enameled cairngorm brooch on the inside of his pilgrim's cloak, using it thus to fasten the hated mantle without calling undue attention to the piece's worth.

Despite himself, he stared at his brooch, at the remnants of the once-fine cloth it held together. His hands fisted, rage pounding through him at the stark reminder of what had been done to her—and at the worse villainies she could have faced.

He stifled a furious oath, hoped the long shadows cast by the nearby yews hid the muscle beginning to tic in his jaw.

Hid, too, the increasing edginess that he had yet to proffer his protection as her escort . . . and under the guise of her husband.

To his dismay, his cheeks began to prickle and burn, and he prayed to any gods who might hear him that he wasn't blushing.

Prayed, too, that her response wouldn't press him into forcing her acquiescence. The saints knew he'd rather march naked through the deepest, darkest glen in a storm of sleet and rain.

Forcing a woman to do aught against her will would break the one code of honor he prided himself on ne'er having breached.

The only corner of his valor he'd kept brightly polished since the very first day he noticed a difference between himself and the fairer sex.

Ill ease closing in fast, he slid a helpless look in Mac-
Fie's direction, thankfully catching the Islesman's eye, but
the bland-faced bastard merely shrugged . . . clearly content to withhold himself from Iain's task of persuading the
two women of the necessity of remaining together.

The need to submit themselves to the farce of pre-
tended marriages.

Feeling more inept by the moment, Iain drew a long
breath before he returned his attention to Madeline.

And the instant he did, a fierce jolt of pure male appreciation shot through him when his gaze defied his best
intentions and flew straight to his brooch, this time seemingly determined to linger there.

And what true man's gaze wouldn't, for the scooped-
neck bodice bore such a jagged tear a full score of
brooches would have failed to repair the damage.

Worse yet—for him—the sight of something of his
resting so close against her skin proved almost more than
he could bear, for her attempt to recover her modesty
only drew the tattered linen tighter across the full swells
of her breasts, emphasizing rather than shielding their
lushness.

One or two irreparable rips gaped wide, giving delicious glimpses no red-blooded man ought be exposed
to . . . lest he be allowed to sate the lust such sweetness
was sure to stir in his loins.

Iain's throat instantly tightened, as did other parts of
him.

Indeed, it'd taken but one fleeting look at a single
coral-tinted nipple, puckered tight and thrusting, for his
body to make short work of his fervent wish not to un-
settle her.

And she thought him a gallant.

Shoving nervous fingers through his hair, he said a silent prayer of thanks for the loose-hanging folds of his plaid.

Nevertheless, if she peered as closely at his lower body as she was studying his face, she'd soon see just what an un-gallant he was.

So he turned away.

And hoped another glance at MacFie's ugly countenance would banish the rise beneath his plaid.

Blessedly, it did, and he wheeled to face her as soon as he knew he could without further compromising her modesty.

"Iain of Baldoon," she surprised him by saying, again seeming to practice its feel.

"So I have said," Iain ceded, amazed his voice didn't crack like a besotted squire's, so enchanting was the way she said his name. The soft lilt of her Highland tongue a sweet balm he'd not tire of hearing, if he lived a thousand years. "But there is more I must tell you."

She peered at him. "Aye?"

A flicker of interest flitted across her face. No coyness or condemnation . . . just a look of simple and honest inquiry.

Iain's heart twisted, then began thumping hard against his ribs.

How long had it been since a lass had eyed him with aught but accusation or pity?

And even *before*, with the exception of his sweet Lileas, it'd been the glitter of MacLean gold lighting every bonnie female face to turn his way.

That, or the titillating thrill of bedding a laird's brother.

The closest many an ambitious lass would e'er come to such a coup.

And Iain had ne'er much cared . . . till now.

Straightening his shoulders, he clasped his hands behind his back. He was almost certain they'd begun trembling and he wouldn't embarrass himself by adding weakness to his long list of faults.

So he stood as straight as he could, waited for her gaze to cease flitting over him, and hoped he wouldn't catch a gleam of calculation hiding anywhere within the depths of her gorgeous, thick-lashed eyes.

"I ken what you want to tell me," she said, her green-gold eyes all innocence and wonder.

Iain arched a brow, waited.

"You are laird," she said, and Iain's heart plummeted to his toes.

Careful to keep his alarm at bay, he steeled himself to rectify her conclusion. "Sweet lass, I would subsist upon naught but bread and water if I could please you by claiming it were so, but I am not laird," he told her. "I am but the laird's brother."

To his amazement, she simply shrugged.

"It matters not," she said, her gaze full earnest. "But I vow your brother is one of the most fortunate lairds in the land."

Iain eyed her carefully. Surely he'd misheard her.

He had to be dreaming.

She reached up to press gentle fingers to his cheek. "I should like to know more of you, good sir," she breathed, and a shadow passed o'er her face. "Aye, I truly wish I could."

Iain stared at her, his skin tingling where she'd touched him. Golden warmth like he'd never known spilled through him, its sweetness cloaking the faint glimmer of regret in her eyes. Erasing, too, the tint of melancholy coloring her last words.

Her *other* words shot straight to his heart and made him want to throw off every cumbersome chain of guilt, yank her into his arms, and claim her lips in a searing, never-ending kiss.

A fine, soul-slaking kiss to make up for all their lost yesterdays and to lend resplendent promise to the many tomorrows lying before them.

Tomorrows that should have lain before them.

A bliss that would ne'er unfold.

Iain blinked away the thoughts, suppressed a frown, and almost succeeded in closing his ears on the voices of a past he couldn't flee.

Indeed, a decidedly gruff-sounding harrumph at his elbow minded him of the impossibility of escape.

"I thought Amicia's *arisaid* would suit our disguise better than a torn and soiled postulant's robe," Gavin MacFie declared, Amicia's exquisitely woven plaid dangling from his outstretched hand.

"Disguise?" Madeline's brows shot up, her gaze flying to her friend, then to Iain's sister's *arisaid* . . . the same one he'd used to wrap around a few of the most priceless pieces of MacLean treasure.

Precious goods stashed in the very bottom of his travel bag.

A fierce growl rose in Iain's throat, his fingers itching to curl around the Islesman's neck.

A neck slowly turning as red as the bastard's beard. "You haven't told her yet," the dimwit stammered, for once having the grace to appear nonplussed.

Saints, he even looked rattled.

A condition Iain would have reveled in under any other circumstance.

"Told me what?" Madeline whirled on him, her wide-eyed paleness lighting balefires of warning across every inch of ground he'd managed to win from her.

He opened his mouth to speak—to say something, anything—but no words came, for his tongue seemed determined to stick to the roof of his mouth. Ramming both hands through his hair, he wished the stony ground would open up beneath his feet.

His blood cooking, he glowered at MacFie.

She blew out a breath and swung on her friend. "What have I not been told?" she repeated, a vein pulsing visibly at the base of her throat. "And what is this about a disguise? Who is Amicia?"

The older woman met her questions with a well-meaning if cautious smile. "Amicia is your shadow man's sister," she said, indicating Iain.

With surprising agility, she plucked the *arisaid* from MacFie's hand and thrust it into Madeline's arms before she could voice a protest.

As quickly, she snatched away the wadded mass of Iain's pilgrim's cloak and handed it to him.

He took it, some unattached part of himself noting that it now smelled faintly of heather before he sent it sailing through the air to join the other cast-aside vestiges of his pilgrim disguise.

"What you've not yet been told," Nella of the Marsh was saying, "is that these two gallants have kindly offered us their escort." The words out, she looked so pleased with herself Iain wondered fleetingly where her loyalty lay.

Madeline looked anything but pleased. Her eyes widened to an alarming degree, and every freckle gracing her proud cheekbones stood out in stark relief against the gleaming whiteness of her skin.

Her companion rushed on, clearly unconcerned . . . or perhaps well used to the lady's wrath. "For propriety's sake and our own good safety, they've suggested posing as our husbands until we've reached our destination."

Sheer panic—and barely contained anger—broke out on Madeline's face. She stared at her friend, nigh white-lipped, her eyes darkening to a deep, mossy green, the lovely golden flecks completely gone.

Iain stared at her, slack-jawed.

Were he not so intimately involved in her vexation, he would have hooted with amusement, for ne'er had he seen a lass come anywhere close to the fury of his own unleashed temper.

Ne'er until that moment.

Her indignant gaze flitted between the three of them before settling on her companion. "We do not need an escort," she ground out, her agitation palpable. "And I'll have naught to do with the husband part of it."

Clenching Amicia's *arisaid* so tightly her knuckles ran white, and with high color seeping onto her cheeks, she looked every proud inch an unconquerable Celtic warrior princess.

She swiped a curl away from her eyes. "You ken we must travel alone . . . and why."

Nella folded her arms, apparently every bit as brave and daring. "And you, my la—" she broke off, her own cheeks flaming. "You cannot say I e'er approved. Two lone women a-traipsing across the land!"

Leaning forward, she braved Madeline's narrow-eyed stare. "No matter the reason."

"And what *is* the reason?" The question slipped from Iain's lips before he could catch it . . . remembering too late the danger of provoking anyone caught in the throes of such white-faced fury.

She rounded on him. "None that I care to discuss, sirrah," she said, the whole sweet column of her throat and the fine upper curves of her breasts wearing the same becoming flush as her cheeks. "Not even in the face of your gallantry, which I shall ne'er forget and e'er cherish."

That last, and the wee shade of regret he'd caught lighting across her face as she'd said it, gave him hope . . . and the encouragement he needed to seize his advantage.

He stepped forward before the courage left him, lifted his hands, palms outward. "I give you my word of ho—" —he broke off to slide a warning glance at MacFie—"my word of honor that no harm shall come to either of you from this hour onward, my lady," he sought to reassure her.

"Not so long as you are in our care," he added, low-voiced . . . and, he hoped, with enough quiet certitude to calm her. "We shall see you safely whither you please."

"Nay." She waved a dismissive hand and began backing away from him, her swift retreat causing her to stumble over a toppled headstone.

She caught herself, but one of the cloak brooches sprang from her bodice and dropped to the ground.

The nipple Iain'd glimpsed earlier popped into view, the tear in her bodice gaping wide enough to display it fully. Wholly relaxed this time, the nipple's unpuckered fullness and the round disk of her surprisingly large areola proved just as rousing as in a tightly ruched state.

Iain's loins clenched at once.

His conscience chided him.

And she gasped, clapping a quick hand over the delightfully exposed delicacy.

"Oh, dear saints, whate'er have I done to be so tested!" she cried, a telltale brightness sparkling in her eyes. "Just leave me be, all of you," she pleaded, and swirled Amicia's *arisaid* about her shoulders.

With a last, furious glance at each of them, she snatched up the fallen brooch, spun on her heel, and hastened out of the kirkyard.

Gavin MacFie whistled and turned aside. Shaking his head, he took Nella's elbow and began guiding her toward his horse. Too flummoxed to move, Iain watched them go, knowing without asking that she'd ride with Gavin to MacNab's.

He also knew he'd not ride anywhere without his particular *bane* sitting securely before him . . . whether she desired to accompany him or nay.

'Twas for her own good, he told himself, starting after her.

He caught up with her in eight easy strides.

"Lass, you have just caused me to break the one code

of honor I ne'er thought I would," he grumbled, and swept her into his arms.

A dark scowl now marring *his* face, he strode back through the kirkyard gate, carrying her toward his waiting garron. With each step of way he tried not to think about the gravity of his deed.

For not only had he just abducted a woman against her will, he'd also rubbed grime all o'er the last untarnished corner of his pride.

Chapter Eight

MANY HOURS LATER AND MUCH incensed, Madeline huddled above a wee patch of heather-free ground, her rumpled skirts bunched about her hips, and blew out a breath of sheerest frustration. She kept a narrow-eyed stare pinned on *him,* her shadow man, and wondered where her dignity had gone.

More than that, she couldn't decide which of her present depredations plagued her the most—her aching feet, her fiercely sore buttocks, or the humiliation of Iain MacLean's refusal to allow her to slip alone into the sheltering cluster of gorse bushes and dwarf hawthorns.

Dangers a-plenty roamed the land, he'd minded her, excusing his overly vigilant shepherding by claiming robbers, rogues, and ravagers bedeviled even this pleasant country of gently wooded slopes and deceptively peaceful vales.

Especially in these times of disharmony and lawlessness in the Scottish realm.

He'd underscored his point by tightening the arm he'd wrapped securely about her middle when, his warning scarce spoken, they'd passed the gutted ruin of an empty cot-house, its fire-scorched walls and blackened roof thatch lending harsh validity to his caution.

In truth, leaving her glad of it.

Unbidden, Silver Leg's hood-eyed visage flashed through her mind, and a torrent of cold shivers snaked down her spine. Lifting her chin a notch higher, she closed her heart to the horrors she'd seen and wished a triplefold plague on the dastard.

Blinked back the tears she'd sworn not to shed for her father until she'd seen his death avenged.

Aye, 'twas glad she was of her shadow man's protection.

But not *this* glad.

Pressing her lips into a firm line, she aimed another barrage of impotently defiant daggers at his broad back and wished the tumbling burn beside her would gurgle and splash with a bit more vigor.

Nay, much more vigor!

Her pointless wish expended, she dug her fingers deeper into the woolen folds of her gathered skirts and longed to make a few blaring noises of her own. A peppered word or two, muttered loudly, or at the very least an indignant, windy huff.

But any such outburst might incite him to wheel about to face her, and, saints be praised, so far he'd kept his word.

As he'd promised, he held a fair distance, and gave not the slightest indication of turning around . . . or even sneaking a glance over his shoulder.

Nor did he rush her.

But he could surely hear her.

And that knowledge blasted heat straight up the back

of Madeline's neck. She bit down on her lower lip, a hot tide of sharp-edged embarrassment coursing through her, making her task all the more difficult.

He appeared perfectly at ease with their rather delicate undertaking.

Not ten feet away, he waited beside his quietly grazing garron. Nary a muscle on the whole tall length of him moved, his entire body arrow-straight and so rigid he might as well be carved of solid, living stone.

He stood with his long, well-hewn legs braced slightly apart, and even his hands bespoke his masterful self-possession, clasped simply and ever-so-casually behind his back.

Madeline eyed him, quite certain he'd becharmed her—for how else could he have haunted her dreams for weeks? Make her look on him in favor, moon-eyed and swooning o'er his bonnie muscles, now, when caught in the throes of such an awkward moment?

Faith, his braw proximity rendered anything *but* gawking at him a feat of near impossibility.

So she resigned herself and used their unique positioning to send her appreciative gaze sliding over every darkly handsome inch of him.

The brisk evening breeze riffled his unbound hair, an unseen caress along its sleek raven spill. Insistent, curling warmth began to pulse low in Madeline's belly. As so often since he'd abandoned his pilgrim's garb, a fierce urge to touch his hair seized her, spiraling through her with ever-increasing intensity until each one of her fingertips tingled with an eager, raging need.

She stared at him, stunned by her overpowering compulsion to feel great silky handfuls of the glossy blue-black strands pouring, cool and smooth, over her palms and sifting through her greedy fingers.

A pleasure she burned to experience . . . if only just once.

And soon, while she still had time for such feminine frivols.

Blowing out an irritable breath, she glanced aside, looked out across endless heather-clad braes to the silent waters of a distant loch, its mirrorlike surface a deep steely blue in the approaching twilight.

So familiar a landscape, so new and bewildering the feelings her shadow man awakened in her.

So frighteningly irresistible.

She looked back at him, and still more shivers spilled down her spine, but delicious tingles this time, each delicious thread spooling together to join the decidedly intimate pulsings already stirring low in her belly.

Scarce recognizing herself, she tightened her grasp on her skirts, her breath catching at her fierce reaction to him. She squeezed shut her eyes, half-wishing the tantalizing sensations spinning inside her, the piercing ache for what couldn't be, would cease when she reopened them.

But they didn't.

If anything, they increased.

The instant she opened her eyes, the sweet throbbing so close to the very center of her femininity sent echoing ripples to every corner of her body.

Even her toes grew warm and tingly.

The intimacy of holding her skirts hitched about her hips with him so near, stirred her, too—regardless of the reason she did so.

She released a quivering sigh, and felt more the wanton than the Abercairn kitchen maids she'd occasionally spied slipping into dark corners with bonnie squires.

Saints, but her Master of the Highlands thrilled her, and in ways no decent woman ought allow.

She drew deeply of the chill evening air, fortifying herself on its comforting earthiness, a bracing blend of damp heather, gorse, and quartz-shot stone, until the prickly tingles ceased whirling through her.

Until she could once again concentrate on what she needed to do.

Or at least focus on one of Iain MacLean's less-distracting attributes.

Such as what a patient man he seemed.

Thoughtful, too, for he'd urged his mount off the road the moment she'd voiced her need, indulging her modesty without complaint and striking ever farther up the sloping moorside despite the rough going.

He'd picked a tedious path, urging his surefooted garron, a Highland beast well used to harsh terrain, across mud-slicked ground and through thickest heather, carefully skirting bog holes and outcroppings of large, lichen-covered boulders until they'd found a thicket dense enough to suit her.

And now that they'd found one, a myriad of difficulties assailed her . . . in particular her dangerously flaring attraction to him. A passion she couldn't allow to flourish even if his heart wasn't hung on another.

Madeline frowned, her palms beginning to dampen. She blew a dangling curl from her eye and shifted her position to avoid the tickling brush of a tall-growing clump of deer grass.

"We still have a good score of miles to ride." His deep voice rose above her shame and ire—blessedly giving her just the cover she needed to complete her task.

"Can you not be quicker about your ... er ... *business?*" he added, his usually mellifluous voice sounding more than a little strained.

Mortification fired Madeline's cheeks. "I am almost finished," she shot back, quite certain her face would soon glow bright enough to illuminate the coming night for miles.

"I am glad to hear it, for I am no wilted dotard, I assure you," came his terse reply, and even she, uninitiated in the baser needs of men, didn't mishear the taut-sounding urgency behind his words ... or misread the reason for it. "I pray you, lass, have done so we—"

"We two do not make a 'we,'" she snapped, tight-voiced and all too aware of ... everything.

All too aware of him.

He merely arched a cynical brow.

She didn't need to see it to know ... it was quite noticeable in the stiffening of his wide-set shoulders and the visible tensing of his hands.

Eyeing him sourly, her vexation at the whole of her plight flared like embers caught in the teeth of a fine and gusty draught. Almost wishing he'd proven podgy-handed and cross-eyed rather than so appealing she could scarce draw breath around him, she kept her gaze fastened on his back—willing him to stay put—and made swift use of the dried clump of absorbent sphagnum moss he'd given her to ease her task.

"I am finished," she announced, relief sluicing off her.

She pushed to her feet, smoothed her skirts. "T-thank you for the . . . *the sphagnum.*"

He turned around, gave her a tight nod. "You will appreciate it even more after I've attended your rope burns this eve." His dark gaze flickered to her ankles, her wrists, lit briefly on her hips . . . or somewhere thereabouts. "Sphagnum moss also works wonders on the soreness plaguing a certain part of you, my lady."

The ground dipped beneath Madeline's feet. He meant her buttocks! "I am not sore."

"Och, nay?" He cocked another brow . . . one she saw this time. "Then why are you standing bent at the waist and with a hand pressed hard against your hip?"

Madeline straightened at once, and so quickly, she couldn't stop a pained wince from slipping past her lips.

His curved in a knowing smile.

Or rather the left corner of his mouth lifted in that odd quirking that seemed to pass for his smile.

She blinked, took a step backward.

He peered hard at her, his expression a curious mix of looking bemused and infuriated. Several long minutes passed before he spoke. "Whether it pleases you or nay, lass, we *are* and shall give ourselves as a 'we' so long as our paths run together," he said, striding forward, his gait smooth and fluid, his voice almost a growl.

A predator's growl.

He towered over her, looming so close she had to crane her neck to look up at him. "As for your soreness . . . and I ken you'll be hurting . . . so long as you bide in my care, I see myself responsible for attending to your comfort as well as your safekeeping."

"I am fine," Madeline blurted, denying the fiery pain biting deep into her buttocks.

And wishing she could deny how thrilling some vixen hiding inside her found the thought of his hands smoothing salve onto her bared flesh.

Any part of her bared flesh, even *there* where such pounding hurt throbbed and burned she doubted she'd be able to sit comfortably for a sennight.

"A sphagnum tincture soothed onto your . . . er . . . *hurts* will ease the discomfort and help you sleep." Looking uncomfortably deep into her eyes, he smoothed his knuckles down her cheek. "You needn't look so stricken. I'll simply prepare the sphagnum for you. I didn't say I would apply it."

"Oh." Madeline swallowed her disappointment, hoped he wouldn't see any lingering trace of it on her face.

"Though some might tell you otherwise, you needn't fear me," he said, and touched one knuckle to the tip of her nose. Stepping back, he held out his hands, palms outward. "I shall look after you as best I can until the hour I deliver you to where'er it is you were heading before our paths crossed."

I was heading to hell, sirrah, but I fear I've already arrived.

Hastening there by the day and dreaming of you by night, she almost blurted.

Instead she lifted her chin. "I do not fear you, sirrah. Nor do I care what others might say of you," she vowed, then added the words she must. "You may leave me at the gate of the nearest convent. It matters not which one."

He angled his head to the side, studied her. "I say you it should, lass."

A sudden shift in the wind wrapped his scent around her, enveloping her in its clean, spicy maleness, and beguiling her senses so thoroughly she swayed a bit. He reached for her at once, grasping her firmly just above her elbows, the warmth of his strong fingers seeping through the layers of her clothes to become fine, tingling currents racing up and down her arms.

"I am loath to disillusion you," he said, clearly unaware of his effect on her, "but vice and debauchery in nunneries has been on the rise for years. Some establishments are little better than joy houses these days."

"Then I shall give care not to enter a tainted one."

Iain shook his head. "Nay, lass, I shall give that care."

Assuring they made a wide bypath around any and all ecclesiastical refuges known to be of sordid repute was the least he could do for her. And for his own sorely dented pride, now that he didn't possess a single remaining fleck of untarnished honor.

He cleared his throat. "If you have no preference, I shall see you to the Bishopric of Dunkeld," he proposed, purposely choosing the last stop on his journey of penance.

If he couldn't keep her . . . he might as well enjoy having her near for as long as circumstances allowed.

Long enough to learn her secrets and mayhap steal a kiss or two.

Such a wee sin couldn't add much more black to his soul.

"Dunkeld?" she fair squeaked the word.

He inclined his head.

"Dunkeld is an ancient and worthy establishment,"

he declared, warming to the idea. "My clan has ties to the bishopric, so I can leave you there with good conscience."

"Dunkeld Cathedral?" she echoed again.

"Is there any other?" Iain looked sharply at her, not missing the slight furrowing of her brow.

Nor the widening of her lovely green-gold eyes, the quicksilver flash of distress momentarily discoloring their beauty.

She knew Dunkeld and didn't want to go there.

Iain was certain of it.

"Dunkeld is as good as any," she acquiesced, with a too-carefree shrug.

The sensitive skin on the back of Iain's neck began to tingle, the fine hairs of his nape lifting. His every nerve end snapped to rapt attention.

He recognized that shrug.

It was the same kind Amicia affected when something mattered greatly to her but she meant to hide its importance.

Certain he'd stumbled onto his first clue to her true identity, Iain rubbed his chin with equally feigned disinterest. He glanced casually at rain clouds banking in the distance. "It will do us no hurt to examine other nunneries along the way," he tossed out, testing her.

He looked back at her, watching her closely.

And she didn't disappoint him.

He could almost see her ears perking.

She pounced on his bait with astonishing speed, nodding so energetically the red-gold curls framing her face bobbed as if they'd taken on a life of their own. "That would please me," she said, a telltale breathiness in her voice. "I am eager to take the veil, good sir."

A lie if e'er he'd heard one.

But she was eager to be about *something*.

Of that he was certain.

Iain sighed. "My route of travel will take us past St. Fillan's and its Healing Pond, for one," he suggested, choosing this possibility because of its nearness. "Mayhap you will find more favor there?"

"Oh, aye," she agreed without the slightest hesitation, her enthusiasm scarce contained. "I have heard of the pond's healing qualities."

Iain fought to keep from calling her on her lies.

As he'd suspected, she received the suggestion of St. Fillan with visible relief, even turning aside to hide it from him. But when she swung back, her own gaze probed, a shadow that could have passed for regret stealing some of the warmth out of her eyes.

Definitely damping her excitement.

She looked at him long and piercingly. "So you *are* on a pilgrimage?"

Iain shoved a hand through his hair, wished again he could flash her a brilliant smile, mayhap even laugh, and then assure her that, nay, he was merely making a foray across the land.

Attending clan business for his brother, the laird.

But if he hoped to hold even a smidgen of her esteem, he could not and wouldn't lie to her.

So he squared his shoulders, gave her one of his twisted smiles, and spoke the truth. "A pilgrimage of sorts, aye," he admitted, before his fear of tainting her view of him could rise in spirited protest. "I am doing a penance, lass."

"A penance?" No accusation, simply keen interest.

"So I have said, and one I deserve, I must say you." He moved to his garron, using the breadth of his plaid-slung back to shield how deeply her lack of shock or scorn touched him.

"But be of sure heart, that I am not a marauder or murderer," he told her anyway. "Worse could befall you than riding with me."

Turning, he gestured her to him. "I shall tell you the reason for my journey after we've paused for the night, but now we must make haste to reach adequate lodgings. It is a lengthy ride to the next township."

She blinked, but came forward. Hesitantly. "Township?"

"Would you camp the night in the roofless shell of yon cot-house?" He looked up at the darkening sky. Even the wind now held the damp smell of coming rain. "A storm brews, lass, and I would see us dry before it breaks."

Taking her lower lip between her teeth, she slid a sidelong glance in the direction of the cot-house's lamentable remains, a speculative glint sparking in her gold-cast eyes. "Nella and I have slept in less welcoming places than a burned-out crofter's cottage."

"Well, you shall not this night," Iain decided for her.

Without warning, he seized her by the waist and lifted her onto the garron's back. Quickly, before she could object.

Or tear off through the heather, costing them both an unnecessary and time-wasting sprint across the rough, uneven ground.

A fool's errand she ought have known would only end with his catching her.

And maybe demanding a kiss as recompense for his trouble.

"I do not want to overnight in a township," she objected, her full lips pursing in such a tempting fashion he was wont to kiss her right then.

Breathing a silent oath, he vaulted up behind her, pulled her securely against his chest. "You have no choice, sweeting," he whispered against her hair as he kneed the horse into motion.

And neither do you, his MacLean heart taunted him.

Not in wanting her.

Nor that, even now, before they'd put the steeply sloping brae behind them and returned to the road, he was already contemplating ways to sneak a kiss from her.

Or that with every passing hour spent with her, he was proving himself less and less worthy of the style she'd bestowed on him.

Frowning as darkly as the fast-approaching rain clouds, Iain spurred the garron to greater speed and chose to ignore the title his conscience tossed at him.

Unchivalrous blackguard.

A heartless scoundrel out to take advantage of an unescorted and helpless lass.

A maid, he was certain.

His scowl returned, settling even darker across his brow when a good hour later he spied a monastery where they would surely have found refuge and succor in a welcoming hospice . . . yet he dug in his knees, urging his mount onward, even possessing the gall to be gladhearted the lass had fallen asleep and couldn't notice.

Instead, he rode on, keeping to the northern road until the rugged moorland gave way to even higher ground, the hills heavily forested and cut through with long, deep glens . . . but eventually sloping down to just the type of village he'd been hoping to find.

Not quite a township, but an unwalled and sleepy cluster of low-browed, thatch-topped cottages built 'round a small, gray-walled kirk. A long-ruined fortalice tower stood dark on its mound some distance away, and a scattering of sheep and cattle grazed on the common pastureland.

Iain felt a twinge of guilt but quickly tamped it down.

Any weary travelers seeking lodgings in such a forgotten hamlet would have no recourse but to spend the night in the local inn.

Such as it would prove to be.

The kind offering pallets of straw on the common room floor, a flea-ridden bed shared by many in a room that hadn't known a gust of fresh air in centuries . . . or a private room, tiny but clean, if the innkeeper was shown a handful of coin.

And Iain MacLean had coin a-plenty.

So he gritted his teeth and kicked his garron's sides, spurring toward the little village and what he hoped would be the most pleasant night he'd spent in ages.

Accepting, too, that his surreptitious machinations marked him for the kind of lout he could no longer deny he'd become.

A self-serving blackguard.

And a greater one than his clan or any who knew him would e'er believe.

Chapter Nine

$\mathcal{D}$EEPENING TWILIGHT, GUSTY WIND, and a thin drizzle of slanting rain accompanied Iain through the sleepy hamlet. The rapidly worsening weather and empty, straw-mired streets soundly cloaked any appeal the village might have held on a bonnier, less storm-plagued night, while low rumbles of distant thunder underscored the futility of seeking shelter elsewhere.

A self-inflicted complication he sorely regretted the instant his garron clattered beneath the arched gateway of the village's sole hostelry and he spied the ale-stake, a long, horizontal pole projecting from above the door.

Its unwieldy length adorned with bundles of leafy, green branches, the fool contraption bobbed dangerously in the ever-increasing wind ... and marked his chosen lodging as an *alehouse* rather than the more commodious and hospitable inn he'd hoped to find.

Dread stalking him, he drew rein beside a towering pile of cut peat not far from the stables. He expelled an irritated breath and glanced around, his gaze flickering over the tavern's muddied foreyard.

Squawking chickens pecked at the soiled straw scattered across the mushy ground and pigs grunted in ankle-deep muck. The noisome beasties edged ever nearer to snuffle at his garron's shaggy fetlocks. Iain frowned, convinced he'd left his wits somewhere on the road behind him.

Right about where he'd spotted the monastery tucked away in a dark wood . . . and ridden on. His hand fisted around the reins, guilt tweaking him.

A goatherd would have known better.

The lowliest sower of grain.

He had, too, truth be told, but he'd so wanted a kiss. Or rather quarters for the night that would have proven conducive to stealing one.

Instead, he'd found a wee scrap of an alehouse. A dubious-looking establishment he doubted could procure a ewer and basin of warmed water and soap, much less a private, vermin-free bed.

A shudder snaked down his spine, and he slanted another frustrated glance at the weaving ale-stake. His every instinct shouted at him to wheel about, spur his garron, and be gone. Ride away before *she* awakened, journeying the whole night through if need be.

Windy mizzle, empty belly, or nay.

But the buttery yellow pools of torchlight spilling from the establishment's half-shuttered windows beckoned and the rain-chased air, misty and damp in the close confines of the inn yard, held the distinct aroma of deliciously roasted meats.

His stomach clenched and growled, and he imagined Madeline's did, too, even though, from the relaxed, pliant feel of her, she still dozed quite soundly.

He looked at her, something inside him softening at the way she leaned so trustingly against him, at how the soft weight of her warmed more than his physical body. She'd pulled Amicia's *arisaid*—a MacLean plaid—over her head, using its woolen folds to shield her from the mizzling rain and that, too, touched him.

Made her seem needful of him, a thought that took his breath away.

Iain MacLean, scourge of his clan, *needed*.

He swallowed roughly, for one moment of fanciful indulgence allowing his heart to thump harder, to climb just a few wee inches up his throat.

The lass made him feel alive again.

And heated, despite the night's chill winds and persistent, misting rain.

He drew a long breath, let the scent of her fill his senses. Sweet as an angel's breath, its clean, heathery lightness chased the dark from his soul and sent hair-thin cracks spreading every which way across the vitrified casing of his heart.

Iain blinked, tried to rid himself of such fool romantic musings. But the more he sought to banish them, the worse they became.

The wilder, more bold, and far too hurtful to allow.

Tightening his jaw, he frowned up at the darkening sky, his resentment at the foul weather nigh as great as his scorn for himself, for the heavy, pewter gray clouds marred how wonderfully right it felt to have his arm wrapped about her slender waist.

And the thin smirr of sideways rain tainted his pleasure in how temptingly the full, bottom swells of her breasts brushed against the top of his forearm.

This time of year, the night should have been limpid, pure, and awash with finest luminosity until the wee hours.

And had the fates been kind, kissed with enough magic to spare him a dollop or two.

But the gods preferred to vex him by ladling a goodly dose of raucous laughter and coarse, upraised voices onto the lashing wind, and upping the ear-splitting screech of the ale-stake as it swung on its rusty hinges.

His conscience hounded him, too. It banded together with the scattered remnants of his chivalry to catch him unawares the instant the tavern's thick-planked door swung open and its errant ale-draper stepped outside, a slop pail clutched in his meaty hands.

She awakened, too, jerking upright with a startled gasp even as the dark-frowning shadow of his conscience watched his every move from a murk-filled recess near the arched doorway.

Twisting around, she blinked at him, her lovely eyes hazy with sleep. "W-where are we?" she asked, her honeyed voice equally slumber-drugged.

And so maddeningly alluring Iain's fingers itched to whip out his steel and slice his glowering conscience to ribboned shreds.

The ruddy-complexioned tavern-keeper, too, if he dared come betwixt such a fine, almost intimate moment.

But he did, of course . . . much to Iain's perturbation.

With a well-practiced flick of his wrist, the portly ale-draper flung the contents of his slop pail onto the muddy ground. He tossed aside the empty bucket and strode forward. "Ho, good sir!" he called, wiping his hands on a grimy cloth hanging from a wide leather belt slung low beneath his considerable girth.

"Lady." He dipped his head to Madeline, his greeting amiable if a mite ingratiating. "Welcome to the Shepherd's Rest," he greeted them, a decidedly speculative gleam in his eyes. "How may I serve you?"

Iain dismounted, then reached for Madeline. He eased her off the garron's back, but kept her in his arms, holding her high against his chest so her dangling feet remained well above the mired ground.

"My wife and I require good victuals, your best ale, and quarters for the night," he said, crossing the inn yard. *"Private quarters."*

The tavern-keeper bristled. "Meals here are praised for miles around, and some claim I brew the finest heather ale in the land," he spluttered, holding wide the door as Iain swept past him into the common room. "But I'm full up for the night . . . lest you wish a pallet on the floor?"

Iain paused just inside the threshold, surveyed the alehouse's crowded interior. Smoky blue haze from a low-burning peat fire hung thick in the air, its pleasant tang well laced with the earthier smell of ale-soaked floor rushes.

He turned to the tavern-keeper, arched a brow. "Have you naught better than the floor?"

"'Tis a busy night, sir," the man said with shrug and a sidelong glance at his roistering patrons. Flush-cheeked and loud, they filled all but one of the rough-hewn oaken tables . . . a smaller one near the door and full in the draught of the cold, damp air pouring through the shutter slats.

Iain frowned, shoved an agitated hand through his hair.

Even the settles flanking the cavernous stone hearth proved occupied. And those were most often left unheeded, the stifling heat thrown off by the peat fire making the hard-backed settles less desirable seating than the bench-lined trestle tables.

"Good sir, we have had a day of long and hard riding. My wife is sore tired," Iain said with an eloquent glance at the black-raftered ceiling. "Are you sure you haven't a wee niche of room hidden away abovestairs?"

The ale-draper gave another apologetic shrug. "Most folks hereabouts make do with sleeping space on one of the common beds in the back room, but even those are spoken for this night." He spread his hands. "Four to a bed."

"Pray let us ride on," *she* breathed into his ear. "I do not like it here."

Something in her tone made the hairs on Iain's nape lift, but he lowered her onto the bench of the only empty table and patted her shoulder in what he hoped she'd perceive as a gesture of reassurance. "The heavens just cracked open above us, lass," he said, and a furious clap of thunder lent truth to his observation.

She jumped, stared up at him with rounded eyes. "But—"

"Sweet lass, we'd be soaked to the bone before we even left the inn yard." Iain leaned close, smoothed a damp curl from her brow. "I will not see you catch ill," he added, raising his voice above the pelting rain and wind. "Do you not hear the storm?"

Before she could answer or worse, reveal their deception, he turned back to the ale-draper. Squaring his shoulders, he assumed his best brother-of-the-laird posture. "Even the humblest establishments are wont to keep quarters for those wishing privacy."

As he'd suspected would happen, a glimmer of interest flickered across the other's face. Encouraged, Iain discreetly lifted a fold of his plaid to reveal the bulging leather purse hanging from his waist belt. "It would be propitious for you if you can procure such a chamber."

"There is one room. . . ." the tavern-keeper owned, eyeing the coin pouch.

Iain let his plaid fall back in place. "Is it clean?"

The man hesitated, moistened his lips. He slid a glance at a harried-looking serving maid replenishing burned-out candles on the tables. "My daughter can change the bed linens. But the room is dear . . ." He let his words trail off, toyed with the end of his drying cloth.

Taking the cue, Iain fished a few coins from his purse. "I'll double your profit if you send up a bath and triple it if you make haste."

The tavern-keeper bobbed his head. "I shall see to it myself as you sup, milord," he crooned, accepting the coins. "You shall bathe in rose water and sleep on swan down."

"See you only that it is private and clean," Iain said, taking a seat across from Madeline.

He reached for her hand, tried to tell himself his conscience wasn't glaring at him from over her bonnie shoulder . . . and that the talk of bathing wasn't the reason for her sudden pallor.

"We need heated water to make the sphagnum tincture," he said, rubbing gentle circles across her palm with his thumb. "And a bath will soothe your aches."

She pulled away her hand, looked aside.

"Mind you, lass, I am a man and a hungry one," Iain blurted before he could think of a less clumsy formulation.

Pinching the bridge of his nose, he heaved a sigh and tried again.

"It has been overlong since I have . . . since I—" he broke off when the tavern-keeper's daughter plunked a brown-glazed jug of well-frothed heather ale and two wooden cups on the table. An older woman, perhaps her mother, set down a platter heaped with brown bread, cheese, and half a roasted capon.

Iain nodded thanks, but knew greater relief to see them hasten away.

"Since you what, sir?"

Her sweet voice caught his ear, the intimation behind the words enough to have set his face to flaming had he not long ago learned to school his features and mask his emotions.

But then he met her green-gold gaze and nearly forgot the technique.

God's eyes, had he truly been about to admit how long it'd been since he'd lain with a woman? That—as he now knew—he'd only ever slaked the burning in his loins, but ne'er come close to quelling his deeper needs? The needs of his heart?

Not even with his own late wife?

Stifling a pained grimace, Iain unsheathed his dirk and placed it beside the platter of victuals.

He inhaled deeply of the night air streaming through

the window shutters, let the chill damp fill his lungs. He looked at her, watched her across the table, and didn't know whether to laugh or cry.

She undid him beyond all belief.

He had indeed been about to look her full square in the eye and announce that only she amongst all women could banish the hunger inside him, heal the ache in his heart and make him whole.

A pronouncement that would have surely sent her bolting from the Shepherd's Rest and into the storm-chased night, never to be seen again.

Truth to tell, were he the gallant she'd styled him, he'd warn her to run miles from Iain MacLean, hot-tempered scourge of the Isles and killer of innocent wives.

Disappointment to all who trusted him.

"Sir?" This time *she* reached across the table to lightly tap his arm.

He near jumped from his skin. The simple touch sent a jolting current of intense sensation shooting through him, unleashing a raging need for more. Clamping his jaw, Iain struggled against a scarce containable desire to seize her hand and drag her bonnie fingers o'er every inch of his flesh.

Frowning darkly, he shifted on the hard bench, every fiber of his being crackling with the urgent need to share *intimate* touches with her. He burned to press the flat of her hand firmly over his heart so she could feel its thunder and know she stirred more than his baser needs.

Much more.

But for now she was peering at him, round-eyed and dewy-lipped, and making him ache simply to hear her call him by his name.

And to learn hers.

Her full and true appellation.

"I told you my name is Iain," he reminded her, lifting the ale jug to pour two cups of the thickish brew. "Not sir or lord, simply Iain . . . even if you have given me a very fine style."

He slid one of the cups across the table toward her. "It would please me if you used my name."

"Iain then," she said, but not easily, for her fingers tensed visibly on the wooden cup. Watching him, she took a careful sip of the heather ale. "You haven't told me what you meant a moment ago, sir . . . *Iain.*"

"Simply that while I am by no measure a frocked priest, neither am I as the stags roaring on the hillside in season," Iain declared, and instantly wished he could cut out his tongue.

Her eyes flew wide, her shock like a dirk thrusting into his breast.

Swallowing a curse, he set to slicing the brown bread. "Forgive my crudeness, I pray you," he got out, his gaze on his task. "I am not known for being glib-tongued."

He looked up, offered her a thick slice of the crusty, still-warm bread. "That you needn't fear sharing a chamber with me is what I am trying to say." He waited for her to accept the bread, then added, "I am not a brute-beast. I will not fall upon you when you disrobe to bathe . . . if such a worry has distressed you."

"You're mistaken." The denial came so swiftly it surprised and heartened him. "That isn't my concern. I have seen and trusted your gallantry," she said, her averted gaze on a far corner near the hearth. "But whether you are chivalrous or otherwise, it is not . . . seemly for us to share a room."

"Then we shall make it as much so as we can," Iain offered, and imagined his conscience nodding in sanctimonious approval.

"I swear to you, I shall not look the entire time you bathe," he promised, and washed down the regrettable vow with a great gulp of heather ale.

"You won't?"

Iain near choked.

Had her voice held a trace of wistful regret?

Disappointment?

Or was he indeed losing his wits as swiftly as his control?

Setting down his ale cup, he dragged the back of his hand across his mouth, and looked sharply at her. But she was still staring across the crowded common room.

"You have my word on it," he managed at last, hoping to assure her of her modesty . . . and bind himself to his pride.

Keeping his word was about all he had left of it.

"I will do naught in that chamber save tend your abraded wrists and ankles, and keep you from harm." He stared at her, at a loss to ease whate'er plagued her. "I do not renege on promises given."

A quick shake of her head was her only response. That, and to wash down a healthy bite of capon with a formidable gulp of ale.

"I do not doubt your word," she said, low-voiced, the trembling fingers wrapped round her ale cup disproving her.

Iain pried her fingers from around the wooden cup and

took her cold hand between his two. Thick tension rolled off her, and while her hand shook, there was a rigid stiffness about the rest of her that tore at his heart.

She feared him.

There could be no other explanation.

And no way to allay her concerns other than to humiliate himself.

Taking a long breath, he began caressing her palm with his thumb again. Slowly and gently. To soothe her, and to let the smooth silk of her skin settle him.

"I told you I was doing penance," he pushed out the words, each one heavy sludge dredged from the darkest, nether regions of his soul. "My sin is but my temper," he confessed. "Naught more sinister than the quick-tindered bursts of an ill humor I cannot always contain."

She bit her lower lip and slid another glance at the far corner, kept her gaze there.

And looked more fraught than before.

Beginning to feel helpless, Iain released her hand and sliced off another choice portion of roasted capon for her. He placed it on her side of the trencher, and he watched her take it, a different but equally fierce ache twisting his gut at the sight.

In addition to her more obvious discomfort, the lass clearly hadn't had a good meal in ages. She'd devoured most of what they'd been served well before he'd taken but a few bites.

Not that he cared.

Not beyond knowing a black fury at whate'er circumstances had made her so needy.

Grasping the table's edge, he leaned forward, lowered her voice. "I have ne'er harmed, nor would I harm a woman," he swore to her, his temples starting to throb when she didn't take her gaze off the far corner. "Nor have I e'er . . . er . . . lavished attentions on a lass who wasn't willing."

"It isn't you, good sir." That, a mere hush, scarce to be heard above the howling wind, the loud rattling of the window shutters behind her.

She turned back to him. "It is I."

"My temper caused me to accidentally topple a standing candelabrum in my family's chapel . . . I set the whole of it ablaze, everything. That chapel was the pride of my clan, and its loss is the reason for my penance, my journey to Dunkeld. To make amends and heal my temp—" He broke off when he realized what she'd said.

"You?" His voice came thick, puzzled.

Their gazes met and locked.

She nodded, drew Amicia's *arisaid* closer about her head and shoulders . . . so close he could scarce see her face for the shadows cast by the plaid's generous folds.

Iain poured himself another cup of heather ale, tossed it down in one gulp. "As I am no ordinary pilgrim, sweet lass," he said, plunging onto dangerous ground but uncaring, "so, too, are you no seeker of the veil."

She made no response, but her silence and downcast eyes proved answer enough.

"How do I know?" he asked, when she didn't. He took her hand again, turned it palm upward.

As if sensing what he was about to say, she tried to yank back her hand, but Iain held fast. He traced the tip of his forefinger first across the exposed underside of her fingers, then down the very cup of her palm.

"Smooth and tender flesh, white and unmarred," he

said, not surprised to see her flinch at the observation. Saints, but he hated having to pry the truth from her. "These hands have ne'er seen greater toil than the plying of an embroidering needle. Or the lifting of a wee votive offering, and that, sweeting, we can discuss abovestairs."

She turned away, and Iain thought he caught the bright shimmer of tears in her eyes. But he had to know who she was, what she was about. And what had brought her to such a dire pass.

Only so could he help her.

And the saints knew he wanted to.

He sighed, began gently massaging the whole of her hand, the base of her wrist. "True postulants fall into two categories," he told her, "and, aye, 'tis your hands that give you away."

"Think you?" she asked, a slight note of rebellion in both her tone and the lift of her chin.

And Iain was glad to see it.

He almost smiled. "Nay, I know it," he said instead, purposely letting a wee note of arrogance into his voice . . . just enough to keep the edge on her irritation.

And hold her tears at bay.

"What two categories are there?" she snapped, and this time Iain's lips did twitch a bit.

Folding his arms on the table, he held her gaze, pleased when hers didn't waver.

"The first," he began, "is the gentlebred maid, matron, or widow seeking sequestered asylum for whate'er reason spurs the need. The second is the less advantaged young woman who seeks a life—any life—away from the hardships of her own."

One fine red-gold brow shot upward. "And why can I not be either?"

"Because you, precious lass, are the third," he said, and hoped to the saints his voice held no trace of triumph.

"The third?"

Iain nodded. "Were you the first, the gentleborn maid sent to retire behind the safety of a convent's impenetrable walls, you would have been under heavy escort. No family of worth allows a daughter to roam the land unprotected . . . regardless of her destination."

"And the second?" she asked, refilling her ale cup.

"The second could ne'er be you," Iain asserted. "A lass of the commonality hoping for a better life would have roughened, work-toiled hands. Yours have broken nails and scratches, but those are merely evidence of the hardships you've encountered on the road."

She took a slow sip of ale. "Meaning?"

"You have the hands of a lady . . . your skin is too soft and white for a peasant's."

She didn't deny him. "And what is this third category you would place me in?"

"A wellborn lady fleeing difficulties," Iain said, now quite certain of it.

"And if I am?" She watched him over the rim of her wooden cup.

"Then I would know why."

"I cannot tell you why." Madeline squirmed on the bench. She almost wished she could tell him. But she'd already revealed far more than she should have.

She couldn't divulge more.

Not when two of Silver Leg's men whiled in a dark corner, speculating about her identity, their whispered slurs and suspicions louder in her ears than the clapping of the loosely-latched shutters behind her.

The men's unspoken glee at finding her—and what they hoped to do to her—pierced her courage more thoroughly than the night's chill damp knifed beneath every loose fold of her borrowed *arisaid,* every rip and tear in the shamefully torn clothes hidden beneath.

"Then—for now—my sweet, at least tell me your name," her braw gallant compelled. He looked at her with such honest concern in his dark eyes that hers almost grew moist again.

Almost, for Drummonds didn't cry.

"Come you," he urged, taking her hand again, squeezing it. "Your name is all I ask."

Madeline sat up straighter, expelled her resistance on a great, quivering sigh. "I am . . ." She trailed off, the letch coming at her in waves from the far corner shredding her nerve, and making it difficult to voice her name even in a whisper.

Iain stood then, coming around the table to join her on the bench. He drew her to him before she could catch breath to object.

Not that she really wanted to . . . the saints knew she'd ached for him, *needed* him, for weeks.

"Your name, lass," he encouraged, fingering one of her curls. The brush of his warm, callused fingers against her cheek nearly undid her. "Tell me so I can help you."

"I am . . . I am M-Madeline Drummond of Abercairn." The truth came out in a rush . . . even as *they* concluded the same. She knew because their triumph squeezed her rib cage and filled her with dread.

"Abercairn near Dunkeld?" Iain MacLean was asking

her, but she scarce heard him. The two men were looking their way, one of them even pushing to his feet.

Madeline gave a jerky nod. "Aye, from thereabouts, but Abercairn is no more," she said, too flooded with panic to mind her secrets. "I—It's been taken, my father slain, and I—I . . . I want you to kiss me."

"Kiss you?"

Rather than oblige her, Iain MacLean pulled away. He stared at her so slack-jawed, his expression so totally flummoxed, she would have laughed outright had she not been so very miserable, were not Silver Leg's minions heading her way.

"Aye, kiss me. Now!" She threw her arms around his neck, and pressed against him, crushing her lips to his in her first ever kiss.

A wild and desperate tangling of lips, tongues, mingled breaths . . . and fear.

Fear of the rank vileness coming at her from the corner, and fear of Iain MacLean, for he'd abandoned his startled resistance and was obliging her with a mastery that melted her and made her ache for more.

Sweet golden heat and delicious, prickling tingles spooled through her until she almost forgot to breathe.

His kiss filled her with a divine sweetness so intense she nearly, but not quite, forgot her troubles.

And the other pressing matter that plagued her.

An issue that had just taken on direst urgency.

The irrevocably damning knowledge that Iain MacLean belonged to another.

Chapter Ten

THE FOLLY OF HER ACTIONS STRUCK Madeline the instant the cold-spinning exaltation of Silver Leg's henchmen swung into something else entirely . . . blessedly not aimed at her, but unsettling all the same. A sharp-edged and twisting lust so lewd in its intensity her skin prickled and her stomach clenched with revulsion.

Her heart began thumping hard against her ribs and her mouth went full dry. She pressed closer to Iain MacLean, winding her arms tighter about his broad shoulders, stretching her fingers ever deeper into the heavy silk of his hair.

She moistened her lips, holding fast to him as if his strength and warmth could shelter her not just from the storm raging outwith the alehouse walls but also from the turmoil whirling inside her.

But heedless of her clinging, gusty winds kept rattling the shutters, and heavy rain continued to pelt the window's stone ledge. Cold damp seeped through the shutter slats, chilling her to the bone.

And each new crack of thunder made it easier to believe the ominous rumbles were God's own voice scolding her.

Chiding her for imagining the floor had tilted beneath her feet the moment her shadow man's lips had touched hers.

For truth, she'd melted, a luxurious warmth settling over her the instant he'd cradled the back of her head with a firm, steady hand and begun raining soft kisses across her forehead, her cheeks, and even the tip of her nose.

Gently caressing her nape, he brushed the lightest kiss of all against her temple. *"Sweet, so sweet,"* he murmured, teasing a loose curl with his breath.

Wondrous sensations cascaded through Madeline upon his softly spoken words, but she needed affirmation he'd actually said them, for the howling wind and raucous din inside the alehouse snatched them away before she could be sure.

She pulled back to peer at him, and his dark eyes met hers in a gaze of such startling intimacy his peat brown eyes appeared almost black. They also commanded a visceral bond between them.

A shockingly deep connection so powerful its potency surged through her, rocking her to the core of her being.

Even the soles of her feet tingled and grew warm beneath his bold and claiming stare.

But then he sighed, and a shadow flitted across his brow. The fleeting sadness stripped away all but a few shreds of his crackling male confidence and laid bare a naked vulnerability so poignant that a wholly different kind of warmth swept Madeline.

An all-consuming burn to soothe and caress him, to banish whate'er troubled him so profoundly.

She cleared her throat, dredged up her courage. "I . . . we—" she began, fully intending to share her own darkest secret, tell what she knew of his heart . . . and how. But he stilled her with a gentle flick of his tongue across her lower lip.

"Do not say it," he whispered against her cheek, his golden voice tight with strain and sounding ragged.

He kneaded her shoulders with bliss-spending fingers, his touch distracting her. "Acknowledging what is between us would bring naught but pain," he cautioned, holding her gaze. "Let it be enough to ken your sweetness could easily undo me, fair lady."

Once more a flicker of sadness glimmered in his eyes. "Aye, precious lass, you could make me forget more than my tattered honor." He traced a finger along her jaw. "Much more."

Honor, he'd said.

The saints knew he'd already made her forget her own.

Madeline almost cringed at the thought, shame spilling through her like sheets of eddying water.

Somewhere a shutter slammed against the wall, its loud banging an almost welcome reprieve from the accusatory grumble of the rolling thunder.

A loutish burst of laughter came from Silver Leg's men, and Madeline shivered. Their debauchery chilled her more than the cold, moist air streaming through the rain-damp shutter slats.

Abhorrence at herself flooded her, too, for their lechery only underscored her own breathless need.

Trickling desire spiraled through her, and it pulsed just

as urgent as the baseness firing the ruffian's blood. 'Twas a keen awareness of him. A thrumming need, that deepened with each darting flick of Iain MacLean's tongue against her lips.

The intimacy of his kiss, and his surprising tenderness, bound her physical body to him as soundly as his nightly visits to her dreams had endeared him to her heart.

She closed her eyes a moment, struggled against the urge to bury her face into his shoulder and inhale deeply. His scent intoxicated her and she drank it in greedily, reveling in its decidedly masculine blend of wet grass, old stone, and softened leather.

Damp leather seasoned with peat smoke and an elusive but utterly irresistible hint of pure, unadulterated male.

Sighing, Madeline combed her fingers through his hair, let the luxuriant black strands slide across the backs of her hands.

Aye, there could be no doubt he befuddled her.

Lulled and bespelled her.

She trembled, the mastery of his kiss, the soft warmth of his breath—the mere nearness of him—overwhelming her senses.

A few stolen kisses sought in a dire moment, and she'd come wholly undone.

Lost herself.

And her scruples.

Abandoning them so irrevocably, she continued to cling to him, molding herself to the solid warmth of his broad chest. Her arms snagged firmly around his neck, she buried her fingers in the cool silk of his hair, even though her every instinct screamed that Silver Leg's hirelings had strayed from their purpose.

Her newly awakened passion banished all coherent thought as it rose to a piercing, mind-dulling degree. A weighty and heated throbbing began somewhere deep inside her, and she parted her lips, unconsciously bidding him to deepen their kiss.

He needed her—at least in that moment—she had no doubt.

Casting off all caution, she savored the astonishingly intense yearnings spooling through her body, willingly giving herself over to the sensations.

Let the storm-chased night send a bolt of lightning to fetch her straight to the gates of hell, but she didn't want him to stop kissing her.

Couldn't bear for him to stop.

Too sweet, too unaccustomed and rare, were the ripples of pleasure spreading through her with each gentle brush of his lips across her own, each velvety sweep of his tongue against hers.

Faith, she'd ne'er dreamed a man could kiss so softly. Or that the mere feel of his mouth lighting over hers could infuse the lowest part of her belly with such a deliciously heavy warmth.

A fine, pulsating heat she suspected no true lady ought feel, much less enjoy.

And gentle birth be damned, she didn't care.

But she *did* care that Iain MacLean was not free.

That undeniable truth weighed heavily on her shoulders and cooled her burgeoning ardor as swiftly as if someone had emptied a bucket of icy water o'er her besotted head.

Her eyes flew wide, the reason she'd hurled herself at him once again foremost in her mind. Pulling away, she broke the kiss and slid a sidelong glance at the two miscreants whose raging letch filled her throat with choking, vile-tasting bile.

She followed their stares, her eyes straining to peer through the haze of bluish peat smoke hanging thickly above the crowded trestle tables.

Her pulse skittered, running hot and fast when her gaze lit on the focus of the men's lust. Worldly-wise, and tolerant, as she thought herself, Madeline gasped in astonishment.

A buxom joy woman lounged in the shadowy entrance to the darkened sleeping dormitory, her heavy-lidded expression and slow toying at the folds of her skirts just where her thighs met, a clear invitation for any man eager to partake of her proffered charms.

Large-boned and coarse, but with an extraordinarily lustrous wealth of rich-gleaming auburn curls tumbling to her waist, the bawd's generous breasts near burst from the lowest-cut gown Madeline had e'er seen.

The top halves of the whore's nipples, rouged and tightly ruched, peeped provocatively above the edge of her plunging bodice. Madeline swallowed hard, uncomfortably aware of the hardened peaks of her own overly full breasts.

And how exposed they'd be without the borrowed plaid draped about her shoulders.

Aware of an audience, the bawd arched her back. The deliberately sensual stretch caused both her nipples to spring free and their thrusting tips popped into full view for any who cared to admire them.

And many did.

Hoots, hearty shouts of masculine glee, and a few poorly veiled sniggers rose above the general din.

Heat inched up the back of Madeline's neck, and she tightened her grip on Iain's shoulders.

She risked a glance at him.

He, too, stared, but unlike the thick cloud of miasmic lust she could almost see swirling around Silver Leg's slack-jawed henchmen, her shadow man's granite-set features revealed naught but cold indifference.

Your breasts are more fetching by far, she thought she heard him murmur, but the words were smothered beneath a burst of tawdriest ribaldry as every man present and not too deep in his cups to notice praised the joy woman's bountiful wares.

A largish man at the next table leaned forward, his eyes near bugging from his ale-flushed face. "'Fore God, if those teats wouldn't harden a dead man's lance!"

"Mine already *is* hard," another declared, his proclamation eliciting a chorus of guffaws.

"And I mean to wrap those curling tresses all around my hardness," one of Silver Leg's men cried, making for the whore.

Madeline stared in horrified fascination. Almost forgetting to breathe, she was only vaguely aware of Iain MacLean's pulling her close again. He eased her head to his shoulder, holding her there, the flat of his hand pressed firmly over her ear.

The beat of his heart pounded hard and steady beneath her cheek, and she didn't need her gift to sense his rising anger . . . the mounting fury inside him.

'Twas a simmering displeasure he strove hard to master.

A vexation that warmed her despite its ferocity, for her feminine instincts told her the reason for his ire was seeing her exposed to such a rife display of sordid carnality.

But depraved or nay, she couldn't tear away her gaze.

As if cast of stone, she looked on as the second of Silver Leg's men, the older one, hitched his loose-fitting trews to accommodate the tentlike protrusion of his arousal.

"You can have *that* hair," he called to his friend's back, starting after him. "'Tis her other hair I'm a-wanting to see. Her *lower* hair."

"Oh, aye, now that'd be a fine sight!" a slurred voice agreed from somewhere in a back corner.

The bawd's painted lips curved in a lascivious smile.

Giving a throaty laugh, she caught hold of her skirts with both hands and slowly pulled apart a hitherto hidden split in the fabric to offer the men a glimpse at the lush nest of dark red curls springing betwixt her fleshy thighs.

Madeline gasped.

Iain MacLean swore.

He shot to his feet, dragging her with him. "I knew that was the style of this place!" he fumed, swallowing back a harsher retort lest he truly shock the lass.

His temper a beetling threat beneath thinnest restraint, he tossed a glance at the door arch to the kitchen. "Where has the ale-draper betaken himself?" he demanded, raising his voice above the cacophony.

Ever careful to keep a shrewd eye on the two men pawing the whore's breasts.

Craven dastards he meant to question Madeline Drummond about at first opportunity.

His malcontent a palpable, living thing inside him, he raked the other carousers with a blazing-eyed glare but harvested little more than one or two owlish stares.

All other buffoons lining the trestles ignored him, their drooling gazes fixed on the whore as she deftly unfastened the lacings of her bodice to fully expose the heavy white globes of her breasts.

"A plaguey stewhouse," Iain muttered, turning away in disgust.

And hoping he'd done so swiftly enough to prevent *her* from seeing the whore's garish performance.

His jaw clenching, he tightened his arm about Madeline's shoulders and kept scanning the smoke-hazed murk for the ale-keeper.

On impulse, Madeline gripped his hand, squeezed it. "I shan't swoon on you, sir. I've heard all alehouses are frequented by one or two such women," she said, glancing at him. "Even fine inns."

He arched a brow at her. "Say you?"

She nodded, her gaze seeking the bawd.

The woman had hooked arms with her newly lured customers and was drawing them into the shadowy realm of the common sleeping room, where Madeline suspected she relinquished a portion of her profits for a well-stuffed pallet in a dark and private corner.

"Whether such women are welcomed in an establishment or nay, a lady ought not be confronted by them . . . or be troubled by the knowledge of their existence."

"I know of much that weighs on my heart, sir," Madeline admitted, pushing away her own troubles before they could seize and crush her. "Greater cares than one joy woman and her night's trade."

She sighed.

And wished for the hundred thousandth time that she *wasn't* privy to all she knew.

Iain MacLean eyed her sharply, his dark eyes brimming with silent questions. A muscle twitched in his jaw, and she touched two fingers to the spot, pressing gently until the jerking ceased.

"As I just banished the twitch in your jaw so, too, does the joy woman serve a need," she said, quiet-voiced . . . and thinking of Nella.

She drew the *arisaid* tighter about her shoulders, repressed a shudder. Not that her common-born friend had e'er trod as lamentable path as an alehouse whore.

But Nella had known her own sorrows, fetched as she'd been at the first bloom of her womanhood to bear sons for a landed man whose barren wife couldn't produce heirs.

A faint echo of Nella's long-ago anguish rippled through Madeline. She shuddered and hugged her waist, grateful the years had changed Nella's pain to numb resignation.

But Madeline's indignation o'er her friend's past had ne'er lessened.

Straight teeth, clear eyes, and a robust condition had decided Nella's fate, thrusting her into a life she'd come to accept and even to joy in . . . until she'd made the grave error of showing too much affection to the young boys she could ne'er claim as her own.

And falling in love with the wellborn man whom she still refused to name.

Her admiration for Nella steeling her own backbone, Madeline cast another glance toward the sleeping dorm. Its low-arched entry loomed empty, but muffled grunts and the ragged rasp of heavy breathing drifted from within its shadowy depths.

She turned back to Iain. "If anything," she said into the hush stretching between them, "such women are to be pitied."

Greatly pitied, but ne'er scorned.

Nor could she condemn a single one amongst their ranks.

Hadn't she, mere moments before, strained against Iain MacLean's chest? Known wonder at the hard-slabbed contours of his muscles, evident even beneath his leather hauberk and the folds of his plaid?

Indeed, she had reveled in the solidness and warmth of his masculine strength, breathed deeply of the essence of him—and still ached for more.

She'd gloried in his kisses, all but begging him to deepen each one. And she'd ached for him to slip his tongue between her lips and let it tangle with her own far more often than he had!

Truth be told, she was nigh onto begging him to kiss her again.

There and then.

Forthwith.

And fully heedless of the flustered-looking ale-keeper hurrying toward them.

The man's half-anxious, half-bursting-with-pride countenance gave him away. Their quarters were ready at last.

Madeline's stomach dropped to her feet, her bravura

evaporating. "Oh, dear saints," she got out, sudden panic surging inside her.

Jerking free of her shadow man's grasp, she looked down, made a bit of a show at smoothing her rumpled skirts . . . anything to keep him from seeing her cheeks flame.

Or noting the desire still skipping along her nerve endings.

Her true feelings for him.

"Aye, most dear," he agreed, his earlier anger gone from his voice. He hooked a finger beneath her chin, lifted her face. "Dear, and far too sweet."

"Too sweet?"

He nodded. "Too dear and sweet for the likes of me, fair lass," he said, his husky tone doing strange things to her knees. "And much too desirable to suffer a life of abstinence and fasting behind convent walls . . . no matter how many bumbling poltroons are after you."

Madeline's gasped. "You knew?"

"My great lacking is my inability to hold my temper, lass. There is not and ne'er has been aught amiss with my wits, I assure you." He gave her one of his lopsided would-be smiles, its very imperfection splitting her heart wide open.

Lowering his head, he dropped a kiss on her cheek. "Or dare I hope you find me so irresistible you couldn't help but throw yourself into my arms?"

"I—I . . ." Madeline stumbled over her tongue. She'd grown too light-headed to think clearly.

"Your pardon," the ale-keeper addressed them, from behind, and cleared his throat.

Iain MacLean whirled to face him. "Our room is prepared?"

"And none too soon, it would seem." The man cast an eloquent glance at Madeline, his words and the look like a knell tolling on her heart.

Iain's hand encircled her wrist . . . as if he sensed her sudden urge to bolt. "Is the chamber clean? I've no great wish to sleep fully clad."

Ignoring the jibe, the proprietor used his drying cloth to mop at his sweating brow. "'Tis full to the rafters we are, my good sir, but I've prepared the room myself and warrant you'll find it well-appointed and"—he slid another glance at Madeline—"privy enough to serve your needs."

Her heart racing faster than the rain beating on the window shutters, Madeline looked away, let the moist air pouring through the wooden slats cool her heated cheeks.

A sharp skirl of throaty, female laughter sounded from the sleeping dormitory, and a wash of ill ease spilled down Madeline's spine.

Iain's brows lifted, his handsome face darkening with displeasure. He turned a keen eye on the ale-draper. "The chamber is not used for . . ." He left the sentence unfinished.

Not a bit nonplussed, the ale-draper took a lantern off a shelf and deftly kindled its wick. He gestured to a narrow, dark stairway at the back of the room.

"None save quality climb those steps, I assure you," he said, his barrel chest swelling a bit. "All others take their pleasure belowstairs. You, my lord, shall pass the night in a blessed haven."

"Then pray take us there," Iain put to the man.

The ale-draper nodded, clearly pleased. "I bid you follow me," he said, and raised his lantern.

With surprising agility for such a well-fleshed man, he turned and struck a swift path through the press, making straight for the far wall and the spiral stairwell cut deep into its thickness.

Iain strode after him, his viselike grip on Madeline's wrist leaving her no choice but to hasten in his wake, her uncomfortable gaze fastened on the looming threshold.

Draughty and dimly lit by a few sputtering wall torches, the stairs wound upward into the dark unknown, though, truth be told, Madeline knew exactly what awaited her beyond the well-worn stone steps.

If she allowed her passions to get the better of her.

But she wouldn't.

No matter how much her lips tingled and ached for more of her shadow man's kisses.

And despite the way her heart clutched at the mere thought of sharing darker, deeper intimacies with him. The kind they'd shared countless times in her most secret, damning dreams.

Fisting her hands, she closed her mind to the lurid images. But they whirled a mad dance across her sensibilities and—were she not careful—threatened to trample everything she held as right and honorable.

Convinced he'd becharmed her, she mounted the turnpike stair behind him, the chaos of conflicting emotions inside her waging a fiercer battle with each ascending step.

"Have a care, lass, the last few stairs are slippery," Iain warned over his shoulder. Releasing her wrist, he laced his strong, warm fingers with hers.

The touch, the warm pressure of his firm but gentle grasp, sent tingles speeding up her arm.

Have a care, he had said.

The words almost made Madeline laugh aloud.

A nervous laugh, for little he knew what great care she already exercised. Even the simple words of caution, issued in his deep, golden voice, melted her bones.

Jellied her knees so badly she could scarce maneuver the *non*slippery steps.

Feeling trapped, apprehensive, and excited in one, she followed him onto the landing, and the moment she set foot on the somewhat slanting wood-planked floor, a cold wave of jitters swept away the last remnants of her fortitude.

She began to tremble.

No longer just her knees, but the whole of her body a quivering mass of jelly.

For good or ill, she was about to spend the night with her shadow man.

Candlelit hours alone with the man who'd branded his claim on her soul the very first time she'd felt him wrapping himself so warmly around her heart.

"That be your room," the ale-keeper declared with pride, his voice overloud in the quiet of the landing.

He gestured toward the end of the short, poorly lit corridor where the merest hint of soft, golden light leaked from beneath a surprisingly stout-looking door.

He started forward, his raised lantern casting weird shadows on the walls . . . each one of them seeming to point long, accusing fingers at Madeline.

Iain MacLean squeezed her hand, but the gesture he'd surely meant to be reassuring only flustered her more.

That wee physical contact sent little bolts of heated flames skimming across her every nerve ending.

As if he knew, he tossed a quick glance over his shoulder, one brow lifted in silent question.

Was she ready?

She gave him an equally mute nod, sparing herself the shame of voicing a lie.

Beyond him, the ale-draper had reached the end of the darkened passageway and was already opening the door to their room. Welcoming yellow light poured from within, its inviting glow banishing the shadows.

Madeline's heart leapt to her throat.

She gulped.

But then she set her jaw and consigned herself to making the best of what she couldn't change.

Retiring was no longer an option.

And only the morrow's rising sun would prove if the long hours between then and now would leave her filled with bitter regret or glad-hearted relief for not seizing hold of what she knew would be the sweetest of bliss.

The same wet and windy night, but in far less commodious quarters deep in the bowels of Abercairn Castle, Sir John Drummond, *true* laird of the castle and all its surrounds, drew a wheezy breath of chill, musty air. 'Twas the best he could hope for in his dungeon cell.

He silently thanked the saints that, as a young man, his first act upon becoming laird had been to abolish use of this selfsame hellhole.

A cramped and dank niche scarce larger than a garde-robe in the lowliest of keeps and equally foul-smelling.

An abomination beneath any man's dignity.

Sir John prided himself on being a just man, a fair and kindhearted one.

And it was his great softheartedness, the lack of steel and fire in his blood, that made him a much-loved father to his people, but a not so notable laird.

A *poor* laird, were anyone callous or outspoken enough to speak the truth.

A truth that had landed him in his present predicament and would no doubt cost him his life.

But not his beloved daughter's.

And for her—to ensure she lived and remained un-harmed—he'd draw on the strengths of the more stalwart Drummond lairds who'd gone before him and, for once in his life, be intractable.

Firm and unbending.

Wholly resolute.

He'd do it for her, for Madeline, even though she'd never know. It would be his last gift to her, the daughter he loved more than life itself.

"Where are the jewels, Drummond? The English booty. All ken your father harvested riches from the slain English after Bannockburn. 'Tis said he spent days gathering English swords and armor, simply to pry away the jewels . . . and with the Bruce's sanction!" Sir Bernhard Logie peppered him with the same questions he shot at him every day. "I've found your treasury stores, your gold and silver coin, but not the stolen English riches. Where are they, Drummond?"

He considered the fingernails of one hand, his face a tight-set mask. "It will go easier on you if you speak."

But his repetitive barrage and veiled threats only

earned him the same blank stare Sir John gave him each time he sought to interrogate him.

Sir John pressed parchment-dry lips together in a bold show of defiant silence that, truth be known, required little strength. Just as his limbs withered by the day, becoming too thin and weak to bid his will, so, too, did his cracked and parched tongue lie dead as a dried autumn leaf in his mouth.

Useless beyond forming a few painfully rasped words which, at the moment, he wasn't wont to attempt.

"Where is your daughter, John? Where would she run to?" Silver Leg began his second assault of asked-daily questions. "Who would harbor her?"

Marshaling what strength he could, John Drummond turned his head to the side. He fastened his stare on the narrow air slit cut high in the opposite wall and hoped Logie wouldn't notice that if the wind caught the slanting rain just right, a strong enough gust could send a burst of fine, wet mist spraying into the cell.

The moisture John gleaned in that way went far in keeping him alive.

And miserable though he was at the moment, neither did he want to die. Unlike most Drummond men, he lacked the courage to look death in the eye and feel no fear.

"Think you can ignore me?" Silver Leg came closer, nudged his thigh with a booted foot. "I see the serving woman brought you a plaid," he said, leaning down to muss the length of wool Morven had so lovingly tucked around John's shackled legs.

"She fretted you'd perish of the cold. I told her she could bring you your own plaid, the one on your bed—

my two greyhounds sleep on it—but she declined, claiming the dog hair would make you sneeze."

And Sir John did.

The mere thought of a greyhound's coat was enough to set his nose to twitching, his eyes a-water.

"That dire?" Silver Leg shook his head in mock commiseration. "A pity to exit this life without knowing the companionship and loyalty of a big-hearted dog," he added, his tone softening as he spoke of his pets.

Sir John kept his face a stony mask. He struggled not to let his tormentor see he'd innocently trod upon another soft corner of John Drummond's heart, for though he could ne'er be *around* dogs, he'd e'er loved the creatures.

"I told the serving wench you'd starve before you'd freeze to death," Sir Bernhard's voice came cold again. He snapped his fingers and a pale-faced kitchen lad entered the cell with a platter of roasted *capercailzie*, the large turkeylike birds so plentiful on Drummond land.

Tasty and much enjoyed throughout the Highlands, its tender, savory meat had e'er been one of Sir John's favorite repasts. He near swooned as its delicious aroma filled the tiny cell.

His empty stomach near convulsed with hunger. His mouth would've watered copiously if only he'd had enough fluid in his body to allow it.

Silver Leg tore away a roasted leg joint and waved it in Laird Drummond's face. "It would be to your best advantage to speak," he advised, bringing the *capercailzie* leg so close it almost grazed Sir John's nose.

But he yanked it away as quickly. "Think hard after

I leave, and you might see the wisdom of being less belligerent."

Recognizing the end of Silver Leg's torments, John Drummond gave heed to his weariness and let his head fall back against the slimed stone wall behind him.

The effort to hold it upright so long as he'd been face-to-face with Logie had taxed him greatly.

Too weary to sigh, he closed his eyes and wished his sense of smell had gone the way of his useless tongue.

The faintest of smiles flitted across John Drummond's haggard face.

He didn't mind his tongue's failings. And he was mightily relieved by his continued ability to repel Silver Leg's attempts to wear down his resistance, for he could make himself understood if he *wanted* to speak.

But he didn't. He'd sooner yank out his tongue.

Answering the dastard's questions would be to damn his daughter to certain death.

Abercairn Castle *did* hold a considerable cache of pilfered Sassunach jewels. And it was true enough that they'd been taken with the late Good King Robert's blessing.

But as war booty.

Due and just reward for Drummond swords and loyalty at the Battle of Bannockburn, the Hero King's most shining triumph over the English.

And once Silver Leg discovered the hiding place of such a treasure, he'd have no reason to keep Madeline alive.

Sir John drew another quivering breath, licked his dry lips.

With the exception of him, only his daughter knew Abercairn's secrets.

So John Drummond kept silent.

And prayed to every saint in heaven to let him live long enough for his daughter to get as far away from Abercairn as her feet could carry her.

Chapter Eleven

$\mathscr{I}$AIN STARED AT THE OAKEN PANELS of the heavy
wooden door, his fingers clenched around its substantial
drawbar, and reached deep inside himself for the courage
to slide the greased bar into its socket-hole.

Doing so would mean locking himself in the chamber
with Madeline Drummond . . . locking *her* in the room
with him.

The latter being the reason for his hesitation.

The ale-draper hadn't lied about the room being well-
appointed. Beaming with pride, he'd ushered them inside, even patted the bed's plump feather mattress, again;
claiming it stuffed with swan down. Iain doubted that,
nevertheless, its sumptuous dressings and great size made
the bed seductively inviting.

The entire chamber proved inviting.

Firmly latched shutters held back the worst of the
night wind and lashing rain, though enough of a draught
whistled through the slatting to ruffle the wall hangings
and tease the flames of whate'er candles had been lit.

A great branch of them flickered on a sturdy table by

the bed . . . along with a platter of oatcakes, honey, and tasty-looking cheese. Two drinking cups and an earthen jug of what the ale-keeper insisted was fine Gascon wine rounded out the tempting array.

And each one of the unexpected comforts banded together to thrust a cruel hand straight through Iain's rib cage to squeeze his heart and freeze his feet to the floor, there before the closed door, where he'd been standing, his back to the room, ever since the proud ale-draper's departure.

Iain MacLean, the great Master of the Highlands, was afraid to turn around.

He winced, closed his eyes briefly. The luxuriously outfitted chamber could have been at Baldoon. Not quite as fine as his own, but similar enough in amenities to hold more than the chill of the storm-harried night and all its inky shadows.

The room was full to overflowing with reminders of his past.

Grim ones dark enough to unleash his demons, even as the undoubted luxuries—the great curtained bed and round wooden tub filled with steaming water—ripped at the thin veneer of his manly restraint.

Squaring his shoulders, he drew a deep, shuddering breath. Damp and heavy with the smell of rain, the cold night air also carried the scent of the thyme and meadow-sweet someone had scattered across the floor rushes . . . and a very light hint of heather.

Her scent.

And saints help him, he could so easily drown in it.

His fingers pressed harder against the smooth wood of

the drawbar, the throbbing need he'd suppressed for hours swelling to a painful degree.

He almost groaned aloud.

He *did* adjust the fall of his plaid.

In a welter of emotion falling somewhere between fury and regret, he counted off the reasons he couldn't—*shouldn't*—keep the lass with him.

Beyond the silly style she'd given him, he had naught to offer her. Too many pain-fraught memories resided at Baldoon for him to take her there, and he worried, too, that he was somehow cursed.

Damned by long tradition to bring grief or death to anyone he cared about.

In particular the women he cared about.

The young lass he'd thought to wed before the Council of Elders pressured him into marrying Lileas perished of a fever not long after his wedding, and Lileas lost her own life not long thereafter.

Feeling very much as if he teetered on the edge of a black and bottomless abyss, he gulped back the hot lump trying to lodge in his throat and wished with the whole of his heart that he were a less troubled man.

Madeline Drummond carried enough burdens of her own.

He couldn't allow himself to add to them.

But with a determined effort and a smattering of good fortune, he might be able to rid her of a few of them.

That admirable purpose strengthening him, he slid home the drawbar and turned to face her.

"And now, my lord?" she asked, her tone and the slight lifting of her brows indicating she meant far more than how they'd pass the night.

The most masculine part of him jerked in immediate answer, for she stood in charming disarray near a brazier of glowing coals, her fingers deftly unbraiding her red-gold hair.

"Now?" Iain echoed, well aware his ungentlemanly stare and monosyllabic retort marked him as either a dim-wit or a callous-minded rogue, interested in naught beyond how the pulsing red glow of the brazier gilded her tresses and flattered the smooth cream of her skin.

He'd thought to query her about the ex-voto, pull it from the leather purse hanging from his belt, brandish it at her, and demand an explanation, but the words withered on his tongue, the pulsing heaviness at his groin pushing him to the brink of madness.

He clenched his hands, determined to ignore the insistent throbbing, and hoped she wouldn't notice the rise in his plaid . . . just as he strove not to notice she'd discarded Amicia's plaid.

His sister's *arisaid* lay carefully folded atop a three-legged stool, and the lush fullness of Madeline Drummond's breasts strained against her torn bodice.

Naught but watery darkness leaked through the shutters, but the brazier cast enough illumination to clearly define all the luscious curves and planes of her tall, slender body.

Especially her breasts.

Iain cursed beneath his breath, molten heat pounding through his veins. Thanks be she hadn't yet removed the two brooches holding the gown together.

Sore damaged as the bodice was, he could already see more than half of one coral-tinted nipple peeking through a tear in the cloth. He stared at it, his blood running ever hotter as the well-sized areola drew tight beneath his gaze.

A ragged moan, husky and low, rose in his throat, and his carefully clipped fingernails dug half crescents into his palms. Prudence chided him, warned him to avert his gaze, but he couldn't.

Not on his life.

Candlelight and the brazier's pulsating glow bathed her in shifting patterns of soft golden light and gilded her hair. Her beauty and something else—something too elemental, too compelling, for him fully to comprehend—bespelled him, searing him to the roots of his soul.

So he continued to stare at the beautifully puckered nipple, looked on transfixed as its hardened peak thrust through the ripped cloth as if to greet the chill night air.

Or, were he more free—or maybe less caring—the warmth of his lips.

But he *did* care, so he tore away his gaze, contenting himself with the sweet glimpse she'd unwittingly given him.

His tongue, though, ached to lave that nipple and, as if possessing a mind of its own, displayed mutinous frustration by affixing itself firmly to the roof of his mouth.

He tried not to scowl. Wished he could flash her a dazzling smile. Or at least a comforting one.

Instead, he looked directly into her green-gold eyes, hoping to regain some semblance of control by focusing on a less blatantly suggestive part of her.

She peered back at him just as intently, wearing a heart-clutching expression the *sennachies* would surely call haunted longing. The look wreaked as much havoc on his heart as her pertly-ruched nipple let loose in his nether parts.

"Aye, now." She broke the taut silence. "I would not overhurry you . . . but the hour grows late," she said, her gaze straying to the wooden bathing tub.

Steam rose off its heated water, curling wisps fragrant with bay leaf, rosemary, and another pleasing scent he couldn't identify.

She looked back at him. "We are both tired, and the bathwater will not stay warm overlong."

"To be sure," he blurted, mentally kicking himself the instant the words sprang from his tongue.

He winced, expelled an agitated breath.

The fool words hung in the damp air, jeering at him, so he turned quickly to the brazier and thrust his hands toward its warmth.

Anything to hide the color he knew must be creeping clear to his hairline.

The two louts belowstairs who'd seemed so interested in her wouldn't stay in place long either, he'd meant to say. Their path would be cold by first light lest they were addled enough to lurk around after seeing her in his company.

To be sure, indeed.

He rammed both hands through his hair. Ne'er he had spouted more insipid tripe than since sliding the wretched drawbar in place.

Now he did scowl.

He'd ne'er possessed his brother's silver tongue, but neither was he wholly inept at stringing words together.

Until now.

'Twas the lass, he knew.

She robbed him of his ability to control his body's re-action to her and limited his capacity to form coherent sentences.

"Sir?"

"Aye?" he jerked, whirling back around, away from the softly hissing brazier.

"The bath," she said, her gaze steady on his as she re-moved the last pins from her hair, freeing its wealth to tumble down her back in a curling spill of glossy, red-gold curls.

Iain's breath snagged in his throat, his hands suddenly burning, *tingling* to know the cool silk of her bright-gleaming tresses sifting through his fingers.

"Bath?" he repeated, his voice thin, wheezier than a graybeard's.

She nodded and slid another gaze at the wooden tub. "I am wondering which of us ought partake first?"

"Why, you, milady." This time the words fair shot from his lips. Not at all ashamed of his nakedness, he *was* shamed o'er its current state.

Naught under the broad, starry heavens could per-suade him to remove a shred of clothing until his man-hood no longer resembled a tent pole.

His plaid in particular was going to stay right where it was.

"I do not mind waiting if you'd rather go first," she of-fered, apparently forgetful of how much of her the ruined bodice displayed.

"Nay, nay, nay." Iain raised his hands, palms facing her. He waved them back and forth in a gesture of un-mistakable refusal. "While you enjoy your soak, I shall prepare the sphagnum moss tincture I promised you."

Her eyes went cautious ... wary. "You promised you'd keep your back turned, too."

"Aye, so I did," he confirmed, "and you needn't fret yourself, for I ne'er break my word, lass."

"Nay, I imagine you do not, Iain MacLean," she said, seeming to accept that.

And because she did, and so unquestioningly, Iain strode to the end of the bed, where his leather travel satchel rested atop an ironbound coffer.

He kept his promises to himself, too, and he meant to get to the bottom of many unanswered questions this night ... even if his unruly tarse grew so rigid it snapped in two.

Scowling, he undid the fastenings of his satchel and searched through its depths until his fingers closed around a small silver flask.

Uisge beatha.

Fine Highland spirits.

Going to the table by the bed, he filled one of the drinking cups with a wee measure. He'd meant to offer her the fiery drink to soothe her nerves and take the sharp corners off any edginess she might feel upon being alone with him.

Now he needed the potent brew to ease *his* nervous state!

He strode back to her, handed her the cup. "Drink," he encouraged, when she only peered at it, her nose wrinkling at its sharp smell.

"Please," he tried again, his voice a mite softer this time.

She took a small sip.

"I' faith!" she spluttered, thrusting the cup at him, her face turning bright pink, her eyes watering.

"'Tis finest *uisge beatha*—water of life." Iain gently pushed the cup back toward her. "Finish it. The heat it brings will lessen the ache in your muscles," he improvised, the half-truth smearing another layer of dirt onto his honor.

Saints, but his lies were growing legion!

While the drink would surely relax her body, it was the loosening of her *tongue* that concerned him.

Feeling extraordinarily unworthy of the fancy title she'd bestowed on him, Iain took the empty cup from her hands and returned to the bedside table where he'd left the flagon.

He poured himself a much greater portion and downed it in one throat-burning gulp.

And a good thing, for when he turned back, she was working the clasp of his cairngorm brooch . . . trying to undo its simple clasp with badly shaking fingers.

Iain began to shake, too, a sick feeling spreading through his gut.

He knew what was coming.

It was writ all o'er her prettily flushed face.

In the way she worried her pleasingly full lower lip.

Though he wouldn't have believed it, *that* part of him sprang even harder. Granite hard and so much so, even the generous folds of his plaid could no longer be counted on to shield his pathetic condition.

"Oh, bother!" she cried then, and the floor pitched and swayed beneath his feet.

She looked at him, her green-gold eyes just a bit glittery from the *uisge beatha*. "I cannot undo the brooches," she said, just as he'd dreaded she would. "You must help me." Iain died. Or would have if doing so were that easy.

Instead, he suppressed a silent groan and started forward. And he prayed every step of the way that her gaze wouldn't drop below his waist.

He reached her in a few quick strides, the wild beat of his MacLean heart hammering so loud in his ears, its heavy thudding rivaled the night's thunder rolls and the hollow pounding of the ceaseless rain.

"Be at ease, lass, I will help you," he murmured, forcing a calm tone he didn't feel. Then he set his hands to the brooch. Quickly, before he could heed his better judgment and whirl away to sleep outside the chamber door.

"I shall help you in every way I can," some still-there shadow of his honor added, the gallant-sounding words in nowise reflective of the turmoil inside him.

Save that he *did* wish to help her.

But who would help him?

Not a damned soul, he answered himself, and the clasp sprang free, his own cairngorm brooch dropping into his palm.

"Thank you," she said, a slight tremor in her voice.

"I could scarce do otherwise—lest you wish to bathe fully clothed," Iain managed, his own voice tight with strain.

He near flinched at the images conjured by his words, cursed himself for splashing them across his mind.

He *did* shudder.

A great, rolling shudder that roared down his spine with such force, he fisted his hands so tightly the pin clasp jabbed into his palm.

Clamping his teeth, he quelled any outward show of pain—in truth, welcoming the distraction from the growing urge to push apart the edges of the torn bodice and bury his face deep in the valley between her breasts.

Or at the very least, take her in his arms and kiss her senseless.

But he just kept his jaw set and lowered his hands before his fingers could brush against the creamy silk of her bared skin even one more time.

Then he extricated the pin from the fleshy part of his palm as unobtrusively as he could.

But maybe not inconspicuously enough, for her eyes narrowed, and something in her expression told him she was just as mindful as he of how wide her bodice now gaped.

How much it revealed.

Not *all* . . . but enough of her sweet bounty to buckle his knees.

The gold flecks in her irises had gone deep amber in the candle shine, and the intensity of her perusal seeped beneath his skin, filling him with keenest awareness of her.

Awareness, recognition, and an irrefutable sense of rightness.

Belonging.

But a wee flicker of doubt—or confusion—clouded her eyes, hovering almost out of sight at the very backs of their green-gold depths, and seeing it made him ache to reassure her.

To draw her close not just for more heated kisses, but to tell her *who* she was and what they were to each other.

If the MacLean bards were to be believed, she'd belonged to him, and he to her, since time beyond mind.

And would for the rest of their days . . . whether he left her at the Bishopric of Dunkeld or nay.

Legend declared the bond between a MacLean male and his one true love could ne'er be severed. Not even by death itself.

They'd simply come together again in the Celtic Otherworld, then repeatedly seek each other until the fateful moment of recognition in as many lives as were to bless them.

But at the moment, Iain MacLean, the latest of the clan to be cast adrift on the runaway tide otherwise known as the Bane of the MacLeans, felt more cursed than blessed.

Unlike other clansmen, long since blissfully mated, *his* tide of destiny hadn't run a smooth course.

Or even a straight one.

He struggled to find other soothing words, ones to calm her without making her think she'd have to add lunacy to his long list of faults. "You needn't feel ill at ease with me, lass," he said at last, opting for simplicity over eloquence.

A sad smile lit across her lips. "But I do not," she said, and touched a hand to his cheek. "At least not in the way I believe you mean."

"Then why do you remind me of a cornered roe-deer ready to bolt at soonest opportunity?"

"I have told you, it is my own self I fear, not you."

"And why do you fear yourself?" he jerked, not at all sure he wanted to hear the answer.

She searched his face. "Be content with knowing I do not fear you," she said, the sincerity in her voice unman-

ning him. "Ne'er you . . . not while life is in me. I have
seen the goodness in you, sir . . . and your valor."

"And keeping that life in you is my sole purpose, dear
lady," Iain said, amazed his voice hadn't cracked on the
words. Her faith in him, justified or nay, touched him
deeply.

It'd been so long since anyone had admired aught
about him, that he felt a mite embarrassed, too. But he
tamped down *those* feelings and embraced the good
ones . . . the fine golden warmth stretching its sweet light
into the deepest corners of the cold dark inside him.

For a wee moment, some of the weight on his shoulders lessened, but then suddenly, he was afeared himself.
Allowing himself to revel overmuch in any such pleasure
might have the fates snatching it right back from his
grasp.

So he cleared his throat and broached a safer, but
equally important matter. "I would hear who those men
were and what they want of you?"

She looked down, brushed a sheaf of gleaming, fire-
bright curls over her shoulder. "I do not ken what they
want or who they are," she said, setting trembling fingers
to work on the second brooch.

"I think you do," he pressed, hating to push her but
sensing she wouldn't speak of them lest he did. "You recognized them."

She stiffened visibly. "Recognizing them or their vile
intent needn't mean I ken their names."

Still struggling with the brooch, she looked up long
enough to shoot a challenging glance at him. Her eyes
sparked green fire, dared him to state otherwise.

"Those men are strangers to me."

"But you know of them," he argued. "Enough to ken their purpose."

"Nay, I do not," she insisted. "You err."

In a flare of surprising temper, she quit fumbling with the pin clasp and yanked hard on the brooch. It came free at once, a good-sized piece of jagged-edged cloth with it. The torn bodice, and the gossamer-fine shift beneath it, fell completely open, the heavy white globes of her full breasts wholly exposed and wearing naught but the chill night air and two deliciously tight nipples.

Iain groaned deep in his throat.

She gasped and clapped her hands o'er her nipples. "Oh, dear saints," she cried, and angrily tossed her hair back from her face. "Like you, Drummond women are known for their tempers, Iain MacLean," she owned, an agitated quiver in her voice.

Looking utterly miserable, she stared at him, her fingers splayed across the bountiful flesh of her well-fashioned breasts. "Now the gown is ruined beyond repair. I've naught else to—"

Iain reached for her, to take her by the shoulders and comfort her thus, but he caught himself and let his hands drop to his sides. "Gavin will have clothes for you when we join him and your friend on the road north on the morrow," he said, glad he could ease some of her distress. "MacNab, at whose keep they are this night, has more sisters than you can count, and Gavin has instructions to secure fresh garb for you."

"So you are kindhearted as well as valiant," she said, considering him in the candle glow. "I am not surprised."

Again, his heart lurched, an unexpected wash of pleasure sweeping him, the golden warmth he was beginning to recognize and crave, filling even the remotest cracks and crannies in his soul.

His heart.

The slightest of smiles tugged at the corners of his mouth, but the pleasurable sensations proved so strange, so unaccustomed, they skittered away the instant he focused on them.

And the more fool he if he allowed himself any such indulgence. So he schooled his features into a noncommittal mask of blandness.

"Until I leave you in the care of the good brothers at Dunkeld, anyone we meet will think you my wife, and with a few obvious exceptions, I shall treat you as such," he said, the cold seeping back through him with each spoken word. "Think you I could sleep a night—even an hour—betwixt now and Dunkeld if I allowed you to walk about in rags?"

To his amazement, she took her hands from her breasts to grip and squeeze one of his hands. "I knew your heart was deep," she said, tightening her grasp once more before clapping her hands back over her nipples.

"You *knew?*"

"I felt it," she said, her voice thick.

Iain eyed her sharply, something about her tone and the bright shimmer of almost-tears in her eyes sending little nips of wariness down his spine.

But she recovered with remarkable speed, standing tall before him and meeting his penetrating gaze with clear, deep-seeing eyes.

Wise, intelligent eyes he found every bit as intriguing as the delectable plenitude of her naked breasts.

More intriguing, in fact.

A simple truth that unsettled him, for it gnawed voraciously at every barrier he sought to keep between them.

"Drummond women are also known for their fortitude," she was saying. She raised the hem of her skirts, let him see the dirk-hilt protruding from her boot. "I am not afeared to face my challenges alone"—she shrugged—"I ken my limitations and thank you again for procuring raiment for me."

Iain scarce heard her, his mind full occupied with the dirk. A one-armed stripling could pluck it from her fine-boned hand with ease, use it against her. "You think to protect yourself with *that?* A wee bairn's blade?"

Silence answered him . . . as did the pink stain popping onto her cheeks.

She pursed her lips and something in the tight-lipped, voiceless way she regarded him made the fine hairs on his nape lift and crackle.

Surely she didn't mean to use the dirk without provocation?

Iain blinked, dragged a weary hand down his face.

The *uisge beatha*—or more likely, the proximity of her bared breasts—had surely turned his brain to mush.

Addled his wits.

The strain of keeping his gaze above her shoulders was giving him a raging headache.

A worse headache than if he'd tossed down the entire flagon!

He was *not* the paragon of chivalrous virtue she took him for, and his ability to uphold such a sham was fast dwindling. Leaving her standing beside the wooden tub, he stalked to the bed, tossed his leather satchel onto its feather mattress.

"Pray have your bath, lass, afore the water chills," he urged her, rummaging through the satchel until he found the sphagnum moss. "I shall stand before the window, my back turned, until you are through."

And if, perchance, the devil got the better of him and he risked a peek, the linen-lined tub looked deep enough to hide her nakedness to her shoulders . . . which was exactly why he wished her in it!

A fool notion if e'er there was one, he decided, the instant his ear caught the first soft rustlings of her hastily stripping off her clothes. But it was her sigh of pleasure as she lowered herself into the scented water that undid him.

That, and the splashy sound of water lapping against her naked skin.

"Jesu Christ," he swore, his supposed gallantry forgotten.

Frowning darkly, he dropped the clump of moss into an earthenware bowl on the table and filled it with water— thanks be, the bowl had a matching pitcher, and someone had thoughtfully assured it held fresh water.

He was *not* going anywhere near the wooden tub.

Not with her in it.

In particular now that she'd helped herself to the little jar of lavender-scented soap. Its sharp-sweet scent blended with her own lighter, heathery one to rise from the heated water and waft about the small room.

Waft directly beneath his twitching nose, beguiling him and increasing his difficulty in playing chivalrous.

Truth to tell, decidedly *un*-chivalrous thoughts laid siege to him from all sides.

Taking great care not to look her way, he carried the

sphagnum infusion across the room and plunked the bowl onto the top of the brazier.

Then he went to stand before the shuttered window, his back to the room, just as he'd promised—and took some grim satisfaction in having found her at last.

Even if he could only enjoy the completeness she brought him for the short space of days needed to reach Dunkeld.

Resting a shoulder against the window splay, he folded his arms and peered down through the angled shutter slatting at the inn yard, awash in drifting mist and slanting sheets of lashing rain.

Muffled bursts of laughter and song drifted up from the common room, testament of the continued drinking and carousing, and not far beneath the window, the ale-stake bobbed and weaved in the gusty wind, an odd and garish protrusion against somber storm-dark night.

And not unlike Iain himself, somehow out of place in the world around him.

The ale-stake's supports creaked and groaned, angry rusty cries against the indignities of being tossed about on the turbulent night wind. But its screeches and moans availed naught . . . much as his own protests brought no relief from a life gone wrong.

Closing his ears to its pitiful wails, and to the softer, sweeter sounds of Madeline's ablutions, Iain let the cold draught blowing through the shutters carry off any residual doubts lurking at the edge of his mind, unable to deny the irrefutable truth of the clan legend he'd ne'er believed.

E'er a man of dark reserve and little jollity, ne'er had he breathed so freely, known such warmth curl round his heart—or felt more alive—than in the few scant hours she'd been at his side.

She'd even brought a smile to his lips a time a two . . . or, at least the fervent wish to form one.

And he held in greatest trust that, given time, she'd fill his life with so much color and richness, he'd not pass a single hour without smiling.

Not a whim or fancy, she was indeed the other half of his heart, and he would ne'er unsay or scoff at legends or magic again.

Leaning harder against the window's edge, Iain drew a rough breath and faced still one more truth.

Mayhap the most vital one of all.

There could be no stepping back.

He could not—would not—walk away from Dunkeld Cathedral without her.

Regardless of what it cost him—and the saints knew he had scarce little to offer her—she would leave Dunkeld at his side . . . and as his bride.

Chapter Twelve

$\mathcal{M}$ADELINE SIGHED, AND RESTED her head against a folded towel she'd placed over the edge of the linen-draped tub. Sinking lower into the blissfully heated water, she concentrated on every shade and ripple of her shadow man's emotions e'er to spool round her heart or drift through her dreams.

Her eyes half-closed, she curled her fingers o'er her bent and raised knees, and recalled them all . . .

An ache that could ne'er be assuaged.

A black void too deep to e'er be filled with joy and light.

A profound love so all-encompassing it burned with a brilliance to rival the light of a thousand suns.

. . . but she failed miserably in her every attempt to forge a new path into his heart.

Or invite him into hers.

Time and again she tried, remembering his every anguish, his guilt. And, aye, the bottomless love he bore a single woman.

But her efforts proved futile.

She could no longer reach the deepest part of him.

Could feel naught but the numbing cold and emptiness inside her own heart.

The hunger and the doubt.

And the two words that seemed to hover in the air between them, elusive as the wispy curls of scented steam rising from her bath and just as difficult to catch.

She thought the words were *entwined destinies*.

And if they were, she knew exactly what they implied . . . a forever bond between her shadow man and the woman who held his heart.

A bond beyond breaking.

Her eyes stinging from tears she refused to shed, Madeline sat up and plunged her fingers deep into the little pot of soft, lavender-scented soap. The languor brought on by the soothing caress of the warm water on her naked flesh marred by the direction her thoughts were taking, she scrubbed first her arms, then her legs, scouring her flesh with a vengeance until it tingled and shone with a fine rosy glow.

And still she couldn't rid herself of the stain of the two words.

They flitted about in the half dark, taunting her from the shadows and reminding her that she had her own path to follow and that another woman accompanied Iain MacLean along his.

But unbreakable bonds or nay, he *had* looked on her with favor, and well more than once!

And he'd certainly enjoyed kissing her.

Of that there could be no doubt.

But how could he feel such desire for her—for the evidence of his arousal had been unmistakable—if his heart belonged so fully to someone else?

Madeline's brows drew together, each unanswered question another reason for her confusion . . . and why she'd sought so hard to catch hold of some revealing filament for a telltale glimpse into his heart.

Fervently wishing that for once she'd been able to make use of her gift at will, she drew a deep breath and held it, then slipped beneath the water to wet her hair.

Long in need of a thorough washing, she soaped her hair and scrubbed her scalp with special care, the fine and fragrant lather making the task an indescribable bliss. A divine treat every bit as enjoyable as the swirl of warm water rippling across the top swells of her naked breasts.

Uncertainty lapped at her, too. If she couldn't probe the depths of his heart to find her answers, she had little choice but to voice them directly.

Aye, she'd simply ask him.

Her decision made, she reached for a pail of clean water to rinse the soap from her hair. The cold water sluiced over her head and down her back, chilling the already cooling bathwater and making her shiver, but also carrying away any last residue of hesitation.

Feeling more in control of her fate than she had in weeks, she lifted her chin and reached behind her to twist her wet hair into a thick rope. But she'd hardly begun to wring out the moisture—or savor her newfound resolve—when a resounding crash shook the walls.

"Of a mercy!" Madeline shot to her feet, her heart slamming against her ribs.

"God and all his saints!" Iain cried, his hand flying to his sword hilt . . . only to lower again as swiftly.

A quick glance through the still-vibrating shutter slatting revealed the cause of the deafening commotion. Gusting winds had ripped the ale-stake from its hinges and sent it plunging to the ground.

"It was only the ale-stake," he said, turning to face Madeline. "The wind—"

He froze, his mouth going instantly dry.

Saints above, in his shock from the sudden crash, he'd forgotten she was bathing.

Madeline Drummond stood in the wooden tub, the glory of her nakedness rendering him speechless. White-hot heat surged through him, shooting straight to his groin, his need so hard and tight he could scarce breathe.

She stared at him from eyes wide with shock, her nude body, wet, glistening, and rosy from her bath. Damp hair, a tangled mass of dark red ringlets, hung over one shoulder, the curling tendrils clinging provocatively to her naked flesh, molding sweetly to each lush curve.

Iain tried to look away, but making his heart stop beating would have proved easier. His blood running hot, he stared back at her, his gaze fastened on the rivulets of water trickling down her breasts. Some snagged on the very tips of her nipples, forming tiny droplets on the hard-budded peaks, clinging there for long, tantalizing moments before dripping off one by one.

Then a droplet fell onto the nest of red-gold curls topping her thighs, and his entire world contracted to the fierce pounding need thundering through his loins.

He stared at the water droplet, watched it disappear into the lush tangle of wet curls, and the instant it slipped from sight, his sanity returned.

Or mayhap his honor, for he lifted his gaze to her face

and saw his own need reflected there, caught the desire burning in her own eyes just before her lashes swept down to hide it from him.

He recognized it, too, in the deeper red of the flush slowly spreading across the upper swells of her naked breasts. A flush that had naught to do with the warmth of her bath and the brazier's luxuriant heat.

'Twas the rosy glow of a woman roused . . . a flush Iain hadn't seen in years and ne'er such a beautiful one.

Turning back to the window before his sore-battered honor slipped back into the shadowy depths whence it had made its timeous appearance, Iain glowered down at the felled ale-stake and crossed his arms.

He, too, had been felled.

At least the throbbing part of him that shared distinct similarities with the long, hard length of the ale-stake.

Aye, she wanted him, there could be no doubt.

A woman's eyes, in particular, never lie. Not if a man looked deep enough, and Iain had, even in that one fleeting glimpse before she'd lowered her lashes.

And much as a *certain part* of him would wish otherwise, his heart and, aye, his honor, wouldn't allow him to touch her so long as shadows of doubt clouded her eyes.

Pain had been there, too.

And rampant frustration.

All harbingers of just the sort of shaky foundation he did *not* want to build a new life upon. The kind of ghosts he did not want looming between them.

He'd started one marriage with a lass whose gentle eyes had held shyness and, aye, fear, too, and though time banished those shadows, even replacing them with love, it'd ne'er been the urgent, all-consuming passionate love he knew he could have with Madeline Drummond . . . if he didn't let the raw lust gnawing at his innards drive him to rushing her.

Nay, that, he would not do.

Even if she danced naked before him and *begged* him to take her.

He wouldn't lay a finger on her—in *that* way—until naught but purest love, shining and clear and untroubled, shone in her magnificent green-gold eyes.

And until the last of his own ghosts were laid as well.

But he burned for her nonetheless. Knowing her naked, wet, and *willing,* if he encouraged her, so near behind him and yet so far, almost killed him.

Raking a hand through his hair, his breath still harsh and ragged, he stared down at the inn yard, watching as someone flung open the door and a stream of shouting men poured out to gather 'round the downed ale-stake.

He recognized two men.

The miscreants who had thought to accost his lady.

And he welcomed their timely appearance, for they took his mind off the sound of Madeline stepping from the bathing tub. They also reminded him of the danger facing her . . . a thought that cooled his ardor in one fell swoop.

They slunk along the lee of a wall, heading toward the stables, their path keeping them close enough to the light spilling from the windows for him to brand their faces into his memory.

For the second time that night, Iain dropped his hand to his sword hilt. But this time he let it linger there. *Caressed it.* As he lived and breathed, those two jackals would not walk away from their next encounter with him . . . if his lady's terror upon seeing them indeed bespoke the kind of villainy he suspected.

And that was something he meant to find out.

Twinges of guilt nibbling at him for the distress he was surely about to cause her, he opened the leather purse hanging from his waist belt and retrieved the little silver leg ex-voto.

"Tell me when I can turn around, lass, for I would speak to you," he said, curling his fingers around the votive, his impatience to get answers from her kindled by the men's appearance.

"I am covered," she said, after several long moments of soft rustling noises.

Iain turned. She'd wrapped his sister's *arisaid* about her and stood watching him from eyes gone wary.

"It is not my wont to distress you, but . . ." He left the sentence unfinished. "Pray believe I wish I were better blessed with words, lass."

She waved a dismissive hand. "I conceive you speak quite fine," she declared. "And I must ask you something, too, and would rather have an easier way with the words."

"I will answer any questions you have for me, milady . . . if first you tell me why you were gathering these"—he paused to hold up the ex-voto—"from cathedral shrines and holy wells?"

She stared at the votive, the color draining from her face. "Where did you get that?"

"Gavin found it," he told her, setting the little silver leg on the table. "He saw it fall from your hand when you ran from Glasgow Cathedral."

"I was not *stealing* the votives," she said, her voice

tight, quivering with pent-up emotion. "I was looking for them, that is all."

"And why were you looking for them? You must tell me," he urged her, his heart wrenching at the pain in her eyes. "Only so can I help you. I cannot challenge a faceless demon."

"No one can help me." She lifted her chin a notch. She was *not* going to cry. So she reached deep inside herself, probed for the crackling anger she preferred keeping hidden away.

One glance at the little silver leg, gleaming bright on the oaken table, helped her find it.

"Can you bring my father back to life? Mayhap turn back time and undo the hideous act that took his life? The lives of innocents?" She spoke past the hot lump swelling in her throat, her voice rising with each word. "A young goatherd burned alive, do you ken? Burned, and just because he happened around a corner at the wrong time . . . can you save him, too?"

Iain stared at her, outrage churning in his gut. "Pray tell me that isn't what happened at Abercairn?" he asked, already seeing the truth in her eyes.

He stepped forward, wrapped his arms around her, drew her close, tried to spend her his warmth if he couldn't comfort such great horrors. "Tell me you did not witness such things?"

She clung to him, her entire body beginning to tremble. "Aye, that is the fate of Abercairn," she said, her voice breaking. She released a long, quivering sigh. "Abercairn, my father, and the young lads Sir Bernhard Logie burned on pyres before the castle gates."

She looked up at him, her face deathly pale, her eyes

bright with unshed tears. "Do you ken how much I loved my father, sir? More than the whole of the world, I did," she said, her anguish ripping Iain's soul. "'Tis true I hardly speak of him, but that is because I cannot bear the pain of thinking of him."

Her fingers dug into his shoulders, her words a swift-flowing current. "And the boys! Logie's men seized them—goatherds, most of them were. T-they threatened to burn them lest my father threw open the gates. He did, and forthwith, but Silver Leg burned the lads anyway."

Iain's breath caught, icy cold slithering down his spine. *"Silver Leg?"*

She pressed fisted hands against her eyes as if to stave off tears, and nodded. "Sir Bernhard Logie is his name, but he styles himself thus for the little silver leg votives. 'Tis said he was lame as a boy and some obscure saint cured him, so he now makes pilgrimages to shrines where'er he happens to be. He leaves the votives as to-kens of his appreciation," she explained, the words flow-ing like a torrent.

"H-he is one of the Disinheriteds, come back from England in support of Edward Balliol, but his own hold-ing—the one he lost—isn't as rich as ours, so he wanted Abercairn, and took it."

Iain's brows drew together in a frown. "And your fa-ther? What of him?"

"My father is . . . *was* an ill man," she said, blinking hard. "A greathearted man and much-loved laird. But he was a man of letters and learning, not a warrior. He made an easy target for one as ruthless as Silver Leg."

Slipping a hand beneath the damp fall of her hair, Iain kneaded the back of her neck, amazed he could move his fingers so gently with such rage pumping through him. But Madeline Drummond needed gentleness.

Dear saints but she needed a tender hand on her.

"You saw your father killed? Burned on a pyre before your eyes?" Bile rose in Iain's throat, fury at the beasts responsible for such heinous acts.

She hesitated, drew several great breaths. "I saw him led to the pyre. The two men belowstairs earlier . . . t-they were the ones who escorted him."

"By the Rood!" Iain swore, the revelation sealing the men's fate. "I should have run them through then and there." His blood ran cold, outrage pumping through him. "Rest assured I shall avenge you, lass, and if I have to track them across the width and breadth of the land."

Horror at what she'd been through churned in his gut, twisting his innards and squeezing his heart. "You saw this happen?"

She hesitated, shook her head. "I did not s-see him . . . see him burn," she admitted, swiping a hand across her cheek, just beneath her eyes. "I couldn't bear to watch."

"God in Heaven." Iain tightened his arms around her, his own heart breaking. He tucked her head beneath his chin and rocked her. "Sweet, sweet lass."

"T-that was the day Nella and I left Abercairn," she said in a voice so small he scarce heard her above the slashing rain.

"The day you decided to join a nunnery?" *A travesty he was not about to let happen.*

She nodded, looked up at him with green-shimmering eyes gone dark as moss. "The day I decided to kill Silver Leg."

Iain's jaw dropped. "So-o-o!" he said, the pieces beginning to fall in place. "That is why you were looking for the votives?"

She nodded again. "I couldn't hope to avenge my father at Abercairn. Too many of Silver Leg's men would be about. So I thought to catch him unawares, at a shrine, and . . . and—"

"And kill him with the wee bairn's dirk you carry in your boot?"

"Aye, that was my plan. And why I meant to enter a convent afterward . . . to atone for the sin of murder in a holy place."

Iain stared at her. "Sweet lass, ne'er have I heard a plan more doomed to failure and ne'er have I seen a lass less suited for life as a nun."

Much to his relief, a spark of anger appeared in her eyes. "And you have a better plan?"

"Och, aye, lass, but I do," he said, setting her away from him.

His mind racing, hope burgeoning in his heart, he took the sphagnum moss tincture off the brazier, snatched up a few small linen towels from the stool next to the bathing tub, and carried them to the bedside table, using the few moments away from her to suppress the triumph beginning to surge through him.

The lass didn't know it yet, but she'd just given him a far better way to atone for his own sins than prostrating himself before moldering bones and bathing in supposedly sacred waters.

He'd help her regain Abercairn Castle, avenging her father's death and gaining time to woo her properly in the process.

Much pleased with himself, he returned to her side and

struck his most valiant Master of the Highlands stance. Thus posed—legs slightly apart and his arms folded—he drew back his great shoulders and gave her what he hoped would appear as a smile of confidence and encouragement.

One he hoped she wouldn't be able to resist.

If he didn't look the fool, which was a distinct possibility, as he was sorely out of practice at smiling. Being anyone's valiant hero was new territory for him.

But he must have done something right because she blushed prettily and gave him a tremulous smile in return. "And what is your plan, good sir?"

Why, to charm and seduce you, sweet lass. And make you mine for all our days, his heart declared.

"I shall tell you of my plan as I soothe your ankles and wrists with the sphagnum tincture," he promised, guiding her toward the bed. "And you have my word I shall tend only those parts of you that are aching."

He almost grinned at that last, and would have attempted it if she hadn't ground her feet into the rushes and tugged on his arm.

"Aye, lass?"

"You no longer wish to bathe?"

He shook his head. "It can wait," he said, and ran the backs of his knuckles down her cheek. "Soothing your hurts, inside and out, matters more at the moment."

She blinked at that. He'd thought she would smile. But she peered at him, the shadows he'd noted earlier creeping back to cloud her lovely eyes.

"There is something I must ask you, Iain MacLean," she said, her chin lifting, her gaze bitter earnest. "And I must ken the answer afore I lie down on that bed for your . . . er . . . helpful ministrations."

"Then ask away, lass, for I shall keep no secret from you," he said, and meant it.

"Are you married?" she blurted, high color spotting her cheeks. "Is there a lady of your heart?"

Iain blinked, for a moment flummoxed, but secretly pleased she'd asked.

It meant she cared.

He took one of her hands between both of his, squeezed lightly. "I was married, aye." He answered her true. "But my wife has long since passed from history, lass. She is dead and has been for o'er a year."

"But she has not passed from your heart?" she probed, surprising him. "You still love her."

Iain's brow knitted, his initial pleasure at the question swinging into confusion. But he'd sworn not to lie to her, so he answered these questions honestly, too. "She will always be in my heart, aye."

But ne'er in the way that you are, that very heart giving the answer he knew she needed.

"You need what?"

Donall the Bold, proud and mighty laird of the MacLeans, crossed his well-muscled arms and peered down at the wee crone standing before him in his cavernous hall at Baldoon.

Slight and black-garbed as a raven, Devorgilla, Doon's resident wisewoman, cleared her throat and drew a self-important breath.

Indeed, she allowed herself a second one, too.

She'd made the long and tedious journey from her

cliff-top cottage on the other side of Doon, crossing roughest moorland and peat bog, even suffering the blast of wind and rain in her face without hardship.

And now that she had the man she needed before her, she wasn't about to deny herself stating what she required.

Especially when her needs would benefit the laird's brother, Iain the Doubter, whom she knew to be anything but a doubter these fine and bonnie days.

"Well?" The laird arched a dark brow at her.

"I need a skilled leatherworker," she began, counting off her wishes on knotty-knuckled fingers. "A goldsmith or jewelworker, a fast-footed gillie, and passage for him on your swiftest galley."

Donall MacLean couldn't quite hide his surprise. "Am I to learn why you need these men?"

Devorgilla pursed her lips, her eyes twinkling as she shook her head. She loved secrets and intrigues, and she thoroughly believed in the divine place of magic and meddling in the world . . . so long as it was done for someone's good.

And she'd done a lot of good in her time, as the MacLean laird ought know.

The slight upward tilt at the corner of his mouth showed her he did. "Does this have aught to do with my brother?"

Devorgilla gave him her most mischievous smile and shrugged. "It might," she conceded, doubly pleased when keen interest flashed in the bonnie laird's dark eyes.

"Have you had word of Iain?" He narrowed his gaze at her. "Is he well?"

"Some victuals and a place to lay my head this night?"

the *cailleach* bargained, well aware Donall MacLean knew the game and would indulge her.

Shuffling closer to him, she touched gnarled fingers to his hard-muscled arm and slid a telling gaze across the darkened hall to where a line of sleeping men already snored on their pallets. "'Tis too late an hour for one of my great years to be a-traipsing across the heather."

The laird nodded and patted her hand. "All the roast gannet and bannocks you can eat. My best ale, too."

"And the pallet?"

"In my own solar abovestairs . . . away from the snores of my slumbering kinsmen."

Devorgilla cackled and rubbed her hands together, mightily pleased. But not so much as to grovel her appreciation.

Such boons were her just due as resident crone.

"And when will you require the services of these men?"

"Soon. As soon as you can spare them."

"Consider it done." Donall gave her a nod, his lairdly assurance he'd grant her requests.

He, too, had his role to fulfill.

But then the hard set of his handsome face softened, his mouth curving in the faintest of indulgent smiles. Just enough for the crone to glimpse the spindly-legged laddie who'd once been too frightened of her to venture anywhere near her thatched cottage for fear she'd make him drink liquefied toad spittle.

Or worse, turn him into one of the slimy-backed creatures.

"I'll send the men with you on the morrow," he promised, the caring warmth behind his words assuring her the boy had grown into a fine and worthy laird.

"Rob the goldsmith can take you before him on his garron," he added. "That will spare you the trek across the high moor and bogs."

"You are kind," the *cailleach* said, more touched than she cared to show.

"And Iain?" The laird pressed his own concerns again. "Have you word of his well-being?"

Devorgilla almost blushed.

She'd had better than *word* of Iain the Doubter, now known in some quarters as Master of the Highlands.

She'd dreamed of him!

And, och, what a dream it'd been, for she'd glimpsed him and his new lady in very fine fettle.

But she'd keep *those* secrets to herself and simply answer Donall MacLean's question with the expected dignity of her station.

"Your brother is more than well. Truth be told—and I have seen it—'tis fair swollen with pleasure he is of late," she said, and allowed herself another wee chuckle.

She'd let it to the laird himself to catch the double meaning of her words.

His knitted brow said he didn't, and Devorgilla wasn't surprised.

Men could be so blind.

Chapter Thirteen

OUTSIDE THE LITTLE ROOM at the Shepherd's Rest, the sliver of a crescent moon shone dimly through racing storm clouds, and the rumble of thunder grew distant. Chill winds still buffeted the alehouse, bringing with them sheets of drifting rain and the muffled sounds of chaos from the ale-yard as men struggled with the felled ale-stake.

Deep blue-gray shadows filled much of the room's interior save the feeble light cast by the red-glowing brazier and the rack of candles on the bedside table. Thick silence stretched and preened in the inky corners, a crouching presence swallowing the patter of rain on the stone window ledge but not quite overlaying the hard and fast pounding of Madeline's heart.

It hammered so loudly against her ribs she could scarce believe Iain MacLean could not hear its racing beat. Truth to tell, it roared in her own ears with such ferocity, she could hear naught beyond its thudding and the echo of the few words that set it to thundering in the first place.

Truths that spent her glorious, blinding hope.

Her shadow man was widowed, not married.

His braw heart given and claimed . . . but by a dead woman.

Closing her eyes for a moment, Madeline breathed a silent prayer of thanks. In her darkest hour, the fates had smiled on her after all, blessing her with a fine and shining ray of hope.

And she meant to embrace that hope with the whole of her heart.

No flesh-and-blood woman held Iain MacLean's affections.

Immense relief, stunning in its intensity, swept her. Ne'er could or would she be any man's leman—the bane to cause another woman pain.

Even at the cost of her own.

But much as she loathed sharing even a wee corner of her shadow man's heart—his *love* if she could win it— sharing him with the memory of a dead wife was a burden she'd be glad to take on her shoulders.

She sighed, his beautiful golden warmth surging through her, sweet and dear. Iain MacLean, her braw and bonnie Master of the Highlands was free.

And so now, too, was she.

Feeling almost giddy in her relief, she stretched most sinuously atop the chamber's curtained bed, full naked but for the gauzy-thin slip of her ruined undershift and the length of rough drying linen she'd wrapped around her damp hair. She watched him, wondered if her heart showed in her eyes.

He stood before the table, fussing with his bowl of sphagnum tincture. "Do you trust me, lass?" he asked suddenly, turning to face her, a deeper question than his words implied mirrored in his dark eyes.

Madeline blinked, confused. "I would not lie here thus, nigh fully unclothed, if I did not."

Stepping close, he skimmed the backs of his fingers across the bared skin of her shoulders, the light caress sending a rush of delicate shivers cascading down her back. "And *that,* your own near naked state, has much to do with what I would ask you, lady dear," he said, a new huskiness to his voice.

A deep, mellifluous note so rich and smooth it did strange things to her belly. *Delicious* things that made her keenly aware of the transparency and thinness of her gauzy undershift.

"Aye, 'tis of nakedness I must speak," he said, and for one heart-in-her-throat moment, Madeline wondered if he were blessed with a similar gift as her own.

Before she could reply, he pulled back the folds of his plaid to reveal his padded leather hauberk and the two belts slung low about his hips, his waist and sword belts. His money purse dangled heavily from the first, his sheathed brand from the second.

"Even Masters of the Highlands do not sleep fully clothed, sweetness." He gave her one of his tilted, heart-clutching half-smiles. "What I am asking, is if you trust me enough to allow me to sleep as I am usually wont to do?"

Madeline blinked. She knew exactly what he meant.

He wanted her permission to sleep naked.

She moistened her lips, hoped her answer would not come out as a croak. *She'd love for him to sleep bare-backed!*

Truth be told, she'd already seen him thus many times over in her dreams. Seeing him unclothed here before her, in flesh and blood and not cloaked by the shadowy wisps of a dream, would be a treat beyond measure.

"Through my duties as laird's daughter at Abercairn, I have seen the bed-nakedness of many men, and shall not mind yours," she said, well aware *his* nude body would prove vastly different than any other man's she'd seen.

Young lads and squires mostly, cavorting in the lochans near Abercairn in the summer's heat. And older knightly guests, come to visit her father. Men she'd been expected to spend the courtesy of assisting in their nightly ablutions.

But ne'er a man even halfway comparable to Iain MacLean.

"So, nay, sir, I do not mind nakedness."

Especially not yours.

He nodded, his eyes seeming to darken a shade as he reached for the clasp of his sword belt, unlatched it.

His gaze slid to the bowl of steaming sphagnum tincture. "And if I tend your aches thus?"

"I will welcome your touch be you fully garbed or otherwise," Madeline said, the trickling heat beginning to pool low by her thighs chasing any other response from her tongue.

Thoughts of his nude body stirred her in most unladylike ways.

Decidedly delicious ways.

"Then so be it," he said, and jerked free his second belt, the intense way he watched her as he did so almost making her forget to breathe.

He discarded his plaid with equal speed, his dark gaze

never leaving hers as he then unlaced his hauberk and drew the heavy leather garment over his head. Tossing it aside, he made short shrift of his shirt and boots.

His trews followed as quickly, leaving him naked but for his loose-fitting, linen braies. Only then did he hesitate, his hands hovering at their waistband.

He lifted a questioning brow. "You have my word I shall not attempt to touch you unseemly," he assured her. "'Tis only that I have slept bare-bottomed since I was a wee laddie, and I doubt I'd find a decent night's rest clad otherwise."

"I—I understand," Madeline answered, hoping he wouldn't notice the hitch in her voice . . . or the excitement coursing through her. "Most men at Abercairn sleep thus. I have seen them about at times."

He lifted a questioning brow, the slight narrowing of his eyes telling her he'd caught the hitch.

Hopefully, he'd missed the excitement part.

"I would not offend you, lady." He turned narrowed eyes on her, studied her face. "You are certain?"

Madeline nodded . . . her mouth too dry for words.

For truth, it mattered not a whit if he removed his flimsy-clothed underhose or nay. She could already see the whole of him in quite bold detail. The thinness of the fine linen of his braies left nary a secret.

"Pray remove your braies as well . . . if it pleases you," she got out, the weighty warmth pulsing deep in her belly almost intoxicatingly sweet.

He inclined his head. "I am indebted," he said, and the underhose vanished.

Seemingly as easy in his nakedness as he was fully clothed, he turned his attention back to the sphagnum preparation. He stood quite unashamedly at the table, the whole of his masculine glory proudly displayed, the sight sending shiver upon shiver tumbling down Madeline's spine.

She took advantage of his preoccupation with the tincture and let her gaze travel over him. Candle glow fell softly across his wide-set shoulders and muscled back, highlighting the hard planes and contours of his well-trained body, but revealing, too, the silvery tracks of several long-healed battle scars.

Badges of honor.

Madeline's already-racing heart skittered a few beats. Her shadow man was indeed a bold and brave man. The kind another man would welcome at his side in battle. The kind a woman could rely on to keep her and their children safe, their home well guarded. His scar ridges, valiant reminders of the daring he'd displayed upon rescuing her at St. Thenew's Well.

And, oh sweet Mother Mary, but her breath quickened just looking at him.

In particular, looking at *that* part of him.

At the thought, her gaze snapped right there. She tried to wrest her attention back upward, but couldn't. Looking away from the thicket of springy, black hair at his groin and the magnificent piece of masculinity cradled there proved impossible.

Thick and long, his maleness hung heavily between his thighs and the large ballocks dangling behind it were equally impressive. Enough so to make her most feminine place explode in a burst of pure, pulsating heat. An intense, shimmering wash of tingles so exquisite they bordered on being painful.

Over and over again, they raced across her woman's flesh, growing in intensity until she almost moaned. The languorous weightiness pulsing in the lowest part of her belly became almost agonizing in how *good* it felt.

"Oh my," she breathed.

"Not quite what you expected?" His voice, so smooth and rich, only increased the tingling.

"Nay. Not at all," she owned, speaking the truth.

She just didn't add how magnificent she found him. How much he intrigued and stirred her.

But she suspected he knew because he'd tilted his head to the side and was peering curiously at her. Flickering candlelight glinted off the sleek spill of his hair, and a breathless craving to comb her fingers through the black-gleaming strands seized her with such force the tips of her fingers itched.

Ne'er had she seen a more beautiful man.

His dark masculine beauty proved even more heart-catching, more scorchingly alluring than in the sweetest of her dreams of them together.

"The tincture is ready," he said then, watching her intently as he dipped a length of folded linen into the steaming bowl. "You shall soon be quit of your aches."

Madeline nodded, feeling almost as inept at speech as he was e'er claiming to be. She'd almost blurted that seeing him unclothed had given her a whole slew of *new* aches.

Aches of a sort she would ne'er have believed existed. But oh had she hoped they did. And now she knew.

Faith, but he stole her breath.

"We shall speak of my plan to help you while I apply

the tincture," he promised, wringing excess moisture out of the linen.

"You truly have one?"

"A plan?" He glanced at her. "I have said so."

"I do not see how you can hope to help me." Madeline curled her fingers into the softness of the feather mattress, suddenly needful of something to *hold.* "I have told you. All is lost at Abercairn."

"But is it, fair lady?"

The words hung in the air, almost a challenge.

Madeline's head shot off her pillow, and she looked sharply at him, something indefinable in his tone making her heart thump heavily. "I do not understand."

To her surprise a faraway look flitted across his handsome face, and his eyes darkened with a trace of the sadness she'd felt with her gift so often in the weeks before they'd met.

"Things are not always as they seem, lass." He covered her hand with his, gently stroked the tops of her fingers. "'Tis a lesson I have learned the hard way. I would spare you such grief if you will but trust me."

"I do trust you."

"Then put away your doubt and disbelief," he said, still rubbing her fingers, his warmth flowing into her, comforting her.

Just as she suspected he meant it to do.

And it worked. She was melting . . . swooning beneath his gentle caress. Her cares drifted away, no match for his tender ministrations.

Golden warmth began spreading through her. She ached to reach for him, to draw him close so his warmth and strength could pour even deeper inside her, wrap itself clear around her. She looked at his face then, and saw compassion brimming in his eyes.

Madeline sighed.

For all his supposed temper and tales of penance, *she* found her Master of the Highlands to be a great-hearted man of much depth and caring.

A man capable of untold tenderness and devotion.

Just as she'd known he'd be.

He lifted his hand from hers, brushed the backs of his fingers down the side of her face, along the sloping curve of her neck. "A sky black with smoke will hide much of what lies beneath it, but that doesn't mean the landscape is no longer there," he told her, and the way he said it made her pulse quicken again.

He was giving her hope.

And heaven help her, but she was blossoming under it. Even if she had little reason to believe *her* world could be salvaged. She'd seen it extirpated. How could it still be there? Waiting for her beneath her pain.

Her beloved Da yet alive.

Mayhap even needing her now, this very moment.

She looked away, her eyes stinging.

"You did not see your father perish." Iain touched her cheek, smoothed a hand down her damp hair, clearly trying to gentle the words he knew would distress her.

"Could it be he yet lives?" he coaxed. "Perhaps held prisoner in his own keep?"

"Silver Leg is too cruel to have spared my father's life," Madeline said, certain of it. "He enjoys inflicting pain, especially on those unable to challenge him. He loves only gold more. Riches and, mayhap, his two greyhounds."

"I would ask you to think hard, lass. Search your mind for some reason he may have for keeping your father alive. Think, too, about why he has sent his henchmen to look for you."

Madeline blinked. "I cannot imagine what he wants of me, nor can I believe he would relinquish the pleasure he'd take in doing what he did to my father."

"Mayhap we ought to find out if it was truly done as you believe?" Iain suggested, seeming to warm to the idea. Sounding serious. "Aye, I think we should. Mayhap it is time Silver Leg meets a worthier opponent than goatherds and older, ailing men?"

"And how do you think to do that?"

"With my sword arm and my wits." He leaned forward to drop a kiss on the tip of her disbelieving nose.

"You are but one man," she said, blushing a bit from the kiss, but still doubtful. "With your friend, Gavin Mac-Fie, you are two. Two men alone cannot effect much against a well-garrisoned castle."

"It is not good to be so beset with doubt, sweeting," he said, stroking his fingers in her hair. "That lesson, too, I have learned. Only recently, in fact."

But she still watched him with disbelief in her lovely eyes, though he did appear to have sparked her interest. He shifted her mind onto other things . . . away from the bad ones. And that, for the moment, was enough.

And it seemed to please him.

'Twas a fine start in the right direction.

"I have two further men with me . . . great brawny lads," he told her, delighted that he could. For once glad-hearted that Donall had sent along the two hulking sea-men.

Now Madeline's eyes *did* begin to glitter with interest. "Two other men?"

Iain nodded. "The sort who'd enjoy naught better than having this Logie dastard for breakfast and gnawing on his bones for lunch," he said. "You will meet them on the morrow when we join Gavin and your friend."

"So you are four."

"Aye, but I could raise more if my wits don't fail me . . . and they ne'er do, as I told you."

"D-dare I hope?" Her voice broke on the words, her eyes glistening suspiciously again.

"Aye, the hope is well-founded, but I cannot promise. Not yet," he told her true. "Chances are good, though."

She smiled at that.

A tremulous, watery smile that seemed to embarrass her because she lowered her head, blinking furiously the instant the smile had curved her lips.

"Oh!" she gasped then, and Iain knew immediately *where* her averted gaze had fallen.

He'd *felt* the gaze, too.

"He is at rest, lady sweet." He sought to ease her embarrassment. "Do not let him trouble you."

But to his great surprise, she peered closer. And the instant she did, he began to fill and lengthen beneath her keen-eyed scrutiny.

Her gaze riveted on him and she watched in apparent fascination as his maleness swelled and stretched beneath her perusal. "Oh dear saints," she gasped, her brows shooting upward.

He wasn't even halfway hard.

Iain smiled.

A wee one, to be sure, but one of the best he'd managed in a long time, and certainly more of a bold smile than any she'd yet seen on him.

And ohhh but it felt good to give it to her.

"Och, aye, *dear* indeed, lassie, and I do not mean what *you* are gazing upon," he said, taking hold of his length, pinching until the swelling receded.

"Forgive me," he said, and shrugged his great shoulders. "I suppose he is not as bone-tired as I thought."

"I did not mind," she blurted. "See you, I have ne'er—"

"Ne'er seen a man full roused?" he finished for her, and she nodded.

The mere thought, speaking it aloud, had him filling anew. The innocently proffered attest to her virginal state swelled his heart.

Pleased by her innocent curiosity and lack of timidity, Iain carefully applied one of the moss-steeped linens across the backs of her lower calves. He pressed the warm cloth lightly around the raw skin of her ankles; her sigh of pleasure when he did so lifted his spirits even more.

He'd forgotten how good it felt to bring someone pleasure.

Even pleasure of such a simple sort.

He shifted himself on the edge of the bed, savoring her closeness but concentrating on the abraded flesh at her ankles lest a certain part of him attempt to heed its own mind again.

"The sphagnum should work quickly to relieve the pain," he told her, adjusting the steaming linen to cover the whole of her lower legs. "You shouldn't notice any discomfort at all upon awakening."

He began kneading the backs of her calves through

the hot cloth, and she sighed again. A soft, contented sigh. Almost a purring sound. Iain's heart tilted upon hearing it.

Ne'er had any lass purred for him.

Not even Lileas.

And if Madeline Drummond did so simply upon having her calves massaged, the saints knew how sweetly she'd sing upon having other, more sensitive parts of her body lovingly caressed.

But for now the summary of her losses at Abercairn weighed heavier on his mind than delving into such frivolous pursuits, tempting though they might be. Aye, he craved words with her that had more to do with extirpating the blackhearted dastard who'd seized her home than the sweet nothings he hoped to whisper against her ear someday very soon.

Pushing to his feet, he fetched more of the hot linens, this time wrapping the steaming cloths about her wrists. Holding them in place with firm but gentle pressure, he silently cursed the heinous deeds that had given her such cause to weep and hoped the plan that was beginning to take shape in his mind would soon turn her tears to smiles.

A thousand of them for each tear shed.

Chapter Fourteen

$\mathcal{L}$ONG PAST GLOAMING THE NEXT DAY, Iain reined up before the massive Fortingall yew, an ancient giant of a tree, and purported to be older than time. 'Twas his designated meeting place with Gavin MacFie.

The yew stood dark and noble against the gathering clouds and a swift wind, ripe with the dampness of coming rain whistled through its gnarled, down-spreading branches.

To Iain's relief, Gavin, the great auburn-haired lout, materialized almost immediately, stepping out of the shadows of a semi-ruinous chapel behind the yew. A sizable enough structure, if in decay, its crumbling stone walls were almost completely hidden by the yew's incredible girth.

Nella of the Marsh came a pace or two behind him, a curiously anxious look marring her comely brow, but MacFie strode forward and slapped Iain hard on the thigh before he could wonder further about the lady's apparent distress.

"I have seen that look on a MacLean before," Gavin

declared, his narrow-eyed scrutiny as piercing as the wind.

"A fine and good eve to you, too," Iain tossed back, dismounting. "And, aye, I suppose you have seen such a look often enough living with MacLeans as you do."

"Where are the others?" Iain didn't give the other a chance to spout the words he could almost see dancing on the lout's waggling tongue.

"You've been stricken with the MacLean Bane," Gavin loosed the words anyway. "I can spot the symptoms ten leagues away."

"And if I have?" Iain eyed him from beneath down-drawn brows, the edge of his temper beginning to unfurl.

Struggling to douse his annoyance, he lifted Madeline to the ground. "Beardie? Douglas? They are here, too?"

"They are 'round the other side of the old chapel tending the horses," Gavin said, jerking his head toward the ruined stone wall behind the yew's red-gleaming trunk. "MacNab sent along mounts for the ladies. Two fine garrons. I promised we'd return them on our journey back to Doon."

On your journey back to Doon.

"Well met of him," Iain said aloud. "Did he provide the raiment I requested as well?"

Gavin inclined his head. "Aye, and a-plenty."

"He is a good friend," Iain said, truly grateful. "He shall be repaid for his generosity . . . especially if he can raise men to help us retake this lady's home."

Gavin's bearded jaw dropped.

A gasp of surprise issued from Nella's lips. Her startled gaze flew to Madeline. "You told him?"

"Aye," Iain answered for her. "Who she is and why the two of you have been traipsing across the heather."

"So it is to Abercairn rather than St. Fillan's Healing Pond and Dunkeld?" Gavin blurted, coloring as soon as the blunder left his lips.

Iain's gaze snapped back to MacFie. "I am done with bathing in sacred pools, and Dunkeld can wait for its relic and gifts." He studied the other's reddening face. "Madeline's father may yet be alive, and if he is, time is crucial. But how did *you* know she hails from Abercairn?"

This time Nella of the Marsh's cheeks began to tinge. She turned to Madeline, the anxious look in her eyes more pronounced than ever. "Your pardon, lady, but I had to tell him. You ken I ne'er cared for—"

"We must speak of Abercairn," Gavin said, and slid a warning look at Nella.

"And of MacNab," Iain said, lifting a hand in greeting to Beardie and Douglas. The seamen were just emerging from behind the chapel ruin, questions on their faces.

"The MacNab is a longtime friend and ally," Iain began, and all eyes turned on him. *He* aimed a sharp gaze at MacFie. "He has enough men to provide a formidable host of fighting men. Do you think he will lend us their strength?"

Gavin had the ill grace to scratch his beard.

His brows drawing together, Iain turned to the seamen. "And you? What think you?"

They looked from one to the other, uncertainly, but after a few moments of feet shuffling, Beardie cracked his knuckles, and declared, "Aye, sir, I vow he will. The MacNabs e'er relish a good fight. As do I."

Douglas bobbed his head in agreement.

Iain gave them a curt nod, pleased. "Then I would that you ride hotfoot back to MacNab and bid his help. Tell him we will use a dual attack combined with a ruse," he explained. "A small number of men will create a disturbance at the castle's rear wall to distract the garrison, while a larger host simultaneously forces entry through the main gates."

Pausing, he reached for Madeline's hand, squeezed it. "I do not believe MacNab will fail us." To the seamen, he added, "Off with you now, and tell MacNab his men ought arrive at the main gatehouse—and with all haste."

"As you wish," they chorused, already going for their mounts.

They'd no sooner swung into their saddles and spurred away, riding fast southward across the rolling terrain of wooded knolls and broken pastureland, than Gavin clapped a hand on Iain's shoulder.

"MacNab will help," he said, giving Iain the assurance he secretly craved. "I feel it in my bones. The only question is if they arrive on time."

"They *must* arrive on time." Iain wouldn't consider otherwise. "Logie will not give up Abercairn without a fierce fight."

"He'll crave Abercairn's riches," Nella put in, stepping forward. "That will be his reason for seizing the castle. Not because its location and strength would benefit the Disinheriteds, but because of greed."

Iain drew a long breath. He glanced at Madeline and hated how tightly she clasped her hands—so fiercely her knuckles gleamed white. "Madeline told me Logie values gold above all else."

"It is true," Madeline spoke up, her face pale as cream

in the soft, gloaming light, her eyes mossy green, their gold flecks gone so dark that they were scarce visible.

She went to stand beside the yew, idly tracing the fluted patterns of its flaky red bark as she spoke. "Abercairn has riches beyond gold," she began, her voice troubled. "There is a secret cache of priceless jewels hidden in my father's bedchamber. They are sealed deep within the posts of his bed."

Moistening her lips, she went on, "He collected them from the gem-studded armor and weapons of the fallen English chivalry after Bannockburn. He harvested them on the encouragement of Robert Bruce himself as war booty . . . the King's appreciation for Drummond sword arms in the battle."

"So-o-o!" Iain looked up at the darkening sky and blew out a long breath. His heart dipped at the trust she'd displayed by naming the location of such a priceless treasure.

It showed the depth of her regard for him, and that warmed him beyond measure.

"That explains why Silver Leg sent his henchmen looking for you," he said, glancing back at her, the two men's faces flashing before his mind's eye. Chilling his blood. "The dastard will suspect you know the whereabouts of any hiding places."

"And as you see, I do." She leaned back against the yew's massive trunk, adjusted her borrowed *arisaid* against the knifing wind. "I would have mentioned the jewels when you asked me for reasons Logie would seek me, but truth be told, I'd forgotten about them."

Iain's brow lifted. "Forgotten? How can such wealth slip your mind, lass?"

She shrugged, looked off to the side, across the low, whin-dotted ridges. "You must know my da to understand. See you, he is . . . *was* softhearted. A great romantic and a very sentimental man. He claimed Abercairn had enough riches to serve us well, and considered the Bannockburn jewels a treasure beyond material worth."

A tear spilled down her cheek, and she swiped at it. "Da loved the Bruce and valued the jewels in his honor. He felt we must safekeep them for the Bruce's memory," she said. "Da claimed that long past our own lifetimes, the Scottish nation would honor them as national treasures. So he hid them and we simply do . . . er . . . *did* as though they do not exist."

She looked at him, her eyes glittery with tears but her jaw set tight. "I feel as my da did about the jewels. That is why I didn't speak of them . . . I'd truly forgotten their existence."

Iain swallowed against the tightness in his own throat. "Your father is a wise man and a good one," he said, his voice rough.

And hoping upon hope he'd used the correct tense.

"If Logie has men scouring the land for her, her father is either dead or refusing to disclose the hiding place," Gavin ventured, scratching at his red beard again.

"The more reason not to delay," Iain intoned, stifling the urge to throttle the bastard for his bluntness.

"Let us assume it is the latter," he added, allowing himself the satisfaction of leveling a glare at the loose-tongued bastard.

Gavin surprised him by cracking a broad smile. "All will be well," he said. "We will arrive timely and with men a-plenty. I've no doubt."

"Say you?"

"I am certain. Do not forget, we have more help with us than the promise of MacNab's men." Gavin patted the leather satchel affixed to the back of his saddle. "The reliquary casket and its precious relic shed blessings on those who safeguard it, my friend."

Iain's brows shot upward. "You think one bejeweled casket and a wee sliver of wood from the True Cross will guard us against a garrison of sword-wielding men-at-arms?"

Gavin folded his arms. "Och, aye, I do believe," he said, and flashed a brilliant smile at the lasses.

A bolt of keenest envy shot through Iain upon seeing the smile.

Had he e'er been able to smile so disarmingly?

He doubted it, and the thought made him scowl all the more.

"You ought believe, too," MacFie was saying. "We have already seen the relic perform scores of miracles. That, you cannot deny."

And Iain couldn't. So he pressed his lips into a tight, hard line and held his peace.

After all, he had recently vowed to no longer discount legends and magic. But he drew the line at MacFie's boastful claims of descending from a Selkie woman.

"You, my friend, are too much of a believer," he allowed, doubly annoyed when the barb failed to rattle the other. "But I admit the reliquary is a true one," he conceded, if a bit grudgingly.

The lout was right anyway.

The MacLeans' prized reliquary *was* capable of working powerful miracles . . . uncomfortable as they'd e'er made him.

He'd witnessed his share.

Time and time again.

And as far back as he could remember.

And so long as he'd postponed the delivery of the relic to the Bishopric of Dunkeld until *after* settling the matter of Madeline Drummond and her castle, mayhap the relic's magic would indeed smile upon them.

He could only hope, and would.

Secretly, he'd wondered if the relic had lessened his temper, for its fire certainly bit into his veins with less frequency of late.

Truth be told, he suspected Madeline Drummond had more to do with that feat of amazement than a wee silver-and-gold enameled reliquary and its sacred contents.

The lass ignited fires of an entirely different sort in him.

And the most persistently annoying such fire began making itself known even now . . . just watching the rise and fall of her magnificent breasts as she leaned against the yew tree!

Lifting a hand, he rubbed the tight knot pulsing at the back of his neck and glanced out across the miles of broom-and-whin-studded knolls stretching toward the horizon.

The winding road they'd taken from the south had vanished beneath ever-lowering clouds and a pall of cold-looking, misty rain shrouded the rolling hills and deep corries.

"Lest we wish a drenching, I deem it best we be on our way," he said, signaling to Madeline as he spoke. "Think you we can reach your cousin's keep before yon rain spills down on us?"

"Hmmm . . ." Gavin mused, hoisting Nella onto the back of her shaggy-legged garron mare. He narrowed his eyes at the distant rain. "Cormac's holding lies halfway between here and the Augustinian Priory of Strathfillan."

Swinging into his own saddle, he added, "If we make haste, we ought miss the worst of it . . . but not all."

"Then let us be gone from here." Iain turned to assist Madeline onto her new mare, only to see she'd already clambered onto the beast.

She held her back straight, but a nervous pulse beat rapidly at the base of her throat, and Iain's heart twisted at how fiercely she clutched the reins, at the thin trace of white edging her clenched lips.

But worst of all was the shimmer of tears in her eyes. He knew she hated to cry.

Cursing beneath his breath, he mounted his own horse . . . and prayed he wouldn't let her down. Nonetheless nigglings of cold-edged doubt crept up and down his spine. Some even had the cheek to plop down right atop the tight, achy knot of tension pulsing hotly at the back of his neck.

Eager for the comforts of a fine-smoored peat fire, frothy ale, and a dry, warm place to rest his head, he dug his heels into the garron's sides and hastened after the others.

They'd already ridden a goodly distance.

But then *she* drew rein. She glanced over her shoulder, clearly looking for him . . . waiting for him.

Iain's mouth curved in a smile that warmed him clear to his toes.

Because she waited, but, too, because her doing so made him smile.

A feeble excuse for a smile compared to MacFie's toothy grin, but a smile all the same.

A wash of Madeline's sweet golden warmth spilled through him. He'd smiled more since having her at his side than he supposed he had in the whole of his life.

Digging in his knees he urged the garron into a smooth canter . . . and smiled again when the beast complied.

Nay, he could not fail Madeline Drummond.

Couldn't bear seeing her lose heart.

But his fleeting smile faded as he closed the distance between them, wiped off his face by questions he couldn't outrun.

What if Abercairn truly was lost? Her father indeed dead, as she believed?

And more unsettling still, what if his own impetuousness brought her an even worse sorrow?

Would she cease looking on him as a valiant? View him differently?

Would she be able to forgive him?

And if indeed things went horribly wrong, would he be able to forgive himself?

True to Gavin's assertions, they reached Cormac MacFie's modest tower-house with only a light damping, having kept just ahead of the front edges of the pursuing rain clouds. The keep's main door already stood wide in welcome, and as they dismounted, a great bear of a man pulled opened the iron-grilled *yett* and came long-strided to greet them, a smile to rival Gavin's own spreading across his equally red-bearded face.

"Friends, Cousin, I greet you!" he boomed, making straight for Iain. He thrust out his hand with a grand flourish. "You are welcome to my hearth," he declared . . . and near crunched Iain's fingerbones.

The smell of peat smoke, roasted meats, and musty floor rushes wafted out from the hall's opened entry, the most appetizing smell—a roasting boar—made Iain's stomach growl loudly, his mouth water. And more than made up for the man's pulverizing grip.

"May the saints smile on you for your hospitality this night," Iain found his voice once the giant released his hand.

Gavin's cousin more times over than Gavin himself could coherently defend, Cormac MacFie greeted the others. Gavin in particular received a ferocious hug that made Iain wince. He could almost hear Gavin's ribs cracking.

"I didn't ken you'd taken a wife," he said to Gavin, releasing him at last and waving them all into the damp-smelling ground floor, a low-vaulted storage area piled high with ale casks, sacks of grain, and a jumbled assortment of rusty-looking weapons.

Iain noted the weapons, but Cormac bustled them so quickly through the dimly lit undercroft, there proved no time for a closer inspection.

Pausing at the arched entrance to a narrow-winding turnpike stair, Cormac snatched a smallish resin torch from its iron bracket on the wall and led the way abovestairs . . . toward the delicious aromas calling to Iain's watering taste buds and toward a warm and dry place to stretch his bones for the night.

Of a certainty not the sumptuously lovely bed he'd

shared with Madeline the previous night—a chaste sleep born of deepest exhaustion, even if they had slept hip to naked hip.

Nay, Cormac's guests would sleep on pallets, but comfortable and clean ones, Iain was sure.

And he ached for his with a vengeance.

Mayhap even more than he craved the savory-smelling roast boar . . . or even his lady's embrace.

Sleep called him, as did an insistent voice at his ear.

An urgent tugging on his sleeve.

"Sir! I crave a word with you."

Nella of the Marsh clutched a handful of his plaid and held fast. "Please." She pulled him away from the curving stairs leading him ever deeper into the shadows of the undercroft. She paused at last near a wildly sputtering pitch-pine torch.

The torch's flickering light played across her comely face, revealing the same anxious look he'd noted back at Fortingall beneath the ancient yew.

Iain cast a longing glance toward the stairwell, his stomach clenching at the delicious aromas wafting down the stair's curving length.

He drew a long breath. "I am sore tired and hungry, lady," he said, turning back to her. "Can you not speak your mind abovestairs? In the comfort of the hall? We can share a cup of ale before the hearth if that would suit you?"

"My pardon, sir, but nay," she declined, shaking her head. "I would not risk having anyone else hear what I must tell you."

Something in her tone sent icy little shivers tripping down Iain's spine. Her gaze kept flitting about, almost as if she feared someone—or something?—would leap out of the shadows and make a lunge for her throat.

"You are troubled. What is amiss, lady?" Iain peered hard at her, and immediately wished he hadn't.

Her jittery nerves and darting eyes filled him with increasing ill ease.

She wet her lips. "Do you believe in ghosts?"

Iain's brows shot heavenward. *"Ghosts?"* he echoed, incredulous.

Now he *really* regretted remaining below with her.

"Ghosts as in the spirits of the deceased?"

She nodded. "I—" she began only to break off and glance away. After a long moment, she looked back at him and sucked in a great, quivering breath.

"I live alone in a wee cottage. Little more than a cothouse really, but, sir, I am well content there and enjoy my solitude, you must understand," she said, the words flowing fast and unchecked. "Because I have oft been harassed by those who do not understand me, I put about a bit of prattle that I receive visitations from the dead."

At Iain's sharp intake of breath, she lighted a quick hand on his arm. "Please do not mis-take me, sir. I did what I did to ensure my privacy and for no other reason. I have ne'er been visited by a spectre and ne'er hoped to be."

Releasing her hold on his plaid, she began wringing her hands. "It was just a sham, you see? A ruse for my protection," she explained. "Such rumors keep people from one's door."

For truth!

Iain slid another glance at the turnpike stair. Sakes, but they called to him!

He folded his arms. "Why are you telling me this?"

"Because . . . because I was visited by a ghost at Mac-Nab's hall last night. A true one."

Iain's jaw dropped. "And you want me to know?"

What was it about him? MacFie and his selkies. Doon's old *cailleach* trying to give him Fairy Fire Stones, and now this woman and ghosts at poor MacNab's!

"Shouldn't you have told MacNab rather than me?"

She shook her head, her eyes round as a full moon. "The ghost, a woman, instructed me to speak to you."

Chillbumps broke out on Iain's flesh. "A woman?"

"Aye, sir, and a very beautiful one, if in a rather delicate, gentle way," she said, and Iain's blood curdled.

"She bid you to speak to me?"

He wasn't about to ask what the ghost wanted of him. In particular since it sounded like his late wife's shade. *Lileas.*

But Nella was bobbing her head, clearly about to reveal all. "She said she was your wife, sir, and that I ought assure you that she is well and wishes naught but your happiness . . . even if that be at another woman's side."

Iain's stomach dropped to his toes.

His knees turned to jelly, and he near embarrassed himself in a way he wasn't about to admit. Not to anyone and not in a hundred years!

He opened his mouth to speak, but his voice failed him.

And in that moment, he decided to become Iain the Doubter again. "I do not believe in ghosts," he asserted, feeling a wee bit better already.

"She also said that although she enjoyed her time with

you, it was her own choosing to go . . . that she was needed elsewhere and had her own path to follow."

"A spirit told you all that?" Iain the Doubter cocked a brow. *If shades did make an appearance, he couldn't believe they held such long discourses.*

"Aye, sir, that was about the whole of it."

"Nothing else you wish to impart?" Iain couldn't quite keep the sarcasm out of his voice. *It made a fine shield against the horror marching up and down his spine.*

"You do not believe me," Nella said, hurt in her voice. "I do not lie, good sir."

"Did she tell you her name?" he probed, pleased when she shook her head.

"Nay, she did not, and truth is, I was too frightened to ask."

"Did she say anything about how she died?" Now he had her. If she said the *ghost* claimed to have died in childbed or of a fever, he would sleep easier that night.

But Nella shook her head again. "She did not mention her death, sir, but I imagine she must've drowned."

Iain's heart stopped.

He could feel the blood draining from his head.

"Drowned?" Saints, he was afraid to ask, but had to. "What makes you think that?"

"Because she was dripping wet and had seaweed tangled in her hair."

"Wet and with sea—" Iain got no further.

The great and newly styled Master of the Highlands fainted dead cold on the floor of Cormac MacFie's undercroft.

Chapter Fifteen

STILL SHAKIER THAN HE'D E'ER BEEN in the entirety of his life, Iain sat on a rough-hewn long bench at Cormac MacFie's high table and clenched his fingers around his wooden ale cup. Nella of the Marsh's flustered revelations swirled through the bluish haze of smoored peat smoke, each blessed word spilling more light into the darkness in his heart than all the brightly flaring pine torches in his unsuspecting host's well-lit hall.

Her own choosing.

Needed elsewhere.

Wishes naught but his happiness . . . even at another woman's side.

Closer and closer they came, teasing, ethereal wisps of the spoken words. Disturbing and exhilarating in one, their portent curled round his neck, slipped down his spine, and finally slid lower to slither round his chest and squeeze his ribs until he could scarce draw a single breath.

Nor could he touch the succulent roast boar and other savory viands Cormac's well-meaning wife had piled upon his trencher. Grateful to be off his feet, he cast a cautious glance down the table to where his lady's friend conversed quite calmly with Gavin and their host.

She seemed to have recovered from having seen a ghost.

Iain's brow furrowed. He couldn't be sure if he'd e'er recover from having *heard* from one!

Even given the special circumstances.

Sensing his stare, Nella looked his way, gave him an almost imperceptible nod . . . her sincere affirmation that, as she'd promised belowstairs after he'd come to, no one would e'er learn from her what she'd revealed to him.

Or that he'd passed out cold on the stone flagging of Cormac MacFie's undercroft.

Despite his jellied knees and still-quivering innards, gratitude coursed through him. He, too, bore no desire to air the matter. Not with anyone, ne'er again. So he returned her nod, pleased to know their pact was sealed.

He just hoped she recognized the magnitude of his relief and appreciation, for Nella of the Marsh had not merely shared an experience that had truly unsettled her. Nor had she merely imparted a message. She'd banished the last of his lingering doubts and gnawing guilt.

The generous-hearted lass had breathed sweet life into his soul again, and the saints knew he could fall to his knees and weep with the wonder of it.

For the moment, though, he contented himself with raising the wooden drinking cup to his lips, draining the frothy brew, a fine heather ale, and hoping no one noticed how badly his hand shook.

Or that he hadn't partaken of a single morsel of the sumptuous array of savory victuals spread before him.

Truth to tell, he'd lost his appetite for meat and drink. He only hungered for his lady.

She sat beside him, her hip and thigh grazing his, and saints but he reveled in the sight and scent of her. He *craved* the feel of her.

Fire glow from the many resinous torches caught in her hair, gilding the braids she'd coiled above her ears and glossing each and every delightful curl that escaped her plaits to rest sweetly against the smooth curve of her cheeks.

Already garbed in a new gown of finest linen, the simple kirtle's low-cut bodice dipped just enough to give him a tantalizing peek, through the opening of his sister's borrowed *arisaid,* at the shadowy cleft between the lush upper swells of her breasts.

And it was the *arisaid* that made his heart smile, warmed him through and through. Held in place at the shoulder by a fine, round brooch of smooth-polished green and amber pebbles, the soft-flowing folds of the MacLean plaid was a gentle caress against her curves.

And looked so *right* on her, the sight of it stole his breath.

By the Mass, but she undid him.

And unlike the untouched victuals spread before him, he *did* hunger for her.

Hungered for her with a ravenous, all-consuming need. A crushing ache to leap to his feet, sweep her into his arms, and carry her abovestairs, mounting the winding steps of the turnpike stair two at a time, claim whate'er bed their host provided, and make her his at last.

Naught else would sate him.

The saints knew he'd waited a lifetime for her.

And now he was free.

Truly and wholly.

And he burned to love her. To lay claim to her so thoroughly, so fiercely, he'd brand her with his heat, not stopping until they were both so satiated that neither could lift a finger, and his name was stamped all over her, inside and out.

He wanted to touch her in ways that went far beyond the physical. Love her until their breaths mingled and became one, their hearts beat in tandem, and their very souls melded.

Pulling in a ragged breath, he allowed himself another sidelong glance at her breasts as he replenished his ale cup and took another long, restorative draught of the potent brew.

Och, aye, he wanted her. For truth, he needed to be so close to her neither one of them would be able to tell where one ended and the other began.

That was what he wanted, and he'd make it happen, too.

This very night.

If he could stop shaking long enough to properly ravish her.

"A ruse it must be, I say!" Cormac MacFie's booming voice shattered Iain's lusty reverie, banishing each sweet image like so many faint ripples against an incoming tide.

None too ready to relinquish them, he glanced toward Cormac. Half-rising from his chair, the garrulous MacFie chieftain held court at the far end of the table. "A proper taking of Bernhard Logie with or without a sizable host would prove harder than making rain fall upward!" he cried, sweeping all present with a keen eye as if challenging them to deny his claims.

Iain cleared his throat, hoped his voice would prove strong enough to carry the length of the long table. "You ken the pernicious bastard?"

Cormac MacFie snorted, dropped back into his chair. "Enough to say he is a cunning fox washed with all the devil's own deceits," he declared, and tossed back the contents of his ale cup.

Slamming it down, he dragged his sleeve o'er his mouth and chin. "God's death, but I wish I didn't ken the snake! But he is known in most quarters hereabouts." He leaned forward, his meaty hands gripping the table edge. "See you, his own holding isn't far from here—or what *was* his holding until the Bruce took it from him for his support of Balliol and the Sassunachs. The place is in ruin now."

"And ne'er was worth a passing glance as keeps go even before he lost it," someone else put in.

A swell of hearty agreement rose from the others assembled round the table.

"Ohhh, aye, Logie's hall was less grand than my own," Cormac said, falling back against his chair. "But he had dungeons cut so deep into the living rock beneath it, 'twas said one night in such a hellish place would curdle the devil's own blood!"

"Pits, he had, and used 'em, too," another voice joined in from the next table.

"He even put a woman or two to rot down there," Cormac's wife said with a visible shudder.

"Rumor was he did that just because he didn't like the

color of their eyes!" Cormac added, shaking his bearded head.

"He ought fret o'er the color of his own eyes and worry if the demons in hell will approve, for he'll soon be standing face-to-face with them," Gavin called out from where he now stood across the hall, his deep voice rising above the general ruckus. "The man's hours are numbered."

Iain tossed him a quick nod of thanks. He knew why the lout had predicted Logie's doom. And a quick glance at Madeline confirmed it.

No longer eating, she sat stiff and rigid, her gaze fixed on some distant point across the smoky hall.

It was time to see her abovestairs.

Time for lots of things.

Iain eyed their host. He burned to ask the MacFie chieftain to spare him a few good men. They needn't even be prime sworders. Those he hoped would cause a disturbance—a distracting ruckus—at Abercairn's rear wall needed but a good set of lungs and the will to clash together any bits of metal that would make a hellish din.

But Gavin had forewarned him that, although e'er bold in spirit and eager to welcome any and all to his table, Cormac MacFie and the few who abided beneath his humble roof had suffered a spate of horrendous hardships in recent years.

Fever, flooding, and failed crops had taken a toll on his numbers and strength.

So Iain stared up at the smoke-wreathed ceiling for a moment and counted his own blessings. They were growing by the day, and he was indeed grateful. Then he pushed to his feet, knowing inexorable relief that his knees no longer felt like wobbly jelly.

He looked down the length of the high table, caught his host's eye. "It has been a long and strenuous day, and my lady grows weary. I would see her abed now," he said, and lifted his glass, nodding to their host.

"Thanks be to you and yours, Cormac MacFie, for making us so welcome," he said, and downed what ale remained in his cup. "We shall be long indebted to you."

Cormac heaved his bulk to his feet. "The pleasure's been mine, MacLean," he declared, and thrust his own ale cup high in the air. "May God go with you on the morrow!"

Madeline stood as well. "I thank you, too, good sir," she offered, her voice sincere if quiet. "The finest of blessings on you and your house for your warm hospitality."

"Your lady wife kens the chamber I've given you for the night," Cormac called after them as they crossed the rushes, making for the turnpike stair. "'Tis humble, but clean and with a fine rope bed big enough for two. Aye, you ought sleep well . . . if you can manage to do so with such a bonnie sweet lass a-gracing your bed!"

"Pay him no heed," Iain whispered above her ear, his voice just loud enough for her to hear above the ribaldry and guffaws brought on by the chief's parting words. "He is deep in his cups."

"Ho, MacLean! Wait you!" Cormac MacFie boomed, halting them before they could mount the winding stairs.

He sounded anything but befuddled.

Iain turned. "Aye?"

Still on his feet, the big man indicated his kinsmen

with a arcing sweep of his arm. "See you, my friend, we are but a few and I cannot field many, but I'm of a mind to help you tighten the noose about that son of perdition's throat," he announced, looking mightily pleased with himself.

"You wish to send along men?" Iain put the question bluntly, hoped he hadn't misread the other's intent. "Do I understand aright?"

Cormac MacFie flashed a bearded grin so like Gavin's own that Iain's gaze flew to where that particular MacFie stood near the simmering peat fire, conversing with a few other cousins and kin.

"God's shame on me if I meant otherwise!" Cormac crashed a fisted hand onto the high table. "When you leave here, my best men ride with you."

"My thanks, good friend," Iain said, his voice thick. "I shall use them well." The excited buzz of Cormac Mac-Fie's kinsmen followed in his wake as he escorted Madeline up the narrow stone turnpike stair, and from the stir of their eager voices, it was apparent they'd lain idle too long and would relish even the thinnest whisper of a good fight.

Iain's heart leapt, his pulse quickening.

He, too, had idled overlong. Lain inactive, withered, and bored. But unlike that of Cormac MacFie's fired-up kinsmen, *his* relief would come before the morn.

At least he hoped it would.

Oh, how he hoped.

"Will you be sleeping naked again?"

The sweet and bonnie Bane of his MacLean heart posed the question the instant he closed the bedchamber door behind them, the tremulous note in her voice snatching his own carefully prepared words right off his tongue.

Iain scowled, his brows snapping together before he could stop them.

She'd discarded the *arisaid* with unbelievable speed, and stood watching him in expectant silence, the top rims of her coral-tinted nipples peeking at him from the edging of her new gown's low-cut bodice.

And the instant he spotted them, his loins quickened in urgent response. Sharp need coursing through his veins, he stared at her, rendered speechless by two crescent-shaped slivers of sweetly puckered flesh.

His best-laid plains came to naught, thwarted by her pert nipples and the multitude of subtle undercurrents rippling between them.

He sighed, struggled against the frustration mounting inside him. She warmed him like a golden sunrise after a cold, dark night, was what he'd been about to say—sakes, he'd even rehearsed the words a time or two throughout the evening.

And now he'd probably start spouting tripe again. But his wits, e'er sharp and alert, leapt upon the truth behind her innocent-sounding query.

Something had changed.

Or, better said, something had intensified into a swift-flowing current no longer willing to be contained.

"Sir?"

There it was again.

The slight tremble threading her voice, the unmistakable hitching of her breath. An invisible dividing line crossed, its breached boundary forever forfeit . . . if only he reached out and claimed it.

"Do you mean to . . ." The tremulous quality stronger this time, her unfinished words shimmered between them in the cool night air.

Their gazes locking, Iain crossed the rushes to where she stood beside the sturdy, feather bed. "I always sleep naked," he reminded her, finding his voice at last.

His voice, and his courage.

His nerve, too, for if the fates chose to be unkind, this could be their last night together.

The one chance he'd e'er have to know the kind of soul-melding contentment he knew he could have enjoyed with her if his life path had been a different one.

So he summoned all the seduction skills he liked to think he'd once possessed, and lifted her hand to his lips, brushed a featherlight kiss across her knuckles. "Mayhap you ought sleep that way as well?"

Her eyes widened at that, and a visible shiver slid through her. He knew because he'd seen it.

She *liked* the idea.

That, too, was apparent. Her own arousal stood winking at him in the quickening of her breath, in the dewy look of her softly parted lips, and in the increased rise and fall of her glorious breasts.

"I might enjoy that," she said, confirming his assessment. Her frank gaze riveted on his as she brought her hands to her bodice, let her fingers play with the lacings.

He burned to play with those nipples!

Lavish sweet attention on them until far into the night. A low moan rose in his throat, and for once he didn't try to disguise such an expression of his need through the ploy of a hastily summoned cough or sudden clearing of his throat.

He wanted her, and meant to have her.

Now, this night.

"This, good sir, is what I meant when I told you I feared myself." She glanced at the feather bed, drew a trembling breath. "It is madness, but I *want* to lie unclothed this night. And I want to be that way with you."

His heart lurching, Iain captured one of her hands and dropped a kiss into the cup of her palm. "Nay, lass, it is not madness," he said, releasing her hand to shove nervous fingers through his hair. "It is . . . *unusual,* but not madness. It is . . ." He let the words trail off, once again unable to find the right ones.

The words that would explain their connection and why it was so *right* for her to want to lie skin to skin with him, to burn to lose herself in the deep bond that had brought them together. The strange ties that bound them so irrevocably to each another.

He scarce understood it himself.

"It is . . ." he tried again, this time ramming both hands through his hair. Agitation made his heart thud hard against his ribs. "You are—" He broke off again, scowling this time.

God's breath, but he could be a buffoon when it came to expressing himself!

He started to turn away, just long enough to regain his composure, but she circled her fingers around his arm. Her grip surprisingly strong.

She stepped closer. "What am I? Pray tell me, for I dearly want to hear."

Warning bells tolled all through him, but he blurted the answer anyway. "You are my Bane," he said, saying the words quickly before prudence could stay the fool-sounding pronouncement.

"'Tis a clan legend," he rushed on, trying to get past the explanation before her eyes widened any further. "The Bane of the MacLeans. A blessing or a curse, depending on how it strikes."

"I am your . . . *bane?*"

She still did not understand.

Confusion clouded her lovely eyes.

"Bane is what the Legend is called by the bards." He placed his hands on her shoulders, kneaded them. "See you, MacLean males are said to have but one true mate," he began, praying she'd believe him. "*One true love.* A woman bound to them from time immemorial according to the Legend. No other love can compare, and a MacLean male will search relentlessly, ne'er finding peace or contentment, until he is joined with this woman . . . his *Bane.*"

"And you believe this Legend?"

"I do now." That said with utter conviction.

She stared at him, her beautiful eyes luminous in the candle shine, the gold flecks in her irises turning deepest amber. "Are you telling me that I am your *Bane,* Iain MacLean? That I am this woman to you?"

Iain heaved a great breath, full drained from his little speech and feeling just a mite . . . silly.

Half-afraid she might laugh.

Or think him daft.

Madeline Drummond was an intelligent woman. She might easily scoff at old Celtic myths and tales.

But she'd voiced a direct question, and he'd answer her with equal candor.

"Aye, lass, you are the Bane of my heart, and I have known it, *known you,* for months now." He told her true. "I recognized you inside my heart . . . knew of your existence the very first moment I sensed your presence."

She gasped at that, her red-gold brows winging upward. "You sensed me?"

The warning bells came back with a vengeance, and louder.

"I *felt* you . . . deep, deep inside me," he admitted, watching her carefully, wondering at her lack of surprise. "'Tis the way of the Legend. When the time is right, the MacLean male becomes aware of his Bane. He will sense her, the *sennachies* claim. He'll know she is out there, somewhere in the great vastness of the world, and so he waits for her."

She tilted her head, her glossy braids gleaming in the candlelight. "He doesn't search for her?"

"He will if he can. Och, aye, lass, if he can, he will search the width and breadth of the land, and tirelessly, until he finds her. For a certainty," he said, and meant it to the roots of his soul. "But sometimes circumstances prevent him."

"And you were one of the ones who had to wait? Who wasn't able to . . . go searching?" She blinked, her eyes bright.

"Aye, I could not seek my fate at will as others have done before me. Nor did I believe in the Legend." He glanced aside, expelled a long breath.

"I don't think I believed any of the tales until that day in Glasgow Cathedral," he owned. "*Then* I knew I could no longer deny it . . . I knew you were inside the instant I dismounted before the cathedral steps."

He traced a finger down her cheek, and that one wee touch blasted heat all through him. His knees began to feel wobbly again, but for a wholly different reason. Jesu God, just standing close to her, seeing those nipples peeking at him, begging to burst free, near unmanned him.

God, but he wanted her, and soon.

"You knew I was inside the cathedral?" She peered at him, her eyes bright with something very much akin to desire, and his pulse pounded harder at the sight of it.

"Aye, I knew, but mayhap a part of me knew even before then," he said, marveling at the silken warmth of her skin, how precious it felt beneath his touch.

How right and dear.

How very much his.

Her eyes widened. "Why do you think that?"

"Because I had been feeling you so strongly inside me," he clarified, toying with a loose curl just above her ear. "'Twas a fine golden warmth that would come unbidden to spool all through me."

And set my loins like granite.

"I have felt you in a similar way," she said, throwing him off-balance.

Delighting him.

Her gaze steady on his, she reached for his hand, laced her fingers with his. The simple contact flooded him with giddy excitement. He shoved a hand through his hair, tried to remember *he* was supposed to be the seducer. The one in charge and control.

"I would feel you this night, too," she vowed, smoothing her free hand down the loose spill of his unbound hair. Undoing him.

"Feel me?" Not that he didn't ken what she meant . . . it was written all over her bonnie face.

The hard throbbing ache at his groin knew, too.

Indeed, that part of him burned to be . . . *felt*.

To feel her as deeply and thoroughly as only that part of a man can feel a woman.

But his old doubts made him narrow his eyes at her. "Do you realize what you are saying, sweet?"

Lifting her chin, she looked him full square in the eye. "I am saying I would share this night with you, sir. Share it fully."

"This fully?" Iain skimmed his fingers lightly across the lush, upper swells of her breasts.

"More fully," she breathed, touching his face with equal gentleness, lighting her fingertips along the hard line of his jaw.

Carefully watching her face, Iain took hold of her hips, drew her close. "I will not deny that I want you," he said, his voice thick with need, well aware she could feel the hard length of him straining against her through the layers of their clothes. "But I will not press you into something you might regret on the morrow."

"It is because of the morrow, sir, and what may transpire, that I want this," she said, pulling away from him to strip back the bedcovering with a resolute jerk.

"It is my wish to open my heart and body to this . . . this *force* between us, lest the fates conspire against us and the morrow finds one of us with cause to grieve."

Grasping her shoulders, Iain turned her. "You wish to lie with me, lass?"

"If you will have me, aye," she declared, her voice firm.

Determined.

"Then so be it," he said, lowering her to the edge of the bed. His dark eyes smoldering, he removed the pins from her hair, and began undoing her braids. His fingers working so gently in her hair and against her scalp sent delicious tingles cascading down her back.

Leaning down, he nuzzled her neck through the waving curtain of her unbound hair. "Saints, but I want you so fiercely I can scarce breathe."

Madeline nodded. "I am not a woman to speak lightly, sir," she said, her pulse racing for he'd somehow not only undone her braids but also managed to untie the laces of her bodice, magically sliding it and the undershift down her shoulders without her even realizing it.

Her naked breasts sprang free, naught standing between her bared skin and his heated gaze but the cool night air streaming in through the chamber's one, half-open window.

"You have magnificent breasts, lady mine," he murmured, his fingers toying at her nipples. He traced slow, featherlight circles around the puckered flesh of her areoles and each new circle sent spirals of exquisite heat winding through her to pool at her very core.

"And your touch is as I knew it would be . . . tender and dear and so sweet it steals my breath," she said, feeling most wanton for having voiced how he made her feel. "I wanted you from the first," she said, lifting her hips as he eased her clothes down her thighs, helping him by waggling her long legs until he'd pulled every last stitch from her body and she sat full naked on the edge of the bed.

Full naked and wholly unashamed.

Needy.

So needy, she was convinced something inside her would soon burst into countless shards of the tiniest of pieces.

"Wanted me, did you?" Iain stepped back so he could look his fill at her, admire her nakedness as he removed his own clothes. Her hair, a glossy wealth of tumbling red-gold curls, spilled in wild abandon clear to her hips, her hardened nipples thrust through the gleaming strands.

"Do you ken what it does to me to see you naked? So open to me?" he asked, now as unclothed as she. Stepping forward, he took each nipple between gentle fingers and just held them, lightly squeezing, every once in a while giving a wee firm tug.

"Tell me how you wanted me, lass, for I would hear the words." He lifted one hand from her nipples to brush her hair behind her shoulders and free the whole of her breasts to his touch. "I would know that you truly need this." He caressed down her sides, splayed his hands on the curve of her hips, squeezed lightly. "That without our joining, you are not whole."

"The way I want you can scarce be described for ne'er have I known the like before I felt you here." Taking his hand, she pressed his fingers against her breast, there, where he could feel the steady beat of her heart. "You flooded my senses and filled me with need the very first time you came to me," she breathed, seeing no need to lie.

"You consumed me and I ached for your caress." She drew a long, slow breath, arched her back, desire pulsing deep between her thighs as he began toying with the tightened tips of her breasts as she spoke. "Aye, touch me so . . . *please*," she murmured, "for even just the few moments you took to smooth back my hair left me feeling bereft for your hands on me."

Slipping her own hands beneath her breasts, she lifted them for him, offering him their fullness. "Aye, bereft," she repeated. "And full, tight, and achy with need for . . . more."

She sighed, melting beneath his heated gaze. She burned to pull him to her, rub her breasts against *his* naked chest, delight in the friction of his chest hair against her bared skin.

"Och, aye, I shall give you all of me," he promised, leaning down to flick his tongue across first one nipple, then the other. "You are purring, sweetness," he added, and drew a nipple into his mouth, taking the hardened peak lightly between his teeth, using his fingers to circle and pluck at the other.

"Do-not-stop," Madeline breathed, the sweetest tension spreading through her belly, pulsing there and deeper.

"Oh, I shall not, minx." He pulled back to look at her. "Not until I have tasted and sated myself on all of you. I mean to drag my tongue through your deepest heat and savor the very essence of you, lass."

Madeline's breath caught at his words, at the determined smolder in his eyes. Heated tingles rippled through her. "Do you mean what I think you do?" she asked, *that* part of her already dampening in delicious expectation.

He nodded, a roguish smile spreading across his face.

"Oh dear saints!" she gasped, excitement humming inside her as he traced the outer swells of her breasts with

his fingertips, then slipped his hand beneath their fullness
to cup and weigh them.

He slid his thumbs slowly back and forth across the
tightened peaks, and each passing glide shot white-hot
bolts of pure, molten pleasure straight to the tingly
warmth pulsing deep between her legs.

"You are mine, sweetness," he murmured, easing her
onto her back and stretching out beside her. "And I am
yours. This night and always, for all time."

He pulled back to look at her, then rained the lightest
of kisses along the curve of her throat, across the sweep
of her bared shoulders. "You are my greatest joy," he
whispered, trailing his kisses lower, once more across the
lush fullness of her magnificent breasts, then lower still,
across the flat of her belly . . . toward the sweet tangle of
abundant red-gold curls at the juncture of her thighs.

"Finding you has made me whole again," he said,
smoothing a hand down her side, caressing her with gentle, looping strokes. His fingertips swirled across her abdomen, brushed fleetingly across the very tips of her
feminine hair.

He teased her there, toying with her intimate curls with
lighter-than-air touches. He slipped one hand over a
breast, settling his palm upon her hardened nipple and
just slowly rubbing until she trembled and gasped with
the pleasure of it.

"And you have made me whole in ways I ne'er
dreamed I could be," she sighed, parting her legs, gladly
opening them so he could intensify his ministrations.

Wanting, needing him to do so!

"Make me yours in all ways this night," she urged him,

sliding her hands over the hard muscles of his shoulders and upper arms.

"You are so lovely," he said, and obliged her, closing his palm over the heat of her woman's flesh. Very deliberately, he rubbed her with the same, deliciously slow circling motion his other hand used on her breast.

"Aye, make me yours so fully I will be able to taste and remember your scent on my skin for the rest of days," she whispered, trembling with need. "Only so could I bear the stretch of my tomorrows if the next setting sun should find me without you."

"Och, aye, I shall claim you, lass," he promised, squeezing and stroking her breast. "But you needn't fret o'er the morrow. The fates would ne'er be so unkind. I have already paid them a goodly enough tithe, I'd say."

Pleased when some of the worry left her brow, Iain shifted his position and lifted her legs, settling them over his shoulders. His own need now an acute, pounding ache, he looked straight into the glory of her, savoring her beauty.

He inhaled deeply of her rousing female scent, pulled in great, greedy gulps of her essence. "Jesu God, but you undo me," he said, his deep voice husky with arousal.

Consumed with the need to possess her, he lowered his head until his lips hovered just above her fragrant heat. His breath coming hot and ragged, he parted her lush curls and touched his tongue to her, flicking its tip oh-so-lightly up and down the soft crevice between her thighs.

"I shall ne'er let you go," he breathed against her silken warmth. He laved her now, dragged his tongue again and again through her pleasure-dampened sweetness.

"I do not want you to let me go, and 'tis you who are beautiful," Madeline whispered, stretching her fingers through the heavy spill of his hair, holding his dark head close to her center. "Ne'er have I— . . . oh!"

She cried out, arching upward, pressing hard against him as he circled his tongue around and over a maddeningly sensitive spot near the top of her woman's mound.

"So sweet, so sweet," he whispered against her pulsing flesh. He licked her slick, female heat with long, wide-tongued strokes, drawing his tongue over her with exquisite, bone-melting slowness.

"Sweet, aye," Madeline gasped, looking down, incredibly roused by the sight of him between her thighs, by what he was doing to her down there, the way he seemed to revel in drawing in her scent, her taste.

Wave after wave of sheerest tingling pleasure streamed through her, and her entire body quivered with desire. Ne'er had she known such languid deliciousness, ne'er had her heart felt more full. Her very soul, for he touched her that deeply.

Her need began to lift and soar, her body tensing, stretching for something bright and beautiful spinning ever tighter deep inside the part of her he was kissing. A wild pulsing began at her very center, an astonishing intensity about to shatter, the pleasure of it saturating her.

"Heart of my heart, I adore you," Iain vowed, rubbing his cheek against the tender flesh of her inner thigh. He rose then, stretching himself atop her, his weight on his arms. Easing her thighs wider, he settled himself between them, let his hardness rest against her as he reached down between them to keep stroking her soft, female heat.

He slipped his fingers into her damp curls, returned to

the tight and throbbing nub there, stroking gently with concentrated, circling strokes. "Ne'er doubt that I love you," he murmured, his passion almost breaking when she parted her legs farther, opening them full wide beneath him. Her soft whimpers, and the gentle rocking of her hips, inviting him to make her truly his.

"And I you," she gasped, reaching between them, circling her fingers around his hardness, guiding him to her. "I believe I have since I first felt you deep within my heart. Mayhap even before. Aye, I shall love you until the end of all my days."

"Our days and beyond, my minx," Iain corrected, at last lowering himself into her heat, pausing only for a heartbeat at the thin barrier of her virtue. "Naught-shall-e'er-part-us," he half groaned the words as he pushed inch by slow inch into her honeyed depths, losing himself in the satiny tightness of her. His heart split wide, cracking full open to absorb everything she was to him and he to her.

Everything they were to each other.

And always had been.

"You-are-glorious," he managed, waves of molten pleasure crashing over him as he moved inside her, rocking gently, and taking her with him to the most wondrous place he'd e'er been.

Unable to withhold himself a moment longer, he drew back, then plunged full inside her, capturing her cry with his lips, kissing her deeply as their hearts and bodies came together in a blinding burst of brilliant, colored need.

She arched high against him, her fingers digging into his shoulders, clutching at him in fullest abandon, her glory in their union stealing any discomfort and banishing any last doubts about the rightness of their joining, as he cried out her name and collapsed against her, fully spent and wholly hers.

This night.

And for all time to come.

Regardless of the morrow and its fast-approaching shadows.

Chapter Sixteen

*N*OT LONG AFTER FIRST LIGHT, on a dark and dreary morning, Iain and those who'd accompanied him drew rein in the shelter of the wooded uplands some distance behind Abercairn Castle. Cloud-cast and gray, the day's imminent threat of rain and drifting sheets of fine, whitish mist created a welcome cloak to shield their number from any observant guardsmen patrolling Abercairn's impressive curtain walls.

Heavily battlemented, Abercairn's strength loomed atop a distant ridge, and even at this early hour, the castle appeared anything but dark and sleeping. Pale, flickering light shone in many of the stronghold's narrow rectangular arrow slits, and glimmered in some of the larger, upper floor windows. Lit beacons blazed on the parapets, their orange-glowing flames eerie in the gray-washed and watery morning, and even at this distance, men could be seen moving about on the wall-walks.

Rolling pastureland dotted with whin and broom bushes stretched between their hiding place and the castle walls, but much to Iain's relief, the only thing stirring about on the ground ahead appeared to be a few fat and slow-moving bullocks.

Turning in his saddle, he cast his gaze over the little band of men who'd accompanied him. Gavin MacFie and approximately twenty of his kinsmen dashed about hacking at the gorse bushes, collecting great bundles of the prickly branches and tossing each armful into three ruined cot-houses set conveniently near the banks of a fast-running burn.

The firing of the heather-thatched cottages would provide a fine smoke screen, yet were too far from the castle walls for any stray flying sparks to catch fire and damage Madeline's home. The rushing burn would provide water to douse flames once Abercairn had been taken.

A feat only possible if Beardie and Douglas succeeded in getting MacNab to send a good-sized host of his best fighting men.

His lady, who unquestionably ought not have sat on a horse so soon after the night's sweet diversions, and her friend, Nella, the lass who apparently had e'er claimed to receive ghostly visitations, and now, thanks be to him, truly had, made up his only other sets of hands until the arrival of the MacNabs.

The ladies helped without complaint, patiently piling bundles of cut gorse and heather, and even gathering whatever rusted farming or domestic implements they found that could be clashed together to cause a din.

Appearing eager to make a ruckus of her own, Madeline crossed the short distance from the three little cot-houses to where Iain sat his garron.

He leapt down from his saddle, bracing himself for

another bout of the ongoing discrepancy of views they'd been exchanging ever since she'd learned she wasn't to ride with him to the castle's main gates.

Reaching him, she planted fisted hands against her hips. "The old smithy's is—"

"—The best place for you and Nella to await the outcome," Iain finished for her. He began counting off the reasons the two women ought best wait at the smithy.

"The forge is abandoned and hasn't been used in years," he cited its first advantage. "You said yourself no one has neared it in years. Its location outside the curtain walls and the village will enable you and Nella to make a swift and undetected escape if aught runs amiss."

If aught went amiss, she'd just as soon not escape.

Ignoring any such possibility, she turned to Nella. "What say you?" she asked, only to regret the bother the instant she saw Nella's annoyingly *practical* eyes.

"I think as little of two women standing about in the midst of a castle siege as I did of us traipsing across the land disguised as postulants," Nella said in a mild and reasonable tone as annoying as her calm expression.

"Ahhh . . . a woman of my own heart," Iain declared, nodding. He folded his arms. "I, too, think little of disguises, my lady."

Madeline whirled to face him. "You were disguised as a pilgrim!" she reminded him. "And a poor one, too. Ne'er have I seen a man less likely—"

He shrugged. "But, lass, I *was* on a pilgrimage of sorts . . . doing penance, as you ken. And the pilgrim disguise was for the protection of the priceless relic I must yet deliver to Dunkeld. You can rest assured I was not fond of donning that fool garb."

Unable to dispute his reasoning, Madeline shot a frustrated glance at Nella. "I suppose you think we should lock ourselves in a musty old forge that is very likely swimming with bats and vermin?"

"Better the dust of steel shavings and the reek of mold than take a fire arrow in the back or to accidentally get in the way of a fast-arcing blade, my lady," Nella said, with a shrug and a grating little smile.

"No man, friend or foe, would harm a lady," Madeline objected.

Iain rested a hand on her shoulder, squeezed lightly. "You seemed to feel otherwise when Silver Leg's henchmen were coming your way in the common room of the Shepherd's Rest, my sweet." He dropped a kiss on the top of her head to soften words he knew would vex her.

"Ho, Iain!" Gavin rode up, appearing suddenly out of the drifting mist. He led the women's two mares behind him, and a great smile split his red-bearded countenance. "MacNab's men have been spotted! A great host of the bastards and riding fast. They ought be here forthwith."

Iain threw back his head and whooped. "All the saints!" he roared, "I knew MacNab would come through." Digging in the leather purse hanging from his belt, he pulled out a length of thin rawhide and, reaching behind him, used it to tie back his long hair.

Madeline blanched.

He didn't want his thick, waist-length tresses to get caught in the path of an enemy's swinging blade.

Or have his unbound locks hamper him in the wielding of his own steel.

Swallowing hard, she watched a transformation take place. Her shadow man, her magnificent and tender

Master of the Highlands, was becoming a *warrior* before her very eyes.

A hard man, ready to spill blood for what he believed in, and willing to shed his own for the same cause if need be.

She glanced at the two garrons, considered defying his orders about the forge. But she would heed his wishes and ride with Nella to the ancient and out-of-use smithy.

And, as he'd bid her, she would stay there until he came for her.

Or sent Gavin in his stead . . . a possibility she didn't want to consider.

Before she could think further, the fast-approaching thunder of iron-shod hooves on dew-drenched and stony turf split the damp air. From the sound of it, a great many horsed men moving fast. Gusty wind carried the rapid jingle of harnesses and the rhythmic creak of saddle leather, too.

But most joyous of all was an indistinct humming . . . the low swell of men's excited voices.

The MacNabs.

It was time.

Only Madeline wasn't ready, especially if she had to wait in a musty old rotting hulk of a forge. Even so, her breath caught in her throat and hope swelled inside her as the sounds of the nearing horsemen grew louder.

Truth to tell, she didn't really care about being spirited away to wait out the outcome. Nor did she harbor any earnest doubts in that regard. Deep within herself, she knew Iain MacLean would emerge unscathed, regardless of what happened.

Shadow men lived on in dreams, and Masters of the Highlands were too bold to be bested.

Nay, 'twas her father's fate that frightened her.

Frail old men did die.

And having to face the finality of accepting his passing a *second* time, now that she'd let a wee spark of hope rekindle in her breast, would be agony beyond bearing.

She *wanted* to believe Iain MacLean, wanted to trust that mayhap her father had been spared. Learning otherwise would be like having her soul ripped out.

Iain turned back to her then, and her heart slammed against her ribs. Something about him was different. A more stunning change than she would have imagined, even if she couldn't see what subtle nuance made the difference.

His dark eyes softening, he took her by the arms and drew her close. "I thought you had faith in me?" His deep voice, smooth and calm, spilled the familiar golden warmth all through her and took away some of the chill icing her veins.

"Did I mistake? You look so doubtful." He cocked his head, studied her. "Have you so little confidence in my sword arm?"

Madeline lifted her chin, forced a little smile. "I do have faith in you," she said, not wanting him to think she doubted him. "'Tis my father's fate that worries me."

"He, too, will be found alive. I know it within me." Taking her hand, he pressed the flat of her palm against his heart.

Releasing her, he took her face a bit roughly between his hands and slanted his mouth over hers in a deep, searing kiss, pulling away from her much too quickly.

Madeline gasped, almost sagging against him. Her entire body trembled. She tried to cling to him, but before she could even blink, he'd hoisted her onto the garron mare's back.

He did the same for Nella . . . only without the kiss, then he gave their mounts a rough slap on the rump. "Off with you, now! And be of great heart, lassies. All will be well!"

Whether from the stinging slap or his resounding order, the two garrons surged forward, spurring away into the shadows of the surrounding birchwoods and bracken.

"Godspeed!" Madeline thought she heard him—or someone else with a deep, rich-timbred voice call after them, but it wasn't until a short while later when she and Nella reined in before the abandoned forge, a semi-ruinous open-sided structure with an ancient stone-walled enclosure behind it, the old smithy's cottage, that she realized what it was that had been so strikingly different about Iain MacLean.

Every last shadow had vanished from his eyes.

The MacNab had outdone himself.

On and on his warriors came, a great host of bold, high-spirited Highlanders approaching at fullest speed. A bloodthirsty lot when raised to battle, they appeared over the crest of the rolling, heathery slopes, a veritable panoply of weapons sheathed at their sides, hanging down their backs, or tucked wherever a place to secure a dirk or mace or battle-ax could be found.

As they rode forward, the impressive array of metal glinted dully in the early morning's gray light and their ruddy complexions and wild-maned reddish hair hinted at fiery tempers and mean-swinging sword arms.

"'Fore God, there is a sight," Iain cried, smiling clear to his foot soles.

"Praises be!" Gavin agreed.

Almost laughing, Iain vaulted into his saddle. If his lady had still been at his side, he would have swept her off her feet and whirled her in a wild circle so that she would become so dizzy from spinning, and so giddy with excitement, she'd have little choice but to fall right into his sheltering arms.

And it was into his arms he hoped to see her running again very soon. With God's good grace, he would, too.

"Well done," he called to the small host of MacFies. Together with Beardie and Douglas, they were already torching the three cot-houses. Soon, they'd raise general chaos and mayhem, their ruse allowing Iain, Gavin, and the MacNab's men to make short work of pushing through Abercairn's main gate.

"Come, MacFie," Iain called, spurring forward. "Let us give those bastards a taste of our steel!"

Already a hue and a cry had been raised within the castle. Garrison men ran along the wall-walks shouting and pointing at the smoke rising from the cot-houses, the orange flames leaping high into the gray, early morning sky.

Muffled shrieks, war cries, and a tremendous clashing and rattling of swords sounded behind Iain as the Mac-Fies set about their task with gusto, and, as he'd hoped, Silver Leg's men clearly mistook the smoke and flames of the burning cot-houses and the wild cries of a small band of bored and eager-for-excitement Highlanders for a great host of attacking men.

Indeed, they made a large enough ruckus for the castle's morning patrol to ride hotfoot back to Abercairn. Iain's heart soared upon seeing their swift approach. The large host of MacNabs neared, too, charging forward at a strong canter.

Iain kneed his horse, riding hard to intercept them. Within minutes, he drew up before their ranks, bringing his foaming garron to a slithering halt. He scanned their faces, raised his sword in greeting.

"To cover in the shadows!" he urged them, already wheeling about. "But stay close to the gate. Keep your mounts still, and when the drawbridge is lowered for the patrol, we surge up out of the shadows and ride in behind them."

As quietly as they could, they picked their way through the half-dark, moving ever closer to Abercairn's looming walls, and trying their best to blend with the shadows cast by large outcroppings of rock near the gatehouse.

They'd no sooner gathered into a dark, silent group, when the patrol went pounding past them, to a man bent low and beating their horses' flanks with clenched fists. At once, the drawbridge dropped in a great clanking of chains and the portcullis rose with a series of metallic creaks and groans, quickly followed by the hollow-drumming clatter of racing hooves on heavy-planked wood.

"Now!" Iain shouted, his own beast surging forward. He dug in his heels, urging the garron to greater speed before the bridge could be lifted.

He tore after the patrol, his own steed now pounding across the wet timbering of the drawbridge. The Mac-Nabs thundered close on his heels, following in a tight-packed arrowhead formation and yelling a series of angry, Gaelic war cries.

Their massed steel drawn and slashing in furious, killing arcs, the whole of them poured into the castle's inner courtyard, cutting down any and all who stood in their way.

The shouting of men and the wild clanking of swords filled the bailey, and within moments its damp cobbles ran red with the spilled blood of a garrison caught un-awares.

Somewhere a dog barked, and the few of Logie's men yet cowering in the shadows of the gatehouse pend lost their lives to a MacNab battle-ax or long sword. Swinging down from his winded garron, Iain near landed on the twitching corpse of one of the two miscreants who'd sought to seize Madeline in the ale-house.

Resisting the urge to spit on the bastard, he stepped over the blackguard's body, not for one instant grudging the dastard a portion of fine Highland steel as his last supper.

Looking around, he searched the faces of the other garrison men. Some still clashed swords with the hot-blooded MacNabs, others stood already subdued.

Gavin MacFie held his own in a far corner of the bailey, his fierce swinging blows sending one man-at-arms after the other crashing to the blood-stained cobbles.

But no matter how carefully Iain scanned the strong-hold's massive curtain walls or the timber lean-to buildings huddled against them, he couldn't locate the second man from the Shepherd's Rest.

Nor did he see anyone who even remotely resembled the description he'd been given of Silver Leg.

All other hapless souls faced the grave danger of meeting a swift and steely end if they so much as batted an eye against the Highland brawn that held well-muscled arms around their necks, and well-honed blades against their throats.

A sea of flame now bathed the morning sky behind Abercairn, streaking the pearly gray horizon with a hellish orange-red glow, and those garrison men still breathing stood flummoxed in the cold smir of rain just beginning to fall.

Stiff-lipped with defiance, their eyes wide with disbelief, and their hands without their swords, the men of Logie's garrison offered little resistance, some even stumbling from the various outbuildings without so much as a nightshirt or shoe.

"Who amongst you will own to being Sir Bernhard?" Iain called out, swinging down from his heaving garron. He gazed around him, and began pacing before the ranks of captured men.

Sensing a movement behind him, he whipped around, his gleaming brand flashing in a deadly arc, the huge sword slashing down on his would-be assailant, striking just at the vulnerable spot where neck meets shoulder, his blade slicing deep into flesh and muscle. His shock-widened eyes still staring, the man toppled sidelong, his own sword clanking useless to the cobbles.

Spinning back around, Iain raked the gaping garrison

men with a heated stare. "Well?" he demanded, jabbing his bloodied sword in their direction. "Who is Logie?"

No one answered, but proud and granite-faced as they gave themselves, none made further attempts at resistance. As so often, the threat of losing their lives overrode their loyalty to their absent liege.

For truth, Iain might have missed the lout entirely had he not spotted the dark-frowning dastard slinking along in the shadows cast by the lee of the curtain wall. Two men and a pair of cowed-looking greyhounds accompanied him. Iain stared, open-mouthed, stunned that a man of Silver Leg's infamy would stoop to such an ignoble flight.

One of the men with him walked somewhat hunched over, his resentful scowl even blacker than Silver Leg's own. His blood firing, Iain recognized him as the second man from the Shepherd's Rest.

But it was the other man, the third, who truly caught Iain's attention, had him sprinting after the other two blackguards, his heart lodged so tight in his throat he couldn't call out for the bastards to halt.

Couldn't shout a warning that their days of nefarious deeds had come to an end. Truth be told, he could scarce see to run either, for a few particles of dust seemed to have been blown into eyes, causing them to burn and water.

Almost as if he had tears in his eyes.

And mayhap he did, for the third man was the reason the bastard from the ale-house couldn't walk upright. The bastard was carrying the third man slung over his shoulder like a sack of coal.

A sack of pathetically unimpressive coal, for the old

man bouncing along against the blackguard's back was quite thin indeed.

A frail old man.

A fine-boned graybeard who looked to be ailing.

Madeline Drummond's father.

"Da!" If he hadn't guessed right yet, his lady's tearful shout told the tale.

Iain's blood froze. He spun on his heel, turning full around in time to see her rein up, then leap from her saddle just outside the shadows of the gatehouse pend.

Shock tying his tongue in knots, Iain stared, slack-jawed, as she streaked across the bailey towards her father. Ne'er had he seen anyone—male or female—fling themselves from a horse's back with such speed.

Nor would he have believed that a lass could run so fast.

Or so brazenly defy such bitter-earnest orders as he'd given her!

Nella of the Marsh burst out of the pend just then, disheveled and breathing hard, her face red from exertion. Nigh collapsing against the side of one of the lean-to buildings, she appeared to inhale great gulping breaths of air.

Catching Iain's eye, she lifted her hands and began shaking her head, but Iain paid her scant heed. Furious at the danger Madeline had put herself in, he tore across the blood-slick cobbles, reaching her in the selfsame instant she hurled herself at the miscreant carrying her father.

"Mercy of God, woman, what are you about here?" he roared, plucking her off the bastard. "Did I not tell you to stay put at the forge?!"

Wriggling free, she ignored him, launching herself

anew at the blackguard holding her father. "Would *you* have sat fast? Helpless and not knowing what was happening?" she shot back, pulling her father from the other man's arms.

"Well?" she snapped, her tone so like his own when riled, he almost forgot his ire. Cradling the old man's thin body against her own, she glared at him, her eyes blazing defiance. "I told you Drummond women are known for their tempers."

Her chin lifting a notch, she added, "We also descend from a long line of warrior women."

And looking at her, Iain didn't doubt it for a minute. But then the anger seemed to drain out of her and she clutched her father tight, more loving daughter than aught else. She made some kind of cooing sounds, wee little *mewlings,* and just stood there, rocking the man, tears spilling unchecked down her cheeks.

As discreetly as he could, Iain dashed his own from sight and thrust the killing end of his blade beneath Silver Leg's chin. Out of the corner of his eye, he caught Gavin MacFie making short work of the other dastard. His gullet sliced clean through, the man went down without a single cry.

Silver Leg deserved a slower death.

His two greyhounds snarled in bristling agitation, but stopped short of snapping at Iain's sword, their white-eyed trembling speaking more of terror than menace.

"So-o-o!!" Iain lowered his blade, but kept its tip aimed at Logie's sizable girth. "I'd say you've been well fed during your sojourn at Abercairn. 'Tis your doom that I cannot say the same of the laird."

Casting a sidelong glance at Madeline's father, Iain

noted the man's skeletal frame and sunken eyes, the waxy pallor of his skin.

Sir John Drummond's sad state made Iain's blood run cold and ripped off all the veneer he'd struggled so hard for so long to paint o'er his fuming MacLean temper.

"This was ill done, Logie," he said, his voice quivering with rage. "I am nigh wont to tear you limb from limb for your villainy."

Silver Leg spat on the cobbles. "God's everlasting curse on you and yours!" he hissed, his glance sliding to a shadow-hung byre hard by the curtain wall.

Following his gaze, Iain spied two sumpter horses, each one heavily burdened with bulging canvas or leather sacks. Logie had been heading in that direction. No doubt to flee with whate'er of Abercairn's spoils he could carry away with him.

"Where were you going, Logie?" Iain pricked the man's quivering belly with his steel. "Do those sacks contain what I think they do? Or simply . . . food. Since that, too, you seem to crave."

"I'll rot in hell before I answer a single of your questions," Logie seethed, his face dark with fury.

"And I would assure you a swift passage there!" Iain vowed, nodding to Beardie and Douglas. "Seize him and hold him fast until I've seen what those sacks contain."

His blood pounding in his ears, Iain unsheathed his dirk and slit the burlap canvas of one of the sacks. Silver plate and assorted Church goods, not unlike the treasures Iain was delivering to Dunkeld Cathedral, spilled onto the bailey's rain-damp cobbles.

Snatching a handful of silver coins, Iain strode back to Silver Leg. "Your life is forfeit, Logie," he said, letting the coins tumble from one hand to the other. "Had those sacks held your own collection of fine-embroidered tunics and knitted braies, I might have given you some degree of lenity."

Handing the coins to Madeline, Iain grabbed a handful of Logie's hair and yanked back the bastard's head so far, his mouth gaped open. "I ought melt down every last of those coins and pour the molten silver down your throat!"

Silver Leg's face ran chalk white.

"Tell me what you were about with Laird Drummond, and I will think on a more acceptable solution," Iain said, and folded his arms.

"He was taking me to the old smithy," Laird Drummond himself spoke up, his voice little more than a rasp but surprisingly strong for a man who'd been through such hell.

"The smithy?" That, from Iain's lady. "But Da . . . are you sure? No one has gone there for years."

His bravura cracking at last, Silver Leg began to tremble.

Laird Drummond eyed him, a look of raw disgust on his haggard face. "Logie has been using the old smithy to melt down Abercairn silver and gold," he said, clutching his daughter's arm, clearly grateful for her support. "But he hasn't found the *true* treasure . . . our jewels from Bannockburn," he saided, a note of pride in his thin voice.

He looked at his daughter then, and the love Iain saw shining there flooded him with an intense wave of sheer yearning and clutched fast at his heart.

Saints, but he'd love to have a daughter or son he could share that kind of love with someday.

"I didn't tell him where the Bruce jewels are hidden," Sir John said, his gaze still on Madeline's tear-streaked face. "That's why he brought me up from the dungeon when the trouble began this morning. He meant to ride away, but keep me with him until he could pry the answer from me . . . or find you."

"No one is going to e'er harm a hair on your daughter's fine head, Sir John. Nor on your own," Iain declared, keeping an eye on Silver Leg. *"You,"* he said to that dastard, "shall receive a most pleasing penance, Logie."

Striding up to him, Iain drew himself to his full height, and smiled. "I shall allow you to return home . . . to your own home," he said, and his smile widened a bit more. "Word has come to me that the accommodations there are most comfortable. I wish you all haste on your journey . . . both to your own home and to hell."

He turned to Beardie and Douglas. "Hie the bastard from my sight," he said, eager to have done with the viper. "And see you he is cast into the deepest pit in his dungeon."

"Ho! That we will do," the seamen chimed in chorus and dragged the spluttering Logie from the bailey.

Iain watched them go, his mind on his own journey. The one he just ended, for of a sudden, he knew with all his heart that he not only wanted to make Madeline Drummond his bride in truth rather than just the Bane of his heart, he also wanted a family.

One of his own.

And mayhap one, too, in which a fragile old man could be nurtured back to good health. Too much love bonded his lady and her father for Iain e'er to consider taking her elsewhere.

If she would have him.

He turned back to her, determined to resolve that matter forthwith, but a surprisingly firm grip on his forearm stayed his tongue.

"Iain MacLean!" Sir John Drummond's reedy voice held a distinct challenge. "My daughter tells me you have reason to make an honest woman of her," he said, peering at Iain from earnest gray eyes.

Iain's brows shot upward, but he caught Madeline's tearful wink and played along.

"Aye, sir, that may be true," he admitted, struggling to keep a serious face.

"I thought so," the old man said, and Iain suspected he caught a wee twinkle in John Drummond's eye. "Young man, am I going to have to challenge you to uphold my daughter's honor or will you do the noble thing and marry the lass?"

Iain glanced away for a moment, stared at a single shaft of morning sunlight breaking through the clouds to shine on Abercairn's massive curtain wall.

Saints, but he needed to swallow . . . and to blink a few times, too.

But when at last he turned back around, he was smiling.

The most dazzling smile Madeline Drummond had ever seen.

"Aye, I will marry her, good sir," Iain said, lifting his

voice so all within Abercairn's bailey and mayhap outwith, too, could hear him.

"I wish to have your daughter as my wife and at my
side," he vowed, placing a firm hand on each of their
shoulders. "Aye, I want her badly, Laird Drummond. For
all the days of my life."

Epilogue

Dunkeld Cathedral, The Highlands
Two Months Later . . .

YOU AND YOUR NEW LADY wife have all our good
wishes and felicitations." The good Bishop of Dunkeld
reached yet again to pump Iain's hand. "'Tis rare to see a
lovelier bride than the Lady Madeline."

Madeline nodded her thanks . . . again.

Iain kept his dazzling smile in place and didn't show a
single sign of agitation.

Even though the rotund Bishop had kept them standing on the cathedral steps for nearly an hour already.

Indeed, if the gregarious church man didn't soon cease
pressing his abbatial hospitality on them, dusk would
soon settle and the great wedding feast awaiting them at
Abercairn would begin without the bride and groom!

Sliding an eloquent glance at her new husband, Madeline tried to catch his eye, but the Bishop looked her way

instead, rewarding her with yet another of his warm and jolly smiles.

Only Madeline's father didn't seem to mind the wait. Much improved in health in recent months, Sir John Drummond strolled about the tree-shaded grounds, enjoying the tail-wagging affections of the Bishop's young hound. The black-and-tan whelp jumped and cavorted about the Drummond laird's legs, and Madeline's heart swelled as she caught her da's laughter at the dog's playful antics.

Such was a joy she'd ne'er tire of, just as she enjoyed seeing Silver Leg's two greyhounds trail her father's every step through Abercairn, adoration in their great round eyes . . . and her da's, too.

John Drummond had always loved dogs, but ne'er been able to keep one, and now it seemed every canine in the realm found its way to Abercairn's door.

Much to the old laird's delight.

None of Abercairn's leeches could explain why dogs no longer made the laird sneeze, but Madeline and Iain suspected it had something to do with Iain's sacred relic having been secured in Sir John's bedchamber for safekeeping in the weeks before Iain was able to deliver the reliquary casket and his other gifts to the cathedral.

"Ahhh . . . here comes Brother Jerome at last," the rosy-cheeked Bishop intoned, his eyes twinkling. "So sorry to have kept you, but the gillie who delivered your gift a sennight ago claimed he'd been told it was of the greatest importance that you receive it on your wedding day."

Iain's brows lifted when Brother Jerome joined them on the Cathedral steps and offered him a large sheepskin-wrapped package. "Here, my sweet," he said, handing it to Madeline. "Today is your day, too."

But the Bishop placed a beringed hand on Iain's arm. "Nay, sir," he said, shaking his head. "We were instructed *you* are to open the gift."

Puzzled, but determined not to let even a puzzled frown mar his brow on his wedding day, Iain took back the package, opened it, and withdrew the most beautifully worked leather sword belt he'd e'er seen.

Of finest leather and exquisitely worked, it was clear the belt was priceless in value. But it wasn't the belt's value in coin that made it so dear to him.

Nay, the gift's worth went far deeper.

Hot pricklings jabbing at the backs of his eyes, Iain blinked several times in an attempt to clear his fool vision enough to admire the belt's craftsmanship.

But most of all to gaze in wonder and awe at the two large Highland quartz crystals set into the belt's clasp. They shone with a magnificent inner light that rivaled the afternoon's bright blue sky and brilliant sunshine.

Indeed, the two stones shone with an almost otherworldly glow. A stunningly beautiful inner fire that seemed to have a life of its own.

And Iain recognized the stones.

They were old Devorgilla's Fairy Fire Stones.

The very ones the *cailleach* had tried to foist on him long months ago, claiming that they'd help him find his MacLean Bane.

His one true love.

Devorgilla had insisted the stones would catch fire and burn with an inner light that would ne'er extinguish . . . the instant Iain and his Bane found each other.

And now that they had, Devorgilla's glittering Highland quartz shone with a light brighter than a thousand suns.

"Oh!" Madeline peered at the belt, its priceless stones. "How beautiful!" Seizing it, she fastened the belt low around Iain's hips.

Stepping back to admire the belt on him, she smiled. "Now you truly *do* look like the Master of the Highlands."

Iain blinked, glanced aside.

He had to swallow again, too, damn his fool throat!

But when he found his voice once more, he placed two silencing fingers over her lips. "I do not care much about being styled Master of the Highlands, sweet lass," he said.

"No?" Confusion clouded her lovely green-gold eyes. "I thought you liked the title?"

"Och, but I do, never fear," Iain admitted, and dropped a kiss on her brow. "It just matters more to me to be the Master of Your Heart."

About the Author

SUE-ELLEN WELFONDER is a dedicated medievalist of Scottish descent who spent fifteen years living abroad, and still makes annual research trips to Great Britain. She is an active member of the Romance Writers of America and her own clan, the MacFie Society of North America. Her first novel, *Devil in a Kilt*, was one of *Romantic Times*'s Top Picks. It won *RT*'s Reviewers' Choice Award for Best First Historical Romance of 2001. Sue-Ellen Welfonder is married and lives with her husband, Manfred, and their Jack Russell Terrier, Em, in Florida.

More
Sue-Ellen Welfonder!

❧

Please turn this page
for an excerpt from
WEDDING FOR A KNIGHT
available soon
from Warner Forever.

Dupplin Moor
August of 1332

AT SUNRISE ON A HOT SUMMER'S day on the banks of the River Earn near Perth, Scotland's new Guardian, Donald, Earl of Mar, and a large army of the Realm's finest men, engaged in a fierce and bloody battle that would last but a few short hours.

By noon, the whistling cloth-yards of the English enemy had decimated the proud Scottish schiltrons . . . sadly no match for the expert aim of English archers and their constant rain of deadly arrows.

The Guardian, two Scottish earls, a handful of nobles, sixty knights, and several thousand brave spearmen lay dead upon the field. The English aggressors and the Scottish turn-coats fighting with them and known as the Disinheriteds lost but thirty men.

Those few Scots who were wounded or simply pinned

beneath the towering pile of their fallen countrymen, wished they, too, had died.

Of a certainty, they did not consider themselves fortunate.

And along with the endless rivers of blood soaking the ground that ill-fated day, each and every Scotsman to walk away from Dupplin Moor left his heart behind as well.

Magnus MacKinnon was amongst the survivors.

But he left more behind than most.

For along with his heart, he lost the fortune he'd worked three years to amass. Monies he'd won in tourneys and hoped to use to restore his clan's destroyed fleet of galleys.

And mayhap a bit of his family's pride.

But even losing such riches wasn't the worst to befall him.

Nay, the most bitter blow of all was the crushing of his soul.

Chapter One

Baldoon Castle, The Isle of Doon,
One month later

A PROXY WEDDING?"

Amicia MacLean shot from her seat at the high table, her high good humor of moments before forgotten. The pleasure she'd taken at having both her brothers beneath the same roof again for the first time in well over a year was soundly replaced by wave after wave of stunned disbelief.

"To Magnus MacKinnon?" Her heart so firmly lodged in her throat she could scarce push words past it, she stared at her brother, Donall the Bold, proud laird of Clan MacLean and bearer of the most startling news she'd heard in longer than she could remember.

Wondrous news.

And joyous beyond belief . . . not that she was about to voice any such admission.

Too great were the disappointments of past promises

of a suitable match, too numerous the empty promises and hopes of e'er having a family—a home—of her own.

A husband to love her.

"You needn't speak his name as if he's unworthy, lass." Clearly mistaking the reason for her wide-eyed astonishment, Donall MacLean raised his hand for quiet when others in the smoke-hazed great hall sought to voice their opinions. "The MacKinnons may be in sore need of your dowry, but Magnus is a valiant and influential knight. You could do worse."

She could do no better, Amicia's heart sang, long-cherished images of the bonnie Magnus racing past her mind's eye, each fleeting memory dazzling her with its sweetness.

Just recalling his dimpled smile and twinkling eyes weakened her knees.

And he'd been but a strapping young lad when she'd last seen him, years before at a game of champions held on the neighboring isle of Islay. He'd won every archery competition, each trial of strength, and turned the heads of all the lasses with his easy charm and fine, quick wit.

Magnus *the man* would no doubt steal her breath.

Of that, she was certain.

"'Tis said he is of arresting looks, ardent, and a warrior of great renown," Donall's wife, the lady Isolde, chimed in from the head of the high table, her words only confirming what Amicia already suspected.

Her pulse thundering ever louder in her ears, Amicia scanned the faces of her kinfolk, stood silent for a few agonizingly long moments, using each precious one to steel her backbone and make certain naught but cool aloofness touched her brow.

Could it be true?

Dear saints, dared she hope?

If this offer, too, proved fruitless, she would die. Wither away inside and plead the saints to have done with her and make her demise swift and painless.

She narrowed her eyes at Donall, moistened annoyingly dry lips. "Be this a true offer?" she asked, hugging herself against an answer she'd rather not hear. "Has Magnus MacKinnon declared himself or is this another of your well-meant but doomed-to-fail attempts to see me wed?"

Her other brother, Iain, set down his ale cup and swiped the back of his hand over his mouth. "Sakes, lass, think you Donall or I can do aught about the troubles plaguing our land in recent years? You ken why it's been difficult to court viable suitors for you."

Amicia squared her shoulders. "I am well aware of the myriad reasons we've been given for each broken offer," she said, her gaze fixed on the inky shadows of a deep window embrasure across the hall. "What I wish to hear is whether Magnus MacKinnon himself seeks this union?"

The words *proxy wedding* and *sore need of her dowry* jellied her knees.

The glaring silence spreading across the dais end of the cavernous great hall answered her question. She glanced up at the high, vaulted ceiling, blew out a nervous breath.

Faith, the quiet loomed so deafening she could hear every hiss and crackle of the pitch-pine torches lighting the hall, the low-rumbling snores of Donall's hounds sleeping near the hearth fire, and even the wash of the night sea against the rocks far below Baldoon's massive curtain walls.

Almost imperceptibly, she shook her head and looked back at her brothers, not surprised to detect faint flickers of guilt flitting across both their handsome faces.

"I dislike being cozened," she said with all the serene dignity she could muster. Taking her seat, she helped herself to a blessedly welcome sip of finest Gascon wine. "Nor will I allow it. Not so long as I have a single breath in my body."

"God's mercy, lass, it ill becomes you to play so stubborn." Donall dropped back into his laird's chair, a great oaken monstrosity, its back and arms carved with mythical sea beasts. He raked a hand through his raven hair, the same blue-black shade as Amicia's own.

"Nay, Magnus knows naught of the union," he admitted, meeting her gaze. "But he will hear of it upon his arrival on MacKinnons' Isle. He's been gone some years, competing in tourneys, as you likely ken, but he is expected home within a fortnight and his father is certain he will welcome the match."

Amicia stifled a most un-ladylike snort.

She *did* rake her brothers and everyone else at the table with a challenging stare. "Old Laird MacKinnon will be desirous of the filled coffers you'll send along as my dowry. All ken he burns to rebuild the galley fleet they lost to a storm a year or so ago."

"That is as may be, but he also loves his son and would see him well-matched and at peace," Donall countered. "And I would be glad of the marriage, too. Our late father and old MacKinnon were once good friends. Wedding you to Magnus would seal our truce with the MacKinnons once and for all time."

Amicia's heart skipped a beat, and a tiny spark of excitement ignited within her breast. She glanced aside, half-afraid all the desperate hope in her entire world must be standing in her eyes. None of the previous betrothal offers had sounded near as solid, as well deliberated, as this one.

None save the relentless endeavors of a chinless apparition of a lordling whose name she'd long forgotten.

Ne'er would she forget Magnus MacKinnon's name.

Truth to tell, it'd been engraved on her heart since girlhood, and sailed through the cold and empty dark of countless lonely nights now that she was a woman.

Pushing aside every warning bit of her good sense, she scrounged deep for the courage she needed to *believe*. To trust that, like her brothers, she, too, could find happiness.

A purpose in life beyond slinking about her childhood home, useless and pitied.

Welcome, aye, but not truly belonging.

A wildly exhilarating giddiness began spinning inside her, a dangerously seductive sense of *rightness*. Lifting her chin before she lost her nerve, she sought Donall's eye. "The old laird believes Magnus will want me?"

She had to know.

"On that I give you my oath," Donall said without a moment's hesitation.

Amicia's heart caught upon the words, all her suspicions and wariness falling away as if banished by a gust of the sweetest summer wind.

"Old MacKinnon even sent you his own late wife's

sapphire ring to seal the pact," Iain spoke up. He dug in the leather purse hanging from his waist belt, then plunked a heavy gold ring on the table. "Sore-battered by ill-fortune as the MacKinnons have been in recent times, you'll ken he wouldn't have parted with such a fine bauble lest he truly wished to see you wed his son."

"'Tis been long in coming, but you needn't suffer doubts this time." Iain's wife, Madeline, gave her a warm smile.

Amicia nodded her thanks, her throat suddenly uncommonly thick. *Hot,* too. As were her eyes. Blinking furiously, for she loathed tears and e'er sought to avoid shedding them, she snatched the ring off the table and curled her fingers around its comforting solidness.

Wee and cold against her palm, it meant the whole of the world to her.

"So-o-o, what say you now?" Donall leaned back in his chair, folded his arms.

Tightening her hold on the little piece of shining hope already warming in her hand, Amicia gave voice to the last of her doubt. "Tell me first why there must be a proxy wedding if Magnus is expected to arrive on MacKinnons' Isle within the next fourteen days?"

"Only because Magnus is returning from Dupplin Moor," Iain answered for his brother. "'Tis the old laird's hope that having a bonnie new bride to greet him will sweeten his homecoming."

"Come you, Amicia," Donall urged, leaning forward to replenish her wine cup. "I swear to you for here and hereafter, I would not give you to MacKinnon did I not believe he will be good to you."

Amicia drew a deep breath, straightened her back. She didn't doubt Magnus MacKinnon would treat her well.

She wanted him to *want* her.

To love her with the same fierce intensity her brothers loved their wives.

Reaching for her wine, she tilted back her head and downed it in one great, throat-burning gulp. She looked around the table, half-expecting to see disapproving glances aimed her way, but saw only well-loved and expectant faces.

"Well, lass?" Donall reached across the table and nudged her arm. "Will you wed MacKinnon?"

Amicia looked down at the sapphire ring in her palm. It had the same deep blue color as Magnus MacKinnon's laughing eyes. Dashing a fool trace of moisture from her own, she leveled her most earnest gaze on her brother and prayed to all the saints that her voice wouldn't crack.

"Aye, I will, and gladly," she said, her heart falling wider open with each spoken word.

And if by chance he didn't want her, she would simply do everything in her power to make him.

Many days later, on the mist-cloaked Hebridean isle known as the MacKinnons' own since time beyond mind, Magnus MacKinnon paced the rush-strewn floor of Coldstone Castle's once-grand laird's solar, sheerest disbelief coursing through him.

Crackling tension, tight as a hundred drawn bowstrings, filled the sparsely-furnished chamber and even seemed to echo off its pathetically bare walls.

An even worse tension brewed inside Magnus.

His brows snapping together in a fierce scowl, he slid

another dark look at his hand-wringing father. "I will not have her, do you hear me?" he seethed, pausing long enough in his pacing to yank shut a crooked-hanging window shutter. "Saints, but I'd forgotten how draughty this pile of stones can be!"

"But, Magnus, she is a fine lass," his father beseeched him. "Mayhap the fairest in all the Isles."

Magnus swung back around, and immediately wished he hadn't because the old man had shuffled nearer to a hanging cresset lamp, and its softly flickering light picked out every line and hollow in his father's worry-fraught face.

Magnus's frown deepened.

"It matters not a whit to me how bonnie she is," he snapped, and meant it.

The saints knew he'd had scarce time for wenching in recent years. And now, since the horrors of Dupplin Moor, he had even less time and inclination for such frivols.

In especial, *wifely* frivols.

Setting his jaw and feeling for all the world as if someone had affixed an iron-cast yoke about his neck, he strode across the room and reached for the latch of another window shutter. This one kept banging against the wall and the noise was grating sorely on his nerves.

Truth be told, he was tempted to stand there like a dull-witted fool and fasten and unfasten the shutters the whole wretched night through!

Anything to busy himself.

And help him ignore the sickening sensation that he'd been somehow turned inside out.

That the sun might not rise on the morrow.

His father appeared at his elbow, his watery eyes pleading. "The MacLeans—"

"—Are well-pursed and rightly so," Magnus finished for him, turning his back on the tall, arch-topped window and its sad excuse for shuttering. "*They* ken how to hold onto their fortunes."

"'Fore God, son, set aside your pride for once and use your head. Her dowry is needed, aye, I willna deny it. Welcome, too, but that isn't the only consideration." Clucking his tongue in clear dismay, his father set to lighting a brace of tallow candles, his age-spotted hands trembling.

Magnus glanced aside, ran an agitated hand through his hair. He would not be swayed by pity. And ne'er would he take a wife to fatten coffers he'd failed to fill.

Not Amicia MacLean.

Not any lass his stoop-shouldered da cared to parade before him.

And if they all came naked and bouncing their bonnie breasts beneath his nose!

The back of his neck hotter than if someone held a blazing torch against his nape, he strode across the room and snatched the dripping candle from his father's unsteady fingers.

"Mayhap your father's idea isn't such a bad one," Colin Grant broke in from where he rested on a bench near the hearth, his wounded leg stretched towards the restorative warmth of the low-burning peat fire. "I wouldn't have minded going home to have my da tell me he'd procured a fine lass to be my bride."

At once, sharp-edged guilt sliced through Magnus, cutting clear to the bone. Colin, a friend he'd made on the tourney circuit and who'd fought beside him on the blood-drenched banks of the River Earn, didn't have a home or family to return to.

The Disinheriteds and their Sassunach supporters had burned the Grants' stronghold to the ground ... and Colin's kinfolk with it.

Naught remained but a pile of soot and ash.

That, and Colin's unflagging determination to rebuild it as soon as he'd recovered his strength. But even if he could, which Magnus doubted for Colin's coffers were as empty as his own, Colin's loved ones were forever lost.

They couldn't be replaced by all the coin in the land.

"'Tis well glad I am to be home, Da, make no mistake," Magnus said, deftly touching the candle's flame to the remaining unlit wicks ... without spilling melting tallow all o'er the table ᴀ ɴto the floor rushes. "But I see you've gone a mite ᴀ ᴘated in my absence. I do not *want* a wife."

"I pray you to reconsider," his father said, his tone almost imploring. He tried to clutch Magnus's sleeve, but Magnus jerked back his arm.

"There is naught to think over," he declared, laying a definitive note of finality onto each word. "I'll have none of it."

Resuming his pacing, Magnus tried not to see Colin's sad gaze following his every angry step.

Nay, Colin's *reproachful* gaze.

He also strove not to notice the chamber's sparseness, tried not to remember how splendidly outfitted it'd been in his youth ... or think about how much of its former glory he could have restored had the fortune he'd amassed over the last three years not been stolen from its hiding place whilst he'd fought a vain battle against the English on Dupplin Moor.

He slid a look at his father as he marched past Colin, and hated to see the old man's misery. But it couldn't be helped. With time and hard work, he'd set things aright again.

He'd also rebuild his da's proud fleet of galleys ... even if he had to work his fingers to the bone and scrape the very sides and bottom of his strongbox to make it happen.

"You need heirs. I . . . I am not well, son."

His father's voice brought him to an abrupt stop.

Magnus swore beneath his breath, squeezed shut his eyes. "I will take a wife and sire bairns *after* I've regained our fortunes," he said, thick-voiced. "You have my oath on it."

"Well you say it, but I . . . I fear—"

"You fear what?" Magnus's eyes flew wide. He wheeled toward the old man, found him hovering on the solar's threshold, his rheumy gaze darting between Magnus and the gloom-chased corridor yawning beyond the solar's half-open door.

Gloomy and shadow-ridden because the once-great Clan MacKinnon could no longer afford to keep its many passageways illuminated.

A sorry state made all the more glaring by the light, hesitant footfalls nearing from the distance.

His father blanched at the sound and crossed himself. "Oooh, sweet Mother Mary preserve me," the old man wheezed and pressed a quavering hand against his chest.

Magnus shot a glance at Colin, but his friend only shrugged his wide-set shoulders. Whipping back to face his father, he was alarmed to note that his da's face had gone an even starker shade of white.

"What is it?" Magnus demanded, the icy wash of ill-ease sluicing down his back making his words come out much more harsh than he'd meant. "Are you taken sick?"

Purest dread, nay, *panic,* flashed across the old man's stricken face. "Aye, 'tis sick I am," he said, raising his voice as if to overspeak the fast approaching footsteps. "But not near so much as I'm about to be."

Magnus cocked a brow. Something was sorely amiss and he had a sinking feeling it had to do with his father's determination to marry him to the MacLean heiress.

Almost certain of it, Magnus folded his arms and fixed the older man with a stern stare. "Does your *illness* have aught to do with my refusal to wed the MacLean lass?"

A sharp intake of breath from just beyond the doorway answered him.

A *feminine* gasp.

And an utterly shocked one.

But not as shocked as Magnus himself when the most stunning creature he'd e'er seen stepped out of the vaulted corridor's gloom.

'Twas her.

Amicia MacLean.

He hadn't seen her in years, but no one else could be so breathtakingly lovely.

Even as a young lass, the promise of her budding beauty had undone him. Saints, her presence at an archery contest had once distracted him so thoroughly, his arrow had missed its target by several paces.

Her presence now, here in his father's threadbare solar at Coldstone, undid him, too, but for wholly different reasons ... even if some boldly defiant part of him fair reeled with the impact of her exquisiteness.

"Christ God and all his saints," his father found his voice, and promptly crossed himself again. "I meant to tell you, son, I swear I did."

"Tell me what?" Magnus demanded, though deep inside he already knew.

The pallor and shock on Amicia MacLean's bonnie face told the tale ... as did his mother's sapphire ring winking at him from the third finger on her left hand.

The lass herself squared her shoulders and lifted her chin.

She met his stare unblinking and her courage in a moment he knew must be excruciating for her did more to soften Magnus's heart toward her than if she'd thrown open her cloak and revealed all her dark and sultry charms.

Stepping forward, she reached for his father's hand, lacing their fingers. "I suspect your father has not told you that you already have wed me, Magnus MacKinnon. We were married by proxy a sennight ago," she said, just as he'd known she would.

Magnus's jaw dropped all the same.

His *heart* plummeted clear to his toes.

Her heart stood in her eyes and seeing it there unsettled him more than any deadly arcing blade he'd e'er challenged.

The image of serenity and grace, she'd wield her weapons with even greater skill. That he knew without a shred of doubt.

And worst of all, his damnable honor wouldn't let him raise his own against her.

THE EDITOR'S DIARY

Dear Reader,

Ever made a plan that's gone awry—all for the sake of love? Then you'll be charmed to make the acquaintance of both contemporary gal Nina Chickalini and noble medieval warrior Iain MacLean—two different protagonists with plans led astray by romance that can both be found in our two Warner Forever titles this August.

Romantic Times claims that **Sue-Ellen Welfonder** "is on her way to stardom" and that her books are "emotionally intense, highly sensual and soaring with romance." All of those elements can be found in her latest Warner Forever title **MASTER OF THE HIGHLANDS**. Iain MacLean's fiery temper has finally gotten the best of him. On the first anniversary of his wife's death, he sets fire to the family chapel out of grief. Facing the wrath of his family, Iain is punished into taking a pilgrimage to deliver a precious holy relic to an obscure monastery on the far side of Scotland. During his journey, he is side-tracked by Lady Madeline Drummond when he comes across her fleeing her home after her parents' tragic deaths. She wishes to seek revenge on their murderers. As he becomes her protector and champion, Iain discovers his true soul mate in the headstrong Madeline, thus mending his wounded soul.

Leaving the Scottish Highlands for Queens, New York, we present **Wendy Markham**'s Warner Forever debut with **THE NINE MONTH PLAN**. *Booklist* has described previous books by Wendy Markham as "an undeniably fun journey for the reader." For Nina Chickalini, Queens is the only place she's ever known—and the only place she's dying to escape from. Being the oldest of 5 kids, she has always had the responsibility for her large Italian family thrust on her young shoulders. Now, at 36, Nina has decided it's time to start her own life away from Queens. But when her best friend since childhood, Joe Materi, tells her he's given up on finding Mrs. Right and wants a baby, Nina decides to be the surrogate mother. She would do anything for Joe who has always been there for her through thick and thin. But Joe has secretly been in love with Nina for years. Dare he hope their baby plan will lead to a happily-ever-after?

To find out more about Warner Forever, these August titles, and the authors, visit us at www.warnerforever.com.

With warmest wishes,

Karen Kosztolnyik, Senior Editor

P.S. Next month Warner Forever offers you two titles with heroes whose fates are decided by very determined women: in **THAT SUMMER** by **Joan Wolf** a hometown man accused of a crime he didn't commit finds his sole supporter is a childhood sweetheart from long ago; and with **THE SECRET CLAN: REIVER'S BRIDE** author **Amanda Scott** brings to life a dashing Scotsman promised to another who unexpectedly falls in love with a woman he's forbidden from.